THE LESSON

Lisa Bradley is a former journalist and now Deputy Head of Journalism at the University of Sheffield. She lives in Yorkshire with her husband and two sons. *The Lesson* is her second novel.

Also by Lisa Bradley

Paper Dolls

THE LESSON

LISA BRADLEY

Quercus

First published in Great Britain in 2021 by

Quercus Editions Ltd
Carmelite House
50 Victoria Embankment
London EC4Y 0DZ

An Hachette UK company

A CIP catalogue record for this book is available from the British Library

PB ISBN 978 1 52940 782 2
EB ISBN 978 1 52940 783 9

10 9 8 7 6 5 4 3 2 1

Typeset by CC Book Production
Printed and bound in Great Britain by Clays Ltd, Elcograf S.p.A.

Papers used by Quercus are from well-managed forests and other responsible sources.

For my mum

CHAPTER ONE

Evie

The accusation

Evie felt like laughing. In that awful way when someone gives you terrible news, or you're at a funeral surrounded by grief-stricken mourners coughing tearless sighs and, as the coffin comes down adorned with flowers, your mouth starts twitching. The woman in front of her was making notes, scrawly, spidery biro notes with escaped blobs of ink, pimply blackheads on the page. She could hear the squelch of the pen against the paper and it sounded like little suction poppers. It was all surreal. The woman paused and looked up. Her left eyebrow, Evie noticed, was coloured in slightly wonky. It reminded her of the time she had waxed Bronte's and accidentally made her look like a stroke victim.

Laughter threatened to bubble up in her throat and hook

the corner of her mouth, stretching it into a wide Joker smile.

Nothing about this was funny.

And yet the twitch still came, and Evie had to stare at the top of her brown boots and concentrate on a black smeary scuff to stop it all bursting out. Her heart raced and her nails were ragged.

The serious-looking woman in front of her was tapping the end of her pen on the desk in a pattern. She paused and then did it again. Evie pictured herself adding in a clap and bursting into 'We Will Rock You'. Then she stared very hard at the scuff again.

She was here, she was actually going through with this. She was doing it.

'OK Evie, what we need to do now, is take an official statement from you.' The woman frowned at her pad of paper as if it were mocking her. Evie bet she had just caused her a mountain of paperwork.

'Now, would you like someone with you? Perhaps from the Student Union?' The woman looked up and Evie forced herself to make direct eye contact for the first time. Her mascara was cheap, she noticed. It had clumped the lashes together and there were bobbles on the end of the stumps.

'No thanks. I don't need someone with me. Do I really need to make another statement? I've told you everything already.' Evie tucked her dark hair behind her ears and crossed and uncrossed her legs. 'Am I in some kind of trouble or something?'

'No, no, no.' The woman – Louise, Evie vaguely remembered her introducing herself as – leant forward. Her jacket was too tight under the arms and the line of it puckered. 'It's nothing like that. But there is a process to go through with formal complaints. We need to make sure we follow the procedures. Make sure everything is done through the right channels.'

Evie nodded and felt something shift in her gut. 'Will he know it's me? I mean, are you going to talk to him, or something? What are you going to say?'

Louise smiled and her face completely changed. Her eyes softened and Evie smiled back nervously.

'We can protect your anonymity at this stage. That may have to change later but, for now, let's schedule a meeting to go through your statement. You can bring a friend, it doesn't have to be anyone official. Or perhaps your personal tutor? But it might be good to have a little bit of moral support. I know it will be a very intimate conversation and I do apologise for that. But just before we proceed, can I please check that you are absolutely sure?'

'Of course.'

'You are claiming that you entered into a sexual relationship, with your lecturer Simon Davidson.' Louise looked down at her pad and read directly from it. 'You say this relationship began in semester one, and ended abruptly. You also say he advised you not to tell anyone about it, that he continued to mark your assessments and did not allow you to switch seminar groups, as you requested.'

Evie closed her eyes and thought of the cheap vodka crawling back up her throat, her hands splayed against the pub's bathroom mirror. Her pale-yellow vomit in the sink.

'Yes,' she said.

Louise looked at her without blinking for so long it must have dried out her eyes, Evie thought. The pipes in the old, high-ceilinged room clanged.

'And, for the record, you say this relationship was consensual.'

'It was just one time. I wouldn't, well, it was kind of a relationship, I mean, that's what I thought it was leading to but . . .' Evie trailed off.

The urge to laugh had gone now.

Louise nodded. 'I understand,' she said more softly. 'You said you'd been drinking.'

'Yes, I had.'

'And you're sure you consented to the incident.'

Evie hung her head. 'I did.'

Another heavy silence and then Louise drew her breath in with a whistle.

'OK Evie. I'll be in touch over the next couple of days and we will take it from there.'

'Thanks.' Evie stood up and wobbled slightly on her heeled boots. She was surprised to note her thighs were shaking.

'It was very brave of you to come and tell us this.' Louise

pushed her chair back and walked her to the office door. 'In the meantime, I will contact the head of English and make sure Dr Davidson isn't marking any more of your assessments or directly involved in any of your teaching for the rest of the semester.'

Evie hooked her bag over her shoulder and followed her to the door.

'Will the head of department know? I mean, will you have to tell him? What . . . we did.'

'He will have to know the nature of the allegation, yes, but no details. Because you claim it was consensual, there's no actual sexual offence, or sexual harassment issue here. But it's an abuse of trust, and a breach of the university disclosure policy. He has marked your work with conscious bias. And I am concerned that he refused to move you out of his seminar group under the circumstances.'

'He said he couldn't, as people would ask questions. He said moving groups was against policy.'

'So is sleeping with your students and not declaring an interest,' Louise said shrewdly, then caught herself. 'Sorry Evie, I shouldn't have said that.'

'Will he be in a lot of trouble?' Evie asked quietly as Louise opened the door.

'If he is, it's his own doing.' Louise paused then drew the door back quietly. 'Do you understand what it means to be coerced Evie?'

'I think so,' Evie replied.

'Before your next statement please think very carefully

about the events leading up to this indiscretion. You may have said yes, but did he make you, at any time feel like saying no to him wasn't an option? Conversations? Emails? Just, please think about it.'

'I will.' Evie looked down, then forced her chin up and smiled. 'Thank you so much. You've been great. I've been so worried about this meeting, and I was dreading it being a man.'

Louise nodded. 'I'll keep in touch Evie. You take care. I'll ensure the department contacts you later today regarding a new timetable.'

Evie walked out into the muted spring sun. She hated spring. It was so delicate and fragile. There was nothing to it. No bite. Bronte was sat on the wall, scrolling up and down her phone. The weak sun caught her ginger hair and she looked as if she was wearing a crown of fire. She looked up and smiled as Evie approached.

'Hey girl. How was it?' She squinted into the sun as Evie's shadow fell across her lap.

'Yeah OK.' Evie shrugged. 'God. I don't know if I've done the right thing.'

'Babe.' Bronte reached her arms up to offer a hug. 'Of course you have.'

Evie leant in. Bronte's body felt squashy and malleable.

'Want to go and get smashed?' Bronte asked, muffled, into Evie's bony shoulder.

Closing her eyes, she rested her chin on the top of Bronte's head. She smelt of cinder toffee and garden fires.

'Can we not talk to any men?'

'You read my mind.'

Evie pulled away and wiped her cheeks. She hadn't even realised she was crying.

'I'm sorry. God. You've been brilliant over all of this. And you've had such a shit few months too,' Evie said. 'I feel like I've made this semester all about me. I'm such a bad person.'

'No. We're not the bad guys here.' Bronte linked her arm and the two began walking across the quad and towards the Student Union, its octagonal windows shimmering above the older buildings, as out of place as an alien intrusion. But that's what the Duke of York University liked to pride itself on. A blend of tradition and modern thinking. Evie knew some students liked the gorgeous old sixteenth-century heritage, fused with sleek chrome and smooth lines, but she just felt somehow it couldn't make its mind up about what it really was. And that unsettled her.

'What do you think will happen to him?' Evie said, pulling her long wool cardigan around her. A boy she recognised from her Victorian Literature seminar group gave her a second glance as he walked past. She gave him a quick smile, embarrassed about her puffy eyes, but he smiled back, even flashing his teeth, before putting his reddening face down and becoming swallowed in the crowds that were beginning to pour from the lecture halls like spilt milk.

'I don't know, hon.' Bronte squeezed her arm. 'A warning, I hope. I mean, he could get fired, I guess, but you can't think like that. He's the one responsible for his own actions.'

'So am I though.'

'Exactly. And you've done the right thing by coming clean. I mean, can you imagine if someone found out and then started chatting about that being the reason you got so many firsts? You don't need that kind of shit. And you want to know you're getting them on your own merit.'

But Evie wasn't listening anymore. She could barely make out the words because there he was.

Evie's breath began to quicken and her chest felt squeezed. She was too tall to shrink into the oceans of students that seemed to flow around him. He stood there in his own circle, no one hustling or jostling him, like Moses in the parting of the Red Sea. She wouldn't have been surprised if the ice-cream-coloured clouds broke and a ray of sun fell upon him like a spotlight.

He was laughing at something a student was telling him. One with full tattoo sleeves and wearing a Stone Roses T-shirt that probably belonged to his dad. Simon gave him a friendly punch on his upper arm and the student grinned in gratitude. His magnetism was indiscriminate.

'All the girls want to fuck him and all the boys want to be him.'

That's what Bronte had told her on the walk down to their first lecture in September. Evie had been new on campus, having had a disastrous first year at Manchester, but had managed to scrape together enough credits to transfer straight into second year. Halls of residence were for first years only, and Evie hadn't fancied another nine months of cramped bedsits and girls squealing down corridors.

She'd scrolled through the adverts on the Duke's house-share website until she'd found exactly what she was looking for, and had pitched up with her cardboard boxes and Tesco kettle at a six-bed terrace in The Groves. Her room was one of two in the attic. The skylight didn't open properly, there were silverfish in the carpet and fresh paint that looked like it had been slapped on to cover up mould in the corners. But it had a double bed, a desk and once she'd hung her pictures and made up her bed with its throws and cushions, it looked marginally less like a cesspit. Her dad had stood awkwardly while she'd hung up her clothes. He'd shoved a few notes into her hand and then left, waving a cheerful goodbye to the other inhabitants, Liam, Finn, Kelly and Bronte, who'd gathered in the kitchen to peer into the backyard and watch the arrival of the other attic inhabitant, Harvey.

She'd been relieved to have Bronte in the house, although not surprised. There was always someone on a campus within a two-metre radius studying English. But everyone had already made friends the previous year and established little packs to travel in. It was much harder infiltrating new groups. House-shares helped. A ready-made family. If you picked the right one, of course.

Bronte had dragged her to the middle section of the lecture theatre. It was in one of the new buildings, with soft blue chairs with a little drop-down rest for a laptop. Evie watched as the girl in front set hers up and immediately logged on to a Facebook page.

Simon was at the front already, powering up the main terminal and Evie watched as the giant projection sprang to life behind him.

'All the girls want to fuck him and all the boys want to be him.

Including you, I'm guessing by the looks of it,' Bronte had laughed, pulling her laptop from her record bag.

'No. I don't think so. Not into necrophilia.' Evie had wrinkled her nose.

'I think the term is silver fox. Anyway, he's not that old. 40-something?'

'That's old!' Evie had swept her hair over one shoulder and pulled at the neck of her T-shirt. It had been an odd temperature. Not warm exactly. Just not comfortable.

'There's even a Facebook appreciation page.' Bronte had motioned to the girl in front who'd been uploading a sneaky pic of him to the group.

'Urrrghh. How gross. I take it he's as arrogant as he thinks he is attractive?'

'Humble arrogance. The worst.' Bronte had grinned.

Evie looked back as the hall had begun to fill with the hums and groans of muted chatter, the occasional loud laugh. He was tall. Taller than her. She could always tell in an instant. A habit from her teenage years when she'd felt so awkward about being, in some cases, almost a foot taller than everyone else.

'How tall are you?' Girls would say with wide eyes, and boys would tease and joke about the weather up there.

'Five-twelve.' She'd lie. Never six foot.

She longed for a man, or a boy, who she could wear heels next to without them puffing their chest out, or having to be the one to bend down for the end of night kiss. She'd only found one in the end. The one, or so she'd thought.

Simon was definitely six three. Maybe even six four. His hair was short, salt and peppery at the temples, and not muscly as such. But solid. There was definition under his shirt sleeves, his shoulders were wide and inviting.

'Welcome to Introduction to Victorian Literature.' The voice from the front was like liquorice. Dark, sweet and demanded attention. Even Bronte had shifted in her seat and put her phone down. 'I'm Dr Simon Davidson. And this is ENG203.'

She'd watched as he'd gone through the learning outcomes of the lecture, made wry, self-deprecating jokes, so artfully woven in that they didn't seem rehearsed.

Gentle waves of laughter, almost melodic, a crescent and a fall.

He'd paused from time to time. He'd swigged water from a plastic bottle. Not the reusable metal canisters everyone was lugging around smugly. An actual shop-bought, one-time use only, plastic bottle.

It was as if he had smeared himself in peanut butter and laid himself in front of a pack of wild dogs.

This man had balls.

Evie had opened her notebook and started to scribble, drowning out the clitter-clatter of everyone else's keyboards. She preferred it this way, the smooth arcs and loops of her pen across fresh paper, as if the points were flowing from her brain and through her fingers.

The lecture theatre was tiered, spot-lit and cruel. The lights would intermittently change brightness or tone every fifteen minutes. A trick, Bronte had informed her when she'd first looked up startled, to keep their attention.

It was then that she'd noticed him looking at her. She'd felt his gaze before she'd seen it. It had only been for a second. A smile. A dimple in his left cheek. Then his eyes had swept away. He hadn't stopped his flow, not even for a moment. When the lecture had finished, the second hand hit twelve exactly, as if time too were not his master.

Evie halted and Bronte yelped as she wrenched her shoulder.

'It's Simon,' Evie said, her voice low.

'Oh shit.' Bronte looked in the direction of Evie's glare. 'Babe. Just walk past. Don't even look at him.'

Evie looked straight at him.

He fist-bumped the student and turned towards the main concourse. His pink shirt sleeves were rolled up, no jacket. Of course, he would wear pink. It wasn't even warm enough for no jacket. But that didn't stop him.

Look at me. Look at me.

He began walking towards them. One hand in his pocket, the other holding his phone. Eyes down. Smiling.

No. NO.

Evie shoved Bronte to the left until they were directly in front of him.

'Evie, no.'

'He's not going to ignore me,' she spat. 'He can't just carry on, like nothing has happened.'

She stood in his path, her heart racing. He looked up and his eyes locked onto hers, just for a second. Then he smiled at both of them with a raise of his brows, as if to say 'Hi girls', and a roll of his eyes, motioning at his phone. Not a care in the world. He carried on walking purposefully into the thinning crowds. Both girls turned, but he didn't look back.

'Oh my God. He just . . . that was worse than being blanked. Did you see that smile?' Evie's jaw dropped.

'Come on.' Bronte pulled Evie by the elbow. 'You need a drink.'

The Student Union was another of the modern buildings in the strange space-age dome. They settled in their favourite corner to the right of the bar under the complicated mosaic mural, some joint project between art and psychology. It had even won some kind of award, but was a bit trippy after a few vodkas.

Bronte tied her mass of hair up in a bun using a pair of knickers from the bottom of her bag, always her favourite party trick, and leant over her pint.

'This is officially the worst year for men. It is the Chinese year of the rat?'

'Or toad, or something?'

'Snake?'

'Well the closest I have had to sex in six months is when that youth in Go Ape strapped me into the harness.'

Evie laughed. 'Oh God. You're better off without it. It just causes stress and bloody turmoil. I'd rather have a cup of tea.'

'Probably hotter,' Bronte conceded. 'Saying that, you . . .' She looked at Evie and grimaced. 'Actually, maybe not.'

'It *was* hot.' Evie shrugged. 'Just . . . stupid. Here's to a man-free few months.'

Bronte clinked her bitter against Evie's gin and tonic. 'For you maybe. I'm still on the prowl. Listen. Do you want to talk any more? Or are you OK? Want to just forget about it for a while? Give me a signal, because otherwise I'm going to start being all me, me, me.'

'No. Although. Speaking of cups of tea. You know that consent campaign? The whole, even if she said she wanted a cup of tea, and then falls asleep, she doesn't want a cup of tea anymore, so don't make her drink it?'

'That film always really makes me want a cup of tea.'

'Well, it's weird. The woman from HR asked me the same thing today. She like, really pushed to make sure I had consented. Even when I assured her that I did, she started using words like "coerced".' Evie took a sip. 'It's like, she automatically assumed something. As if the only reason I would have made that choice was under duress. Like . . . I shouldn't have wanted it. It made me feel a bit like a victim.'

'She's just doing her job. Imagine the press if she didn't,' Bronte said. 'It's a good thing she checked.' She paused. 'So what did you tell her?'

'What do you mean?'

'I mean, I know you didn't say no, but you didn't say "Yes Dr Davidson I will have sex with you" either, did you?'

'See! This is what I mean. Do *you* say yes every time you have sex? What was he meant to do? Get written permission or something?'

'Well. No. But, he should have at least made sure. I mean, how stupid can you get?'

'What in the throes of passion? Wouldn't that be, what did you call it last week? Knicker-drying?'

'Actually. NO. He shouldn't have done it AT ALL. Because he's a lecturer and you're a student and it's gross.'

'It's not like I'm at school, Bronte. We're both adults. And it wasn't gross. It was . . . Bronte it was *great.* I have never had sex like that before. With someone, who, well, knew exactly what he was doing.'

'Yeah I bet he did,' Bronte said. 'He probably had his eye on how many Jaeger bombs you'd ordered. Why are you defending him?'

'I'm not,' Evie said. 'But you can't call him a rapist either.'

'I didn't use that word.' Bronte's voice went higher.

'OK. But I was complicit. So if he is gross, then so am I.'

'I didn't mean it like that.' Bronte took a massive gulp of her drink.

'What a fucking mess.' Evie bent towards the table, rested her forehead on her fist. 'God. I hope I've done the right thing.'

'You have.' Bronte rubbed the top of her arm. 'Remember why you wanted to do this in the first place. It's an abuse of power. You can't let him do this to other girls.'

Evie nodded and wiped her eyes again.

The click of the toilet door. His cheek against hers. The cigarette smell on his breath. Did he remember it like she did? Those details. That moment. Would it all come flooding back?

'Hey guys.' Evie looked up at the sound of a chair being dragged over and Liam sat down back to front, jigging his legs. He always reminded Evie of a Labrador with his shock of toffee hair and massive brown eyes.

'Have you seen my post on The Common Room?'

'Which one?' Bronte leant over the table and pinched a crisp from his packet.

'The one about Josh's memorial. It's going to print tomorrow but thought I should get it out there ASAP.'

Evie dropped her eyes and Bronte paused, the crisp half-way to her mouth.

'Good idea. Is it all sorted now?'

'Yeah. It's going to be on May 2, the anniversary. We'll hold a candle-light tribute in the quad at dusk, and we're getting some speakers. Jenny's doing a speech to raise awareness and the SU is thinking about widening it out to anyone who wants to come and light a candle in memory of someone they've lost to suicide.'

'That's a really wonderful idea.' Evie gulped. 'I'm sorry I never knew him, Liam. It's just . . . there's no words.'

Liam gave her a thin-lipped smile. 'I hope you come. The more support we get the better. I'm hoping we can get the local TV down.'

'Of course. And, let me know if there's anything I can do to help. Posters, you know, whatever.'

'Yeah thanks. That would be great. I still can't believe you didn't know him.'

'Me neither. I feel like I did.' Evie smiled.

The ghost of Josh was always there. In the house, in their pictures they'd pinned all over the walls. In her room. The room that was meant to be his.

His bright blue eyes followed her everywhere.

'Anyway, see you at home. Tuesday is buy-one-get-one-free at Pizza Republica?' Liam stood up.

'Sounds good.' Bronte smiled. 'I can't be bothered to cook tonight.' She waved as he trotted off through the double swing doors.

'You OK?' It was Evie's turn to reach over the table and squeeze her hand.

'I just can't believe it's been a year.' Bronte shook her head. 'A whole year. It's like, it's like he was just here yesterday. Signing for the house. I keep thinking about that day. Was he thinking about it then? It was such a great day and the sun was out and he seemed so happy. I just . . .' Bronte pulled the knickers out of her hair and let the red waves cascade round her face.

'I'm so sorry, Bronte.'

'Let's just get drunk and make bad choices.' Bronte downed the rest of her pint.

'I thought that's how I ended up in this mess,' Evie said dryly, and then went back to the bar.

www.thecommonroomDoY.co.uk

Hundreds are expected to gather in the quad to mark the first anniversary of the death of Josh Peterson.

The Student Union and the Duke of York University Student Support Services have joined forces in the hope of uniting the campus to raise awareness for student mental health.

Josh, an English Literature student, 19, died on May 2 last year after falling from the roof of the arts tower.

Following a fundraising campaign by the English department and Josh's family, the university will be erecting a steel memorial sculpture in the centre of the quad, to be known as the Joshua Tree.

Josh's personal tutor, Jenny Summers, who led the fundraising efforts for the sculpture and who has campaigned about the huge rise of mental health issues in universities and the lack of support for students, will also be speaking.

Josh had been on a waiting list for counselling but was not deemed to be at 'serious' risk of harming himself or others.

CHAPTER TWO

Jenny

An hour before

His office door is closed. The glass panel in the middle, the one for students to peep through, eyes sticky and fingers gnawed, is blocked up with posters, so I can't see what he is up to. That irritates me.

I don't want to knock. That's like asking his permission. And I know he's in there. I saw him stroll down the corridor with my Pride and Prejudice Penguin mug. It's the only one without any chips because I hand-wash it every afternoon rather than put it in the staff dishwasher. He knows it's mine. He's doing it on purpose. Either that or he is just completely oblivious to mug etiquette and I don't even know which one I think is worse.

I should just walk in. He does that to me. Knocking, while he's already opening the door. I actually find that more insulting than if he just barged in. Nevertheless, I give the door a light tap and clear my throat.

'Yep.' I hear a shuffle and the wheels of his chair scrape across the floor as I open his door. His office is horrendous. Piles of paper everywhere, mouldy coffee cups. A dead spider plant on the windowsill.

That's what makes the Pride and Prejudice mug such an insult. I see it there. Perched on the edge of the desk. I'm going to just take it back.

'Jen! To what do I owe the pleasure?' Simon swivels round in his chair, all smiles and dimples. I feel my cheeks sucking in.

'I've still not had your assessment details for next semester,' I tell him and force a smile. 'I've emailed you three times now. Stop ignoring me.'

'Oh shit, yeah, sorry, sorry.' Simon ruffles the back of his hair even though it's too shorn to be dishevelled. It is definitely greying more. 'Here, shall I just tell you them? Do you want a Post-it? You know me and email . . .' He smiles sheepishly in the little boy manner that I assume I am meant to find endearing.

'No,' I reply and raise my eyebrow. 'I don't want a Post-it. I want you to input the details into the Google form please, like everyone else. The committee meeting is tomorrow.'

'OK. I'll do it now.' Simon reaches out and takes a big slurp of tea from my mug. I feel bile bubble in my throat. 'Fancy a drink later? I've got a late seminar. We've not had a catch-up for ages.'

'I can't, sorry.' I have the courtesy to smile again. 'Too much prep to do for tomorrow.'

'Another time? I hope . . . are . . . well, are we OK?' He leans forward, elbows resting on his man-spreaded knees.

I shrug. 'Why wouldn't we be?'

I turn to go and then pause, feeling suddenly very large, as if I have swelled and the office has shrivelled. It is cramped and airless. But I realise I am being surly and that won't do.

'Have you heard about Josh's memorial?' I turn and ask, in a much softer tone.

'Of course,' Simon says in that earnest way of his. His eyes try to lock onto mine but I won't give him the satisfaction. 'Yes. Absolutely. I assume you're speaking?'

I nod. 'It's good that you're coming. We should all be there.'

'How are you holding up?' The chair inches forward and I reach for the door handle. I shouldn't have let the door close.

'I'm fine. See you later. Fill in that form.'

It wasn't always this way.

There's nothing like old buildings in the spring. The ivy is still alive, wrapped around the honey stone walls of Grove Hall. The magnolia tree in the courtyard has started to blossom and the air smells of old ink and damp cotton. It's not far from the English department to the main bank of lecture theatres, just off the quad. I don't even bother with my coat. The air has lost its bite and there's no redness to my fingers anymore, apart from the ones wrapped around my coffee. I can't lecture without a hot drink in my hand. I never look at the clock, just how much coffee I have left. We are in perfect sync.

It's busy on campus. Some of them scuttle. Heads down but eyes forward. Others prance, like fauns, others flock in herds. But they all move as one, like the swell. I watch them from my office window sometimes. I can't hear them properly. Not really. They sound more like the way you hear the sea in a shell. But I see them. I could pick out each and every one of mine in a crowd.

They take each step like no one has walked there before them. It makes me smile. New undergraduates, barely eighteen. Just weeks ago, they were still in school uniform.

They always trill when I drop the c-bomb in the lecture hall. Never to shock, nor to offend. I teach contemporary women's literature and depictions of sexuality in Victorian prose. It's a little gesture of mine. This is a safe space. There are no rules in learning, no boundaries in critical thinking. No wrong. No right. As long as someone else has said it first of course. God forbid we nurture a culture of independent theory.

I can feel my heart race a little and the backs of my heels rub against my new mock-crocodile three inchers. It's worth it though. I need the height or I'll be peeping over the lectern like the narrator at a primary school nativity.

'Hi Jenny.' A girl with straggly pastel pink hair tucks it behind her ears and gives me a one-handed wave, slowing her pace.

'Oh, hi Elodie.' I smile back. 'Are you coming to small group later?' I nod at the ugly, prefab concrete tower opposite us. 'I can't talk now, I'm just about to teach.'

'Yeah, yeah. Sorry. See you then?' She grins and hugs her notebooks to her chest and then stumbles as a lanky boy knocks into her shoulder.

'Shit, sorry,' Elodie says and the boy holds both hands up in the air in some kind of silent 'don't worry about it' gesture. He keeps walking though.

Sorry for just being there? I decide to pick this up with Elodie later.

As I swipe my ID card and take the lift to the fifth floor, I know the lecture theatre will be already two-thirds full. We all have to swipe in now. Staff and students. They didn't say it was because of last summer. But then again, they didn't really need to.

The entrance is at the back. I walk down the steps in the middle of the rows, feeling like a bride without a father. I have never mastered that effortless jog, the unaware strut. Thank goodness for the coffee in one hand and my notes in the other, otherwise I'd have become very aware of my own arms. They are watching. Still mumbling, pretending to each other not to notice I'm here. The person teaching before me has helpfully left the computer running, so I quickly log in and pull up my slides.

My breathing begins to steady. The door swings open, back and forth like a Wild West saloon, and the last of the benches fill as the final clumps of students file in, until they are one big hive.

I take a sip of my coffee and open my mouth to begin, when I see him. Middle left. Where he always sat. Ironed shirt. Open collar. He is looking at me too, expectantly. Like he always did. Waiting for me to speak. To soothe. To coax and to navigate. With his crooked smile and his bright blue eyes that shone even on his blacker days. I stare back for too long.

I know it's not really Josh, I'm not a madwoman. But I know the image of him will be gone too soon, so I savour it until his face morphs into another. And then I am back, staring at the theatre in front of me.

'OK everyone.' I give my brightest smile. I spend my money on expensive lipsticks and buy my shoes cheap. 'So, I am naturally going to assume you have done the reading. And not just watched it on Netflix.'

A guilty titter. But eager eyes.

'Because, as daring an adaptation as it is, we are studying *The Handmaid's Tale* in its novel form and today our lecture will discuss whether the structure tends towards an apex of power of both sexes or a political feminist statement.'

As I talk the words roll around inside my mouth like lozenges. My cheeks prickle and my tongue never dries. It slips and slides fluidly, and my voice ebbs and flows in the room until I have persuaded every single one, first one way, and then the other. My coffee is cold though when I take a sip. I am off my game.

I take a big gulp, and then another, before coming to my last slide. My eyes search again for Josh's face, but he's gone.

He is gone.

After the lecture, I watch them filter out of the hall, I consider going back to my office but decide there's not much point. My friend from the department, Cate, texts and wants to know if I fancy a drink. I do, but I've got an email list the length of a bible to get through. While I was teaching, I could hear my phone buzzing in one long monotonous drone as the messages kept coming in. It's nearly assessment time, and they are as unsettled and fractious as if it were reaching a full moon. It wouldn't surprise me if one day I looked out into the auditorium and their bodies were bending and stretching, convulsing. Clothes shredded, hair sprouting. A writhing mass of hungry wolves.

My neck cracks as I stretch it from side to side. I could just have one drink, I reason with myself, and then catch up with my emails on the train. We're not supposed to work outside office hours anymore or email students from home at night.

It's called managing expectations.

It's not that I don't understand their point. They come in, waving their cheques and demand, demand, demand. They want service 24/7. They don't get a first, and they demand to know why, when that's what they paid for. Why weren't they told exactly how to write this essay, why weren't they given ten mock exams with intense and explicit guidance on how to ace the next one? Why won't you answer me at 2 a.m.? My tuition fees pay your wages. I am buying this degree. I am buying you.

I own you.

Power balance. How it makes me laugh.

But then again, I see them working double shifts in coffee bars, serving five-pound rounds in nightclubs, getting in at 4 a.m. and up for a lecture at 9 a.m. Just to afford to be there. The loan system is a joke. You can only really be sure of financial support if your parents are rich, or if your family is poor, and you're entitled to it from the government. It's the middle children that nobody loves, they're the ones who can't access the full loans but can't afford the rent. They are not hung-over in lectures, they are just exhausted. They work their fingers to the bone for a career they will never get and a future that won't allow them to jump the queue just because they have a certificate in their hand.

Thank God I don't have children.

I used to get depressed about it. The futility of it all. Their naive anger. Mine. But I don't know anything else. In some ways I am a prisoner here. To quote the best film ever made, 'You've never worked in the private sector. They expect results.'

Most people think that as an English lecturer my favourite film would be something more highbrow than *Ghostbusters*.

And I would challenge Dan Ackroyd there. Perhaps his university didn't expect results in the eighties, but they do now.

I quickly fire off a text to Cate and head back into town.

The streets are busy, this city sneers at the students but they're the ones who keep it afloat. The NUS discounts in the windows, the early meal offers. Happy hours that stretch until midnight. The colours on the cobbles, the laughter and the squeals under the shadows at the Cathedral. It would merely echo with tourists without them.

I head down to The Rose. It's usually reserved for old men and their farting dogs. Cate is already there with a bottle of red next to a split-open packet of thick ridged crisps. There are no designer gins and olives in here, and no chance of bumping into a student wafting an essay draft under your nose.

'Ugh.' I relax into the chair. 'Good idea.'

'Well. I saw the stuff on The Common Room. Thought you might need a drink.'

The wine glugs as it's poured and my jaw aches as I take a deep mouthful.

'No, I knew it was coming. I think it's a great idea and I'm honoured they've asked me to speak. It's just . . . God, it makes my mind rake over it all again.'

'I can imagine.' Cate rests her hand on her chin and leans forward. 'It must be so tough. No one supports their students like you.'

I suddenly wish I was alone with this entire bottle. At home. Fire on and a laptop full of marking.

'It's a full-time job. I don't know how I actually have time to teach.'

'Rod. Back.' Cate raises her eyebrow and I slump back in my seat. I can't argue with her.

Three years ago, Cate had been hauled up in front of a panel after encouraging a student to talk to her mum about the fact she was on anti-depressants. The mum had flushed the pills down the loo and put in a complaint about Cate. And then the student had put in a request for extenuating circumstances which claimed that Cate's direct advice had led to mental anguish and to her getting a 2:2. It had been a year's worth of paperwork and meetings.

She doesn't advise students on anything anymore.

It's strictly sentence construction and referencing in her office.

Then last year her module evaluations described her as cold and uncaring about mental health and personal issues. One called her a robot.

We'd drunk a fair amount of wine that night. So much that I hadn't even caught the last train home. I'd slept on her sofa and been woken up by a small child with crusted green snot round one nostril demanding I make a hippogriff out of play-dough. I'd sworn not to let myself get that drunk ever again.

'Ok. I know. I know I'm my own worst enemy. I never seem to be able to clock off.'

'You're telling me.' Cate sits back in her chair. 'I feel like I've barely seen you recently.'

'Sorry. Things have been tense. I'm so busy. This plagiarism role is taking up so much more time than they said it would.'

'You know why they keep giving you roles? It's because you keep doing such a great job. Just fuck something up now and again and you'll find your workload diminishes significantly,' Cate says.

'Well, you know what they say. You want something doing, ask a busy person. Or a woman in the office without kids.'

'Touché.' Cate fluffs up the back of her hair. 'So, seriously, how are you feeling about the memorial? Ready to make a big "O Captain! My Captain!" speech?'

I flinch and Cate looks down.

'Anything I say just feels like I'm shouting into the void.'

'Nothing you ever do or say is in the void,' Cate says and I detect a touch of, if not jealousy, something in the bitterness family. 'I saw you got nominated again for a teaching excellence award. Congrats.'

'Thanks. We all know they mean nothing though.'

'Only someone who has won three of them can get away with saying that.'

I take another sip and roll my eyes. 'God Cate. What are we even doing?'

'What do you mean?'

'The hours, the emails, the round-the-clock care. I don't resent it. They need it. But who are these children? Why are they so . . . broken? What's happened to them?'

'I've told you. Use Boomerang on your office emails. STOP replying outside office hours. You're your own worst enemy. You're like a new mum picking up her baby every single time it cries.'

‘I think most new mums pick up their baby every single time it cries,’ I point out.

‘Well. More fool them.’ Cate tops up the glasses. ‘Both mine were sleeping through the night from six weeks.’

‘You’re a freak of nature.’

‘Thanks.’

We both smile but a touch of frost has settled over our glasses. We drink the rest of the bottle, idly gossiping about our colleagues, how the men never empty the dishwasher or bother to find out why the photocopier isn’t working. They just leave it flashing aggressively and expect a woman to deal with it. Once we’ve bitched about the new faculty officer and how often the new lecturer works from home, we both start making a show of gathering our bags.

I know it would be easier if I could feel a little warmer towards Cate. She really is the only real female friend I have. We WhatsApp at night, have after-work drinks and occasional weekend trips to the cinema. I wouldn’t call her my best friend, because I know I’m not hers. But that’s OK, I don’t want to be anyone’s best friend. It’s too much pressure. The job description is overwhelming and I have too much responsibility elsewhere.

We walk down to the station and as soon as the cold air hits me I realise I’m a bit drunk. I remember I didn’t have time for lunch and that breakfast was a banana I’d scoffed on the walk to the office. Cate and I air-kiss and she heads off to her platform, her boots click-clacking and her smart black jacket moulded to her skinny frame as if it were custom-made. Two children and she still finds time to compete in ironman competitions and never returns her marks late.

Her phone's already out, she's probably texting her perfect husband for a lift from the station. He coaches the U9s football and is a solicitor who works half the week from home so he can share the pick-ups and drop-offs.

Smug bastards. If she didn't have a family would she be getting award nominations too?

I hope not.

The screens on the big wall tell me I've just missed a train, so I nip over to the station pub for a quick one. I might as well carry on now. The wine here is bitter and much less palatable, but it passes after a while. I get some nuts and let each one roll around in my mouth, the chilli salt rubbing the acrid taste of the wine off my tongue.

I scroll down my emails and make sure there's nothing urgent. I've learnt that now. You can't take your eye off the ball else you'll be hanged, drawn and quartered with your entrails splattered all over Twitter or The Common Room blog.

The usual from the staff, a few students panicking over marking criteria, but nothing too serious. Nothing to make my nerves tingle and my heart race. The platform is busy. The students who commute are all here, with one wireless earbud nestled in an ear. I didn't understand what they were at first. I thought we'd had an influx of students with hearing impairments.

'I'm definitely drunk,' I confirm to myself as I finish the last of the wine and check my emails again. Then I refresh the page and check again.

Outside the pub the tracks rattle and I imagine the steam of the trains from the past, the dirty air and the hustle and bustle of porters in a time when travel was considered romantic.

I think I see you for a second. I know it's not you.

But they are all you. Every student. Every time I look at one, they all have the same pain in their eyes.

I see my train pull in early so I get my January-sales elbows out and hustle to the platform. My mouth is dry and I would kill to grab some water but I really don't want to have to stand, and unless I get there soon I know I'll have my face in someone's armpit all the way to Harrogate. I manage to trample over a snogging couple with matching lip piercings. I wince at the thought of the metal getting all tangled up, and throw myself down in a coveted table seat. I slide over to the window seat, possibly not looking my most graceful, and smile at the kid who shuffles into the same seat opposite. I don't take much notice. He's chav couture, baseball cap and huge jacket. I don't get the student vibe but he looks about the right age.

I check out the spectre of me in the window reflection. My thick, long dark hair is misshapen and static, and I wonder just how many times I have run my hands through it while sitting in the pub. I should have it cut shorter, something more applicable to a 39-year-old lecturer. I see in the reflection the boy with the cap is looking at me. I stare down at my lap so he doesn't think I'm preening, then chastise myself for caring. I get out my gloss and smear it across my lips. Somehow, it makes me thirstier.

The train is full, but not rammed. There are a few people standing in the doors, but the odd empty seat is littered about. No one else is sat at our table. I suppose it's actually a bit late for the commuters.

We haven't moved yet. I look up and the kid catches my eye. He has a faint moustache and fluff on his chin. I can't work out if it's deliberate or he just hasn't shaved. His eyes are hazel and they crinkle as he smiles at me.

'Alright.' He pronounces it without the 'l'. Aww-ight. I want to draw all over his tongue in red pen.

'Hi.' I flash him a proper smile. One with teeth and the slight dimple in my left cheek. The one many drunk strangers have claimed will be the un-doing of them.

I'm still waiting.

'Where you been?' He kind of does a back to front nod at me, his chin jutting upwards.

'Work. Then for a quick drink. You?'

I only ask out of politeness. I actually want to close my eyes and rest my head on the window and let the purr and buzz of the tracks send me to sleep.

Of course, that will not be how it works out. I already know.

'Spoons. Then Alpha. Early spin set. Wiv some mates.'

I have no idea what he's talking about.

'Early night for you? It's only . . .' I check my phone. 'Bloody hell how long have we been sat here? Are we delayed?'

'Dunno.' He shrugged.

I feel warm all of a sudden and wriggle out of my black coat. The top button on my bird print blouse has come undone, and although I'm hardly flashing cleavage, my entire throat and décolletage is exposed.

I decide not to bring attention to it by faffing about with the tiny buttons.

I do not love the company of wolves.

I'm thinking about Angela Carter and tomorrow's seminars when the train fires to life.

'Finally,' I say out loud.

'I'm Callum,' the kid says. Of course he is. He looks like a Callum.

'I'm Jenny.' He offers me his hand, which is both sweet and unpredictable, so I shake it briskly. His handshake is far too limp and his palm is calloused. He has a lot to learn.

'So Callum, are you a student?' I ask, already knowing the answer. 'Or have you got a job? Year out?'

'I'm not a student. Do I look like a fucking student?' Callum rolls his eyes and looks out the window like I've just accused him of being a kiddy fiddler.

'No need to swear.' I raise my eyebrows. 'And I don't know. What does a student look like?'

'Not like me. Soz.' He sniffed and unzipped his jacket. It was taking up at least a seat and a half.

'What are you apologising for?' I ask. 'Not looking like a student?'

'Nah. Swearing. Not used to ladies.' He cracks a smile at this and raises his eyebrows. I give a little snigger. I can't help myself. 'You, like, a teacher or summat?'

'Wow. Almost.' My mouth feels fuzzy and all my spit has turned to chewing gum. 'I'm a lecturer. God, I'm thirsty.'

'Here.' Callum unscrews a water bottle in his pocket and offers me some. 'If you don't mind my germs.'

'Oh, thank you,' I say gratefully and take a huge gulp, swilling it round my mouth and trying not to think of the plaque and disease floating about in the water. I feel the cack in my mouth start to melt away. I take another sip and pass it back. 'I really needed that.'

'Awww. See. Good for summat.'

'Have you got a job Callum?' I am speaking slower. I can tell.

'I'm a sparky. For me dad, like.'

'Really? That's great,' I say. 'Is that something you've always wanted to do?'

'I dunno.' He shrugs his shoulders and looks everywhere but at me. 'Just like the pay, me.'

'I'm sure there's more to it than that. What made you interested?'

'Nowt else to do. I'm thick.'

'I very much doubt you're thick,' I say. 'Otherwise people wouldn't trust you, quite literally, with their lives.'

'What you mean?' He wipes his nose with the back of his hand and I try not to curl my lip.

'Well. I can't even change the fuse in my plug. I guess you rewire entire buildings? Make it safe so families don't get electrical fires? Doesn't sound like a stupid job to me.'

He shrugs again, but meets my eye this time.

'I was shit in school. Just couldn't be bothered like. Just wanted out of there. I bet you're an English teacher aren't you?'

'Why do you say that?'

'I was shit at English. Failed my GCSE.'

'How old are you now Callum?'

'How old do I look?' He grins and leans forward.

'No, I'm not playing that game. You're what? Nineteen, twenty?'

'Yeah.' He sits back.

'And what's it like, working with your dad? Are you close?'

'He's aww-ight.'

'Just the two of you?'

'Nah it's like, his company. Travel round. Building sites. I was in Edinburgh yesterday. London next week.' He swigs out of his water bottle and offers me some, but I shake my head. It feels too intimate now.

'You must love that it's not the same every day?'

'Nah, it's dull as fu— Dull as.'

'What do you like about it?'

'Nowt. The pay.'

I try not to roll my eyes.

'What if you got a job that you loved that paid just as well?'

'Like what?'

'You tell me.'

'I dunno.' He looks back out the window. 'What the fuck is wrong with this train?'

'What did you want to be when you were little?'

'Dunno.'

'Don't say that. Everyone remembers.'

'Dunno. Fireman, maybe.' He looks at me, then looks down, his cheeks a faint pink.

'That would be amazing. Don't you still want to do that?'

'Nah. Can't anyway. You need like, a GCSE in English and Maths.'

'Have you thought about re-sitting?'

'Aren't I a bit fucking old for school? Anyway, got a job han' I?'

'You can do it at night college. So you can still work during the day.'

The train roars to life and we move with a jolt.

'Can ya?'

I smile and pull out my phone. By the time we reach his stop I have texted him links to the local college pages on adult education and to the Firefighters UK home page. I also could have sworn I felt his fingers tracing my knee where it crossed over my leg but I decided to leave that one alone and hope to God I was imagining it.

'This is me,' Callum says as the train slows and he pockets his phone. 'Thanks. You've been mint. You on Insta?'

'No, I don't do social media.' I smile. 'Who needs that anxiety?'

'That's a shame.' Yes, it was definitely his fingers.

'OK Callum,' I laugh, 'take care of yourself.' I wave as he unfolds himself into the aisle. His trainers are so white it blinds me. He gets off the train and I deliberately look away from the window, and catch the eye of a man in a grey crumpled suit.

'That was really nice of you,' he says.

He looks a bit pissed. But then, so do I.

'Ah. Not really.'

'Totally was. They just want to be heard don't they?'

'Don't we all?' I ask ruefully and lay my head back on the seat. I close my eyes and let the warm, familiar buzz wash over me. What if he becomes a firefighter and goes on to save the lives of children? Or the life of the person who discovers the cure for cancer. I'm enjoying my fantasy when my phone buzzes.

I open my messages.

And there it is.

A dick pic.

A huge erect penis in the hand of Callum. I know it's his because I recognise the Sheffield United tattoo on his wrist.

I let out an involuntary groan. Three dots flash up.

Ur so sxy. I wanna fuck u all over.

I don't understand what he means by this. All over where? In my ear? I consider asking him to work on his sentence construction but decide better of it and start flicking through my emails.

I don't block him though. It might damage his confidence.

CHAPTER THREE

Simon

Half an hour after

The Police are playing somewhere. I can hear the tinny noise coming from someone's halls of residence room over the lecture theatre, or maybe from someone's ear buds. But it's definitely the dulcet tones of 'Don't Stand So Close to Me'. The original. Not the re-mix. I can't believe this song hasn't been banned by the feminazis. Fem Soc should be clawing at their door.

And for this one, well I wouldn't blame them. How can they get their knickers in a twist about 'Baby, It's Cold Outside', and then this goes under the radar?

If you listen to the lyrics, that creepy teacher is giving her lifts home in his warm dry car, and yet all the blame is pointed at this young Lolita-like seductress. That whole song is pinned on the daily struggle and terrible predicaments of a poor young male teacher and how hard it is to be worshipped by teenage girls and keep your lad in your pants.

I'm sorry. But it's not hard to not fuck under-age girls.

It's not hard to not fuck over-age girls either.

Just. Don't. Do. It.

I wish I'd not left my coat in the office – I'll have to go back now when my car is much nearer. Turning sharply into the throng, a lad from my workshops, I think he's called Reece, stops me. He is waffling at me about some band I recommended. I nod and grin but I'm not really listening because I can sense a pair of eyes on me and I know before I even look that it's her.

She's there. Here. Right now. Evie Richards. Stood in my path. Flanked by her ginger mate, who made some bitchy comment last year on Twitter saying that I was warmer to the male students than the girls.

If only she knew.

The first thing they do is add me on Twitter. That's safe, it's public. A forum for open debate. After a while, they start sending me Facebook friend requests. I have a separate work one so that's OK too. Creating Facebook groups for teaching is a valid learning community. But then the direct messages start. I'm careful to ignore them. But when you've been drinking, or you just forget it's not an email, you reply. Casually. And then you're suddenly in a conversation. And then before you know it you get a selfie and she's in a club with her tits bursting out of her top and you have to ignore it, and go back to square one and feel like a prick for replying in the first place.

Best to keep it on email. If they DM you, you email them back.

Jenny told me that. Mind you, I'm pretty sure she's not got nineteen-year-olds sending her dick pics. I wonder where her firm resolve would be then.

I'm not stupid.

Twelve years ago, when I was twenty-eight, it was like I'd been dropped cock-first into a ball pit. They'd bat their false eyelashes and turn up to one-to-ones in tiny skirts showing off their endless legs. Now I always make sure to set the timer on my phone. Keep my door open and not spend too long in one-to-ones.

It's easier to banter with the boys. I ask them about their bands and go to their gigs. We compare guitars. They dish the dirt on the girls on the course. We talk Netflix and I give them bar recommendations. We laugh.

I'm a cool guy. Yeah, I know about the cool girl phenomenon. You think that shit doesn't apply to men?

It's exhausting. I can't tell a female student she looks nice, but I can like a male's new ink. And it's everywhere. Cool guys, we have to have a job that isn't for a tax-dodging palm-oil-guzzling company, but equally we need the same kind of salary as if we did. We have to be able to cry at the John Lewis advert and be able to unblock the drain. Not allowed a dad bod, but also not allowed to spend time at the gym. If we lift weights we are misogynistic posers, if we run we are aggressive. If we declare ourselves as feminists we are stealing their thunder. We have to be vegan but not enough to make you feel guilty. We have to be climate change advocates but having an electric car makes us tossers. We are permanently confused, wandering around like toddlers learning how to run, with a slight fear that at any point someone is going to club us over the head with a cricket bat because smashing the patriarchy is always trending.

Working in a university, it's constantly thrust down our necks. Microaggressions, diversity courses, pro-feminist language, just-be-better courses.

Modern man. I don't want to be one. I just want to be left the fuck alone.

I nod at Evie and Bronte but they both have weird expressions on their face. I hope Evie is OK. She didn't turn up to her last one-to-one. And she's asked to switch seminar groups. I can't take these things personally, but I'm only flesh and blood. I suspect it's something to do with what happened in the pub, but I didn't think she was the type. She seems a damn sight more mature than the rest of them. Maybe I called it wrong. Wouldn't be the first time.

I pull out my phone and call Becky to tell her I'll be home on time, and as I walk past the girls I try and smile but I'm not sure it comes out right. I can feel my breath start to rattle. I take a deep gasp and tell myself not to be so stupid. But I have a sense of doom knotted in my stomach and I don't know why. I woke up with it a week ago and I can't shake it. It's like there's a black dog following me out of the corner of my eye and every time I turn around to try and catch it, it's gone. I keep seeing single magpies and I start waving like a maniac, saluting, asking how its wife is.

My wife Becky thinks I'm anxious because my new book has gone out to publishers, and it's true that I'm checking my email every ten minutes, desperately hoping that one, just one, will take a chance. This book is different to the others. It's got to be. If not, I am pretty sure my agent will drop me.

I get to my office and my machine springs to life. I haven't done that email form Jenny was banging on about. I really don't get why she can't just type it in herself if she is that desperate for it. It would only take me two minutes to scribble it down for her. I don't know why she has to make everything so complicated.

My heart leaps when I see there's a new email there, but it's just from HR. I can't even be bothered to read it. It'll be about the new promotions round and I don't want to have to sit on the panel again.

I grab my jacket and walk to my car. It's much quieter now, the kids have filtered back to halls, to their digs in town, shoving the buy-one-get-one-free pizzas from the mucky campus takeaway down their beer-crusted necks.

I'll admit it. I keep my eyes out for Evie. I don't want her to hate me. I don't want anyone to hate me. But I get it. She's probably embarrassed.

I close my eyes for a second and rest my head against the

seat. It's like having a naughty cigarette. Every minute of my day is accounted for, apart from this time. This time when dusk is coming and I can sit behind my steering wheel for the few precious moments before I turn the ignition and my thoughts are allowed to be mine. Just mine. Not my students', not Becky's, not Jamie's. Mine.

My head shuffles the memories like a deck of cards and one falls out of the pack.

We are in my twentieth-century dramatic texts seminar. Room G03. It's my least favourite room to teach in because the desks are all in rows, like a classroom and I can't gather everyone in a circle. One entire wall is windows, floor to ceiling, and the autumn leaves ripple over the paths outside, all russets and gold, like a giant rugby strip. The clock tower casts its shadow over the quad and I can see the eyes of the students watching the second hand tick, tick, tick.

It's hard to get a discussion going, so I swing my legs over the first table in the centre and beckon the back row to do the same, until we're all higgledy, on different levels. Some stand leaning on the edges of the tables, some are still on swivel chairs, others are sat cross-legged directly on the desk tops. We look like an Escher painting.

'So, what do we think? Have you watched the Oleanna *video clips? Where would you like to start?'*

I lean forward, my elbows on my knees. I am manspreading. I know I am.

Evie is sat to my left. Legs crossed.

'I read online that when the professor attacks Carol, people in the audience started cheering. I thought that was shocking. That's so misogynistic,' Bronte pipes up.

I stare at her. I am sure she is not meant to be in this class. But then neither is Elodie, and I let that slide. The faculty has such ridiculous rules and policies. I really don't give a shit which group they come to. As long as they turn up. I moaned about it once to Jenny but she went on and on about attendance registers and keeping group sizes consistent, then she suggested a horrendous red tape exercise where seminar swap requests had to be entered in a form and considered by a panel. I felt like ripping my own arm off just so I had something to throw at her.

'Yes, you absolutely can read his character as sexist. Elitist. His views on higher education are condescending. Do you think he would have treated her any differently if her socio-economic status was different? Or if she were male?' I offer.

I cast my eyes around the group. I can normally tell who has something to say but is too afraid to speak up. They have a sheen in their irises. A twitch of a smile.

Evie has both.

'What about you?' I nod towards her. 'What feelings do you have about that?'

'I actually don't think gender has anything to do with it. It's not a battle of the sexes, it's a battle of power. They both want it, and it switches all the way through.'

'And do you think that's conscious?' I ask her. 'Is the professor deliberately trying to exert power in the first act?'

'He's too egotistical to think he needs to.'

'Very good,' I say and move on, drawing in a guy who is stooped like a willow tree from the back of the room.

*

I shake myself like a wet dog, and drive home.

Becky is wiping the kitchen counters when I walk through the back door. She's in a faded Kiss T-shirt and her hair is piled up on top of her head, with curly bits dangling out. No make-up. This is how I think she looks her most beautiful.

'Hey babe. How was your day?'

'OK.' She shrugs. 'We went for a walk in the park to get some air. Jamie is watching something totally inappropriate through there.' She nods at the open living room door. We are slack about stuff like that. To be honest anything that makes him happy, we give him.

'Ah, OK. I'll go through and watch it with him. What's for tea? I tried calling to see if you needed me to pick anything up.'

She looks tired. More than usual.

'Curry. It's in the slow cooker. Sorry, I was changing the sheets in your bedroom.'

'Oh, thanks.' I rub the bridge of my nose.

'No problem. Any news today?' Becky opens the cupboard and brings out a packet of microwave rice.

'No. Tumbleweed.'

'They've only had it a couple of weeks. Give it time.'

She smiles and winks and God I love her. Her generous curves in that faded T-shirt. I love the fact her skin is sallow and her hair needs a wash because she has been taking care of Jamie all day, and will do again tonight so I can write. I love her for everything she has sacrificed for us.

One day I'll pay her back.

This is my third book out there, my first go at children's books. I'm pretty sure this is my last chance saloon. It could mean everything to us.

It was Becky who convinced me to try something different after my last thriller, *The Spitting Games*, didn't sell. Great writing, they'd said, brilliant twists. But not enough empathy for the characters. Not quite vivid enough.

I'd gone into a sullen slump after that one. Writers think getting an agent is the hard bit. They are right. It's tough. All those query letters. Just hoping, someone, anyone, will like it enough to read the full thing. But it's just the first rung of a never-ending rickety ladder with missing rungs and a wobbly right side.

Becky had said I should write something closer to my heart. And she was right. I wrote *Blink* over the summer. Start to finish in eight weeks and I don't mind admitting I'd had tears in my eyes when I wrote 'The End'.

It's about a ten-year-old boy with a super power. When he blinks he can teleport through time. Only he doesn't know where and when he will land, but it's always a great moment of historical significance. Then he has to work out why he's there, and how to make history happen the way it should.

Becky read it to Jamie as I wrote it. He's the harshest critic ever but he loved it. Well. He would, I dedicated it to him. If I could sell it and if the series took off, then I could drop my hours, help out more here. Becky could even think about going back to work. I know how much she misses her classroom.

I accept my plate of lamb and spinach. It smells of cinnamon and cloves and my stomach rumbles.

'Right, if you're going through there with Jamie, I'm going to go and have a bath.' Becky rolls her head around and I hear at least three cracks.

'Sounds like you need it.'

'Yeah,' she says ruefully.

I go into the living room and my heart burns when I see Jamie in his chair. Every time. It never goes, or fades away. He can't turn and look at me but I know he knows I'm there.

'Hey mate.' I bend down and kiss him on his cheek. 'Your mum says you're watching something inappropriate.' I look at the screen. There are some buildings being blown up and a blonde woman screaming, dirt streaking her face.

'Any good?'

I look at Jamie's eyes and he swivels them to meet mine. He smiles with his eyes. I actually see them change. It's beautiful.

Jamie blinks and I translate the pattern.

We are on a waiting list for a computer now that speaks for him. Becky can't wait. But I will miss it. Communicating with him through his eyes. Like when he was first diagnosed. After the accident, we had no idea he was still in there, locked in there, his mind still fully aware, growing, reaching, expanding.

Until I looked into his eyes and he was there. My boy. I saw it all. Can still see it all. One blink for yes. Two blinks for no. It's how we talked. For weeks. Months even. Other patients, they could spell things out. Those with locked-in syndrome. But Jamie. He hadn't even learnt to read. So that's how we did it. One blink for I love you. Two blinks for take me home.

'I love you too buddy,' I reply.

Then I settle down on the sofa next to his wheelchair and we watch an unknown city burn.

Later, when it's time for bed, Becky comes through with Jamie's medication. She looks all fluffy in her over-sized grey shirt and pink socks. For a minute I miss her so much I can't breathe. To curl up with her, bury my face in the back of her hair and smell the pretentious shampoo she claims she needs to tame the curls. To hook my leg over hers and smell her morning breath. All these things I took for granted. Even when I hated her I loved her. Now I love her because I have no other choice.

'My night,' she says, kissing Jamie on the cheek. 'Can you get the aroma thing on, Simon?' She begins to wheel our son through the living room and into the downstairs bedroom.

I fiddle with the sensory lamp, and the lights flicker softly and cast constellations on the ceiling. The aroma diffuser puffs and glows in muted, sweet tones. This is not the bedroom of a ten-year-old boy.

We get Jamie changed, a comforting routine. Our eyes don't meet, and we each carry out our own tasks until he is moved into bed and his chair is pushed up against the wall. Becky sits on the edge of his bed with a glass of water and a toothbrush and I massage his feet.

'You all set?' I ask Becky.

'Yep. Night.' She looks over her shoulder and smiles so quick I almost don't catch it.

The bed for her is on the other side of the room, its duvet crumpled, meaning it was me who slept in it last night and didn't bother making it. I feel a pang of guilt. Tomorrow, when it's my turn, the pillows will be plumped.

I bend over and kiss my son on his cheek. It's wet and his breath smells of Colgate.

'I love you Jamie, best boy in all the world.'

'Love you dad,' he blinks and I rub my thumb in circles on his palm and remember how fast his little legs would run in the garden when I chased him, pretending to be a monster. So fast the devil couldn't catch him, my mum would say.

But the devil did.

I go upstairs with a cup of tea and climb into bed even though it's only 10 p.m., but Jamie doesn't need the TV blaring next door. I open the iPad and scroll to Netflix. It's still set to *Glee* from when me and Jamie binge-watched season three a couple of weeks ago and I let it spring to life.

I always thought he'd sing.

The dark-haired girl reminds me a bit of Evie. But not as tall. I snap it closed.

I'd cried after the first time, because for a second I'd imagined Becky finding out. Becky screaming and thumping my chest and throwing me out.

And it would be over. And I'd be living my life without her . . .

And I'd cried because, for a second, all I'd felt was relief.

CHAPTER FOUR
Evie

The day after

The dead rabbit was leaking.

Stale blood was dripping from a hole at the bottom of the Tesco carrier bag on the windowsill and the stench was overpowering.

Evie dropped her bag on the kitchen table and put her hand over her mouth.

'Jesus!' Bronte gagged. 'Harvey. HARVEY!' she hollered into the hallway.

'This is sick and wrong.' Evie turned away from the carrier bag as Harvey opened his door a crack at the top of the hallway stairs.

'Harvey!' Bronte stood with her hands on her hips. At 5 ft 3 ins to his 6 ft, she was little compared to him, but fierce. 'It's like an eighties horror film in there. Throw that rabbit away. It stinks. It's going to get maggots.'

'I'm letting it bleed out,' Harvey said in his monotone voice. The smell of his room drifted out into the hall. Oven chips and oil.

'You can't seriously be thinking about cooking it,' Bronte said. 'You'll be ill.'

'Finn ate that cod head after it had been down the back of the radiator for seven weeks,' Harvey pointed out.

'That was for a bet and he got £150 and a night in hospital.'

Evie retched in her mouth. She hadn't even been there but it was legendary. Apparently.

'How did you even think it was OK to kill it? I'm pretty sure you're not allowed guns in this country.'

'It's an air rifle. I'm licensed.'

'Fucking mentalist.' Bronte shook her head and stood to the side, nodding to the kitchen. 'Now, please! Or I'm calling the landlord.'

Harvey sniffed and lolloped down the stairs. Evie ducked out of his way and lowered her eyes. It made her nervous the way he didn't join in with the cooking or Netflix nights, or even have a late-night Saturday beer with them in the kitchen, talking about nothing and saying everything. He didn't have a games console or anything so why was he spending so much time in his room? Probably polishing his rabbit shooting gun like some farmer whose crops hadn't turned.

Harvey hadn't known anyone in the house either before this year. He'd taken the room meant for Tommy, Josh's best friend who'd taken a year-long leave of absence. But, unlike

Evie who had bent over backwards to fit in, Harvey had pretty much nailed his door shut. He ate tins of Stagg Chilli cold from the can and disappeared at weekends to young farmer conventions or shooting parties. Bronte couldn't bear to even breathe the same air as him. She said it stank.

Evie watched him as he picked up the Tesco bag one-handed and drops of russet liquid splattered gruesomely across the floor.

'Jesus, Harvey.' Bronte retched. 'You're going to have to clean that up.'

He didn't answer but stamped on the bin pedal with one heavy-booted foot.

'No, not in there.' Evie coughed up, and pulled the neck of her T-shirt up to cover her nose and mouth. 'Sorry, Harvey, but Bronte is right. We'll get maggots.' The stench was worse now that the carcass was swinging in the air, even in its plastic shroud.

''Sake!' Harvey looked up at her from underneath his tatty baseball cap. 'Where am I meant to put it then?'

'You'll have to take it to the outside bins,' Bronte said, reaching for the mop. 'Just take it before it bleeds out more.'

Evie felt her breakfast oats erupt into heavy bubbles deep inside her gut.

'God, what is his problem?' Bronte shook her head as she squirted cleaning fluid onto the floor. 'What kind of loon shoots rabbits in the park?'

'Do you think he's a bit unhinged?' Evie hugged herself and peered out of the kitchen window to the back alley.

Harvey swung the bag into the big black bin then took a packet of cigarettes out of his back pocket. 'Why can't he vape like a normal person?'

'I have no idea how he even affords to smoke.' Bronte was putting some serious elbow grease into the floor. It was looking shinier than it had for months.

'Do you want a hand with that?' Evie said.

'No, but I might as well do the whole floor now.'

'You should have made Harvey do it.'

They both looked outside to watch Harvey perching on the back wall and lighting up.

'I can't cope with it congealing on the floor. He won't do it properly.' Bronte went back to scrubbing.

'He's a minger. I'll wash up then. God, I wish people wouldn't leave dirty plates in the sink. Can't they just stack them up on the side? I can't get in properly. It's like a nuclear holocaust in here.' Evie ran the tap and squirted washing-up liquid over the plates. It was so cheap it didn't even foam.

'Next year, maybe we could look for a flat just you and me?' Bronte said. 'Off campus maybe.'

'Sure,' Evie said, after a few seconds.

'I mean, just a suggestion,' Bronte said quickly.

'No, yeah, let's take a look at some options.' Evie smiled. 'Oh hey, I forgot to tell you. I've been moved seminar groups, I think.' She turned off the tap and fished her phone out of her back pocket. 'Look, it's showing up on a Monday now.' She scrolled to her timetable app and flashed it in front of Bronte. 'I've got Jenny instead.'

'Oh that's good.' Bronte pulled her glasses down from the top of her head and squinted. 'Oh, you know what? Maybe I should ask to be moved too? I mean, obviously I know all about it. I feel uncomfortable.'

Evie felt her chest tighten. 'Yeah. I mean. I guess you could ask?'

'OK. I will.' Bronte pulled her glasses back onto the top of her head. 'Can you still help me dye my hair tonight?'

'Absolutely.' Evie pushed down her thumb cuticle until her skin was peeling back from the flesh. 'I'm going to head over to the commons this afternoon and get a head start on my contemporary women's lit essay.'

'Do you know what question you're doing?' Bronte asked. 'I might actually head over with you.'

Evie turned to the sink and closed her eyes, taking a deep breath. 'Yeah, great. Actually, I've devised my own. Jenny and I discussed it and she said it's OK.'

'You've written your own question? I didn't even know you could do that? What is it?'

Evie paused. 'It's to do with how *The Handmaid's Tale* isn't a feminist dystopia at all, but an apex of power, with both sexes at either end.'

'Cool. Oh I might do something like that. Maybe we can research together?'

'I had to get permission first,' Evie said apologetically. 'It's because some of the modules this year have crossed over from my old uni. So I'm trying to make sure I'm doing different stuff.'

'Oh, OK. Anyway, I'll walk with you.'

Once they were outside, Evie took a deep breath and let the air fill her lungs and body. Her ribcage felt tight. She was aware she was only offering one-word answers and the occasional nod to Bronte's babble, which only seemed to make her talk all the more to fill the gaps. After a while it became a dull hum and thud in her ears. She needed quiet.

They scanned themselves into the commons, a hybrid glass building next to the library that served as a study space, with work pods and plug-in points, breakout spaces and online resource screens. You could even check out a real-life book with ink on it from the library next door and have it delivered via some drop-down system to the cluster desks.

Evie was looking forward to burying her head in some Atwood for a while, and blocking out the noise.

She'd checked her email on the walk and Louise from HR had emailed her. They'd spoken to the head of English, confidentially, and she no longer had any more classes with Simon. Lectures still, but no small group teaching. She'd also reassured her that while procedures were being followed, he wouldn't be marking her work.

Evie still wasn't sure exactly what those procedures were.

Her stomach churned for the second time that day.

'Oh no.' Bronte came to a standstill. 'Someone's at my desk.'

Evie followed her gaze to a group of international students on the left-hand side of the wide, open layout first floor, sprawled in the little nook that Bronte favoured.

'We can sit upstairs.' Evie nodded at the next level and the wide spiral stairs that joined the two. 'It's always quieter.'

'No, no.' Bronte nudged Evie. 'Oh God. I NEED my spot.'

'Bronte, just come upstairs,' Evie said impatiently and shifted her laptop bag to her other hip.

'Maybe we could see if they are leaving soon?' Bronte chewed her bottom lip.

'For God's sake,' Evie snapped. 'I've got to get on Bronte. Either come with me or stay down here.' She marched towards the staircase ignoring the hurt in Bronte's eyes.

'Hey.' Bronte grabbed her arm. 'What's up? Did I do something?'

Evie turned round and took another deep breath. 'No, I'm sorry, I'm just a bit tense. I'm worried about Simon. About what's happening. I just want to get lost in some studying for a while, block it all out.'

'Oh hon, I'm so sorry.' Bronte grimaced. 'What a twat. Me, I mean. Of course. Look, you find a spot and I'll go and grab us a couple of lattes OK?'

'Thanks.' Evie smiled. 'That would be great.'

She watched Bronte turn and scan herself out. It was like suddenly losing two stone in weight and she felt her shoulders come down from her ears. It wasn't that she didn't appreciate Bronte. She really did. But the suffocation could be draining. She just wasn't used to it. She couldn't even walk to the shop round the corner for milk without Bronte wanting to come. Finn and Liam joked that they were joined at the hip, and Evie would laugh it off and ignore the hurt in Kelly's eyes. God, female friendships were so complicated. She'd been in a relationship for most of secondary school so those dramas had barely touched the sides. She'd struggled to even believe that they happened and thought they must only exist in young-adult books and tween films. Last year all the pictures on Bronte's Insta were of the two of them, her arm wrapped round Kelly's neck, selfies in the Sugarhouse, filters with rabbit ears in pyjamas. She felt like she was intruding to start with. When they asked her to watch box sets with them, she assumed it was sympathy. But when one night she was putting on her lipstick to go down to the union for Friday Fizz, Bronte seemed genuinely surprised when Evie asked if Kelly was coming too.

'Oh I dunno. I'd better text her,' Bronte had said with a grimace. Kelly turned up an hour later. She'd been in her room the whole time.

Soon Kelly had become quieter, less involved, started to spend more time with her law department friends. Evie wasn't sure who was moving away from who. Would she get ditched in the same way? Did she want to be?

The second floor was quieter and she got settled in a four-way booth, spreading out her books and firing up her laptop. The silence was precious. Just the rustle of papers, the muted hush of group chatter, the scratch and scrunch of pen on paper and the tapping of keys. It was almost like whale music.

Evie let her head fall into her hands and for the first

time since she'd been in Louise's office, she let herself think carefully.

Coerced.

The word was still there, niggling, piggling, as Bronte would say.

'Fairytale of New York' had been playing and the smell of mulled wine and cheap multi-coloured fairy lights were rousing the Christmas spirit. That was the first time Simon had said her name. The last night before semester ended and they were all packing up boxes, if parents were picking them up. Bags, if like Evie, they were catching a train.

It hadn't been like this the Christmas before. Then, Evie had been too heartbroken to go to lectures, horrified at the mere thought of going home to the Lakes in case she bumped into the boy who, until a couple of weeks ago, had sworn she was the love of his life and that being at different universities wouldn't change a thing.

She'd not made as many friends as she would have if she'd thrown herself into freshers' events and joined her flatmates on retro nights out held in clubs where sweat dripped from the ceiling and five-pound rounds resulted in rainbow puke clogging up the toilets. Instead she'd visited him. She'd thought he would be pleased, surprised.

He'd certainly been surprised. He'd still been gentle though, warm and kind as ever. But there'd been something not quite right that she hadn't been able to put her finger on. She'd left his uni awkwardly two days in. But by the time she arrived back at hers, then she had missed the first-night bonding sessions and couldn't join in with the jokes.

She'd got herself a part-time job at Tesco and saved up for train fares. She'd only managed to visit him one more time. He'd been distant. Cuddly. But there'd been no dinners out. He'd kept her away from his new pack of friends that he'd told her about over Facetime, even though she'd been desperate to meet them, to be the cool girlfriend. To be involved in his new life.

The sex had been dry and half-hearted. She'd had to stop herself from crying as she'd stared over his shoulder at his mixed martial arts poster collection and realised the look he'd tried to hide in his eyes. But it was nearing Christmas and she'd known what that did to him. It wasn't her. It was the Krampus.

His kiss goodbye at the station had been agony. She'd wanted to scream out, to cry 'don't do this'. If he'd done it then and there, she would have begged. She'd have ugly-cried. There would have been no grace, no dignity.

It had come later. A phone call. After four years. A phone call. And her life as she'd known it was over.

The girls in her flat had been sympathetic. They'd shown up with ice cream and DVDs. But she'd not bonded with them early enough. She'd felt embarrassed by their clumsy attempts to comfort her. Somehow it had made her feel lonelier. She'd felt even lonelier when they'd left, boxes in the boots of cars, heading home to parties and school friends they could brag to about their new lives.

Evie hadn't been able to bear it. She hadn't wanted to slink home with her tail between her legs and listen to the I-told-you-so's. Especially after she'd accused her old bestie of just being jealous when she'd questioned the longevity of their relationship once university had started. She'd lied and said she had too much work to do until the morning of Christmas Eve, when she hadn't been able to bear the silence any longer.

She'd caught a rattling, freezing train to Kendal and her dad had picked her up at the station before early doors. He hadn't remembered to order a turkey, so on Christmas Day she'd cooked them a chicken she'd bought from the petrol station. She hadn't called her friends, or him. She'd watched her dad drink too much whiskey and changed his damp bedsheets. She'd batch-cooked and cut Buddy the terrier's toenails.

Her dad had been asleep on the couch as the clock approached midnight on New Year's Eve, so she'd taken Buddy for a walk around the village, and when the fireworks lit up the black sky all she could see was grey.

She had thought it couldn't get any worse.

She'd thought wrong.

A week later she had driven out to Ullswater, towards Aira Force. She'd known it would be packed with tourists, even on a drizzly, miserable Wednesday. Hikers in their primary coloured pac a macs. Pulled-up woolly socks and sticks. But she knew the paths and the crags, the crannies, the short cuts. She'd been scrambling up here since she could walk. There was a little cave formation, off the beaten track, where if you braved a sheer drop that cracked between two rocks, you could clamber up, almost right behind the waterfall. There, you could smell the mud in the water, listen to it crashing over the elephant grey of the slippery, shiny stones and cliffs. Hide behind the white spray. A perfect cove for first and last kisses.

Evie had traced their initials they had once carved in the rock, the crudely jagged heart, and let the falls drown the screams in her head. It had almost been dark when she'd climbed back down, although it was still only late afternoon. There had been no sunset, no mellow sun kissing the rocks, just a sharp descent into evening, as if someone had slammed a door shut and blocked out the light.

She was careful with her footing and stuck to her regular route back to the car park, it had almost been empty, with the occasional walker marching towards their car. She almost hadn't seen him, but then the amber glow of a car's headlights had caught him. In the thicket. He'd squinted and held his arm up over his eyes. But she'd seen him. Kissing someone else, kissing someone that wasn't her up against the tree.

Evie had dived out of the way, and ducked behind her car, squinting. Once the car had driven off it was dark again and all she could see was the purple shadows of two people, whispering frantically. Angrily almost. Their lips had been close together, passionate, angry kisses.

She'd watched until the darkness had covered them

completely. And then she'd driven home. That night she'd opened a fresh box of Hugo Boss, the aftershave she'd bought him for Christmas. She'd dowsed herself in his smell. The loneliness had been suffocating.

And now, even with the chatter around her, a real group of friends, she felt like an imposter. Like she would be caught out at any second. That they would discover the real her. Vapid. Shallow. Always getting the joke a few seconds too late.

Simon had sat next to her that night. The night before she caught the train home for Christmas.

'Sorry, it's Evie? Yes? I'm still getting used to everyone's names. I know, I should know them by now.'

Evie smiled. 'Yes. Don't worry about it. You've got a lot to learn.'

Simon raised his eyebrows and laughed. 'Oh, have I now?'

Evie turned pink. 'That came out wrong.'

'And Bronte. Now you're an easy one to remember from last year.' He rested his elbows on the table.

'I've heard it all before.' Bronte rolled her eyes good-naturedly. 'Is Jenny coming?'

'I shouldn't think so.' Simon shrugged. 'She doesn't usually. She thinks drinking with students is asking for trouble.'

'What do you mean?' Evie cupped her chin in her hand. She widened her eyes.

'Well. One drink leads to two drinks, two leads to three, three leads to the Jacuzzi . . .'

Evie laughed. 'Seriously? You've been in Jacuzzis with students? I'd have thought that would land you in hot water.'

'Ahhh, I see what you did there!' Simon pointed. 'No, of course not, I'm only joking. I'll be out of here before things get lairy but we're all adults. And I like talking to you all outside of lectures. Probably had some of my best teaching sessions in the pub. Easier to get the debates going. Ah, brilliant, Robert's here.' He nodded to an older lecturer everyone assumed was pushing retirement, given his no-fucks-given attitude and his tendency to glaze over in seminars. Even when it was him talking.

'So Robert's not worried about Jacuzzis then?' Bronte looked back over her shoulder.

'Ah don't let him fool you. He was quite the devil in his day.'

Simon waved Robert over.

'Tell, tell.' Evie grinned.

'No.' Simon winked. 'I'm good at keeping secrets.'

And Evie felt as if the floor had tilted.

'Here you go.' Bronte now put a cardboard cup in front of Evie, pulling her to attention. 'Hey, what's wrong? Are you crying?'

'No. No.' Evie rubbed her eyes. 'I'm just really tired. Thanks hon.' She sipped her latte and winced as it burned her tongue. Bronte was frowning at her, so she quickly hit enter on her laptop, and tried to look busy.

She didn't really have that much research to do for her essay. She'd already done half of it. What she really wanted was the quiet. So she dawdled for a while, checking her emails, her socials, and noticed there was a new post on The Common Room by Student Village Vixen, the university's answer to Fleet Street Fox. Her posts were always good, if near the knuckle. Her posts over the strikes last semester were hilarious, digging into students who demanded their tuition fees back, yet hadn't been to a single lecture all term.

Evie clicked. And then her hands started to shake.

It was only a matter of time before the Me Too movement hit campuses. Lecturers sleeping with students is hardly anything new.

It's just like people sleeping with their bosses to get up the career ladder. Oh how very eighties. I'm sure some women, and some men, have decided a quick blow job wouldn't hurt their grades.

Excuse the pun, but what leaves a bad taste in my mouth is when they then go running to complain about it.

I am not victim-blaming, or slut-shaming here. You want to shag your lecturer? Go right ahead. But don't then play the sexism card or claim you were forced into it – unless of course you actually were. Then nail their balls to the wall.

Yes, as Ross in Friends *said, it's frowned upon. Shagging your employees when you're the boss is also frowned upon. But it's not because it's 'an abuse of power', it's because you're leaving yourself wide open to claims of favouritism and rightly so.*

Be an adult about it. Stop line-managing them. In this case, swap seminar groups. But don't play this Bambi wide-eyed innocent card. It's an embarrassment to women. You get propositioned by someone you don't want to sleep with? Say no thank you. Move on. Just like you would in any bar or club or on Tinder. Swipe left.

Don't go running to HR because you felt you weren't in a position to say no. Come on Tess of the D'Urbervilles. We've moved on since then.

Let me be clear. If any lecturer sexually harassed you, used sex as a bribe, or tried to force you into anything, I would be baying for their blood.

But just for entering into a consensual act, or relationship with another ADULT, and being hung out to dry for it because of a job title – anyone else think there's another victim here? Me too.

'Holy Shit.' Evie's hands flew to her mouth.

'What's wrong?' Bronte looked up sharply.

Evie opened and closed her mouth like a fish.

'What?' Bronte pushed back her chair and came round to Evie's side of the table. 'What . . . Oh!' She leant down over Evie's shoulder. 'What . . . the . . . hell?' Her breath came out in a hiss.

'Who wrote this?'

Evie gulped. Adrenalin shot up and down her limbs and her heart was racing.

'It's Student Village Vixen. How . . . Oh my God. How do people know? Do they know it's me?'

'I'm sure it's just a coincidence.' Bronte put her hands onto Evie's shoulders. 'Babe, don't give it another thought. Look at the comments. Everyone's calling her out. She's like Katie Hopkins, she only says stuff to get hits.'

'It's like this has been written about me.' Evie sat back in her chair. 'Bronte. Oh my God. I can't do this.'

'Of course you can. Come on.' Bronte rubbed her back. 'Like I said, it's a coincidence. This stuff's in the news at the moment. Just wipe it from your mind. Pretend you never read it.'

Evie snapped her laptop shut and stared straight ahead.

'Want to ditch the studying and grab a drink?' Bronte said.

She shook her head. 'No. No it's OK. You're right. I just need to think about something else.'

'OK.' Bronte went back to her chair and opened a book, but every couple of minutes Evie could feel her darting little worried looks. Each one was like a hammer to her head, so she opened up her laptop again to block the view.

'Don't read it,' Bronte hissed.

'I'm not,' Evie snapped. 'I'm ordering some books.'

Clicking onto her university account, she noticed another email from HR. This one was from the generic address though. Not Louise's direct one.

It was an invitation to an official meeting on Monday. She could bring someone with her. There were some attached policy and procedure documents.

She clicked back onto The Common Room and scrolled down the blog, looking for any new comments. Most were horrified. Accusing Vixen of never having the guts to say something so crass if it wasn't anonymous. Calling her a rape sympathiser.

Evie wondered if she was sat at a computer, tears pricking her eyelids, scrolling down these comments and wanting to scream back, you've got it all wrong. That's not what I said.

She remembered Simon's eyes on her in the lecture theatre the day after it'd happened. The way she'd walked out of the bathroom into the banging noise. Sore, humiliated. She'd felt vomit in her throat.

Inspired, pushed, challenged. Even angry. That's how she should be feeling towards these people she was landing herself in such colossal life-changing debt to have the privilege of being taught by.

Not degraded.

This was all for the greater good.

A couple of hours later and she was feeling much better. HR had already told her that no details about her would be made public at any point. She was anxious. Tired. Her brain was buzzing. She even enjoyed Bronte's mindless chatter about what they should cook for tea on the walk home.

When they got back to the house she was even getting hungry and eager to smell the garlic and hear the fizz and pop of the onions softening as Bronte started to prepare a Bolognese. She popped on the kettle and then gathered up her books.

'I'll just clear these up and then I'll come and help' she promised Bronte as she went out into the hall. The kitchen fire door slammed shut behind her and made her jump. It always did. But this time, it wasn't just the noise. There was something else. Something wrong.

She breathed in and a foul smell hit her in the back of her throat, so much it made her stomach turn. Her first thought was that the rabbit was back, but Harvey's door was closed. And the smell was so strong it had to be something closer. She looked down at her feet to make sure she hadn't trodden something in with her, and her eyes swept up the stairs. It was a livery, rotten smell. Like something her dad would throw out from the fridge after forgetting about it for weeks.

Almost metallic.

'Eugh . . . guys what's that smell?' she called out, trying to juggle her books to cover her mouth and nose. There was no reply. The kitchen door was too thick and no one else seemed to be in.

She put one foot on the bottom of the stairs and then another. 'Jesus,' she whispered, as she started up the threadbare maroon and yellow swirled carpet. It never smelt great in the hallway, but it was always more the aroma of damp and seventies carpet rather than this.

It smelt of death.

Evie carried on up the stairs, but the smell became even more intense. She didn't want to turn the corner at the top of the landing in fear of seeing yet another shot bunny, splayed out in front of Harvey's door, its eyes glassy and black, seeping blood into the carpet.

Her fingers reached round the corner and flicked on the light. And there, at the end of the hallway, she saw it. Her door.

She jumped back, not even understanding for a second what she was seeing. Just a scrawl and colours. Bad colours. Something red and purple and slimy, something belonging on the insides rather than the outsides, dangling from her door handle.

She screamed in horror, the kind of scream that infiltrated even the heaviest of fire doors.

'Evie, Evie?' Bronte sprinted up the stairs, spatula still in her hand.

Evie was stood rooted to the spot, staring at the word LIAR written in blood across her door, and nailed next to it was what looked like a thick, long tongue dripping a putrid, bile-like fluid onto the floor.

CHAPTER FIVE
Jenny

The day after

I put a cup of herbal tea in front of Elodie. Lavender and liquorice. The smell is calming and I see her inhale and let the steam soothe her damp, raw face.

'It's all going to be OK Elodie. But you have to come and see me next time, OK? Don't get yourself into this state again.'

Elodie nods and sips her tea. 'You've been amazing Jenny. I can't thank you . . .'

I wave it away. 'You put yourself through so much. Did you have a read of those links I sent you?'

'I did, but I just don't think mum will want a stranger in the house.'

'And I don't think your mum would want you to risk not getting your degree. If she knew what you were putting yourself through . . . Look, I'm really not meant to do this, but would you like me to talk to her?'

'No. You've done enough. Honestly. Thank you. And I promise nothing like this will ever happen again.'

'Just, think about getting some help. Promise you'll look into some options? You can't look after your mum forever.'

'I will.' Elodie nods and we chat and idly gossip about who is going out with who on the course, who said what on WhatsApp and we try to decipher who wrote what on the snarky module evaluation forms that Cate had got last year.

Children finding their voices but so, so off-key.

Once her eyes have de-puffed, I hug her and send her on her way. I feel great when I see her with the hint of a smile and a wave as she trots down the corridor, looking a few inches taller than she did went she slunk in.

Some people run, some people meditate. But honestly, the calm I get when I see this. It centres me.

I have an hour before my next small group, so I reply to some emails, and see that I've been nominated for another award. For outstanding pastoral care. My smile falters when I read the email in more detail and see the nomination came from the department rather than the students.

There's a knock at my door and I look up and smile. It's Cate, looking pristine in her bright body-con dress and tidy hair.

'Congratulations! No surprise though.'

'Hi, what are you doing over here?' I smile.

'Meeting upstairs.' She rolls her eyes upwards to where

the main faculty offices are. 'Don't change the subject. Two in a month.'

'Oh.' I try and look as humble as I can. 'No. Actually, it feels a little weird to be nominated for something so . . . well, awful.'

'Hey. You held those kids together after Josh. You started a conversation.' Cate reaches up and pins an escaped lock of hair back into place.

I give her a thin-lipped smile. 'Bit too late though wasn't it?'

'We've been through this.' Cate comes in and shuts my door. 'How's that memorial speech coming?'

'I feel like a fraud.' I shrug. 'I'm no mental health expert, am I? And I'm not saying anything we haven't all been saying now for years.'

'And that's the point. We're not trained for this. We should never have had this amount of pressure put on us. Ohh gossip. Did you hear there's been a complaint from a student in East Asian Studies because her tutor asked her what she was planning to wear to an interview?'

'Male tutor or female?' I asked.

'Female. God can you imagine the furore if it had been a man? Anyway, the student reckoned she was being sexist and not valuing her as a person, and was only thinking about how she'd look.'

I shook my head. 'That's ridiculous.'

'I know, right. We can't win.'

'I just wish we could be human.'

'Don't be silly. You're not human. You're a lecturer. Got to run, wine soon?'

I nod. There's some truth in what she says. Sometimes I think that's why I'm here. Like the hard egg-like toys I used to play with when I was small. You can wibble them and wobble them but they won't fall down.

Cate goes to leave and I turn back to my desk.

My inbox is full to bursting and I hate making the students wait so I tap at my machine and watch my monitor spring to life.

'Oh, I forgot to ask.' Cate bobs her head back round the door frame. 'Any idea what the deal is with Simon?' She looks back out into the corridor over her shoulder and drops her voice.

'No.' My heart does a little jump. 'What do you mean?'

'I've been asked if we've got any research students free to cover some of his teaching. Is he taking a leave of absence or something?'

'Not that I know of,' I say honestly. 'That's odd. He hasn't said anything. I hope everything is OK with his son. Maybe it's hospital visits?'

'Probably. God. You wouldn't wish it on your worst enemy, would you?'

We both fall silent and do the little shake of our heads. There but for the Grace of God. It's not enough. This laughable attempt at a reverie. But we all do it. Every time.

Cate smiles thinly. 'Anyway, see you. Congratulations again.'

I wait until I can no longer hear the dull thump of her Mary Jane heels, then cross over the corridor. Simon's office is locked and dark.

I take a deep breath and go further up the hall and give a gentle rap on the head of department's office door.

'Come in,' I hear. Peter is the only one of us whose door doesn't have a huge glass panel. He tells us it's so he can hide from students, but we all know he means us. He's not the fondest of making decisions or dealing with much outside of his research.

I open the door and walk in. He is there, hunched over his desk, glasses on the end of his nose, all round and smooth and cuddly. He reminds me of Mole from *The Wind in the Willows*. There is beautiful music playing very softly from a radio on his shelf and a smell of pipe tobacco that reminds me instantly of my granddad. Of wellies and newt fishing and corned beef sandwiches.

'Hi Peter.'

'Hello Jennifer.' He looks up and smiles. 'Congratulations on your nomination.'

'Well, thank you very much for putting me forward for it.' I feel almost like curtseying, like a Victorian child being brought to see her papa.

'Oh I had nothing to do with it,' he says, not unkindly. 'You know me, I never know what all these things are,' waving his hand in the air like he was swatting a bee. 'It was Simon, I think.'

'Well.' I feel slightly crestfallen but keep up appearances.

'Actually, I was just wondering about him. Simon, I mean. Is everything OK? Cate just mentioned that she's been asked to cover some teaching and I wondered if there was anything I could do to help.'

Peter sighs and looks down. 'Yes. Well. There might be. I'm hoping it will all blow over sooner rather than later. I've asked the office to sort out immediate cover.'

'It's nothing to do with Jamie is it? Is he OK?'

'Who's . . . Oh his son. No, no. Nothing like that.'

I feel my heart start to canter.

'That's good. I was worried. But is Simon OK?'

Peter puts his pen down and took off his wire-rimmed glasses.

'There's been a complaint Jennifer. He won't be teaching or researching while it's being investigated.'

'You mean he's been suspended?' I say and feel the floor tilt a little.

'I'm trying not to use that word,' Peter says and wipes his lenses with the little cloth he kept by his keyboard. 'But I think he could probably do with a friend right now.' He looks at me meaningfully and I nod, taking the hint.

'Of course.' I do a little bob of my head and then feel stupid, like I am some kind of servant.

I leave the office with his words ringing in my ear.

Oh, Simon. Are you my friend?

By the time I get home, I notice it's lighter than usual and there's a tease of a sunset over the railway. Enid, my obese and narcissistic tabby, opens one eye lazily then looks towards her food bowl, as if I might deign to carry it over to her.

'Tough day, princess?' I stroke her head and she tips it back and lets me rub her throat with my fingers, the ultimate display of trust. 'More lying about, listening to jazz? Doing lines of cat nip?' I drop my bag and head into the kitchen to pour myself a glass of wine.

I thought about calling Simon. Once. Twice. On the train I was so close to texting, I even wrote one out but deleted it.

If it goes as far as I think it will, I may well be called as a witness. Better to keep my distance now.

My glass is full but I have no stomach for it. I stare around the room. I love this house, nestled between two other town houses, I feel snug and cocooned. The ceilings are high and the hallways narrow and I often feel like the house is holding its breath. I mortgaged myself to the hilt for it, but with its view of The Stray and its atmosphere of old romance, I was swept off my feet.

The commute is a bitch. I always get the train though and when I leave the city behind me and the train dashes back through the towns and villages, I feel like I can leave work behind, and go home to my other life.

At least, that's what I thought it would be like. Giggling with friends over suppers around my kitchen table. Movies, art, the fancy cinema where you get an armchair and prosecco delivered to your seat. A spaniel to throw sticks for on the vast stretches of green that surround Harrogate like a lake.

Except there is no spaniel. And there are no friends.

It didn't occur to me that I couldn't have a dog without a dog walker when I work the hours I do, and my salary won't stretch to it. I moaned once at work about the cost of doggy day care and was given Paddington Bear stares by all the parents paying a second mortgage to nurseries for the luxury of being able to work.

And the friends. I don't know where I thought I would find them. I have them at work of course. Cate. And it's true that I don't want a best friend. That I want my own space. That I have enough in my life. But the house is so quiet, and so beautiful, like a locked-up maiden in a castle that no one will ever see. My shelves are becoming dusty. My fridge is always empty. I haven't changed the spare room sheets since I moved in four years ago. There is emptiness here that I don't understand. I open my laptop and pull out a bar stool. I don't have a garden, just a little back patio that catches the last of the evening sun. It's dribbling across my wooden counter top, so only my extractor hood lights are needed. It's a weary tone.

I open my work email and take a deep breath. There are so many. All marked help! All marked urgent!

I am relieved not to find Evie's name on the list. Fishing my other phone out of my bag, I open WhatsApp. And it's there.

A message from Evie.

He's been suspended. OMG Jenny I'm scared.

I type back quickly.

It's OK. Don't worry. Remember what we talked about. This is about making sure he doesn't do this to anyone else.

Poor girl. Stupid girl.

There's another message, from Elodie, thanking me again.

I delete it fast.

Then I start on my emails. By the time I have soothed and stroked and fed back on drafts, read over CVs, sorted out timetable clashes, I am absolutely exhausted. This is why I don't have a social life, friends round to drink wine and eat olives and watch *Strictly*, why I don't go on Tinder, why I don't date. I mean, I don't really want to. When I am with people, it's such an effort. I feel like it's another job, another part of work. Something I think I have to do. I actually think my hymen may have grown back.

I shudder just thinking about it and go to run a hot bath. My bathroom is tiny, but it has a lovely black and white tiled floor and a tub with clawed feet. It was the dream. A bath with feet. I'd wanted one ever since I was a little girl and used to watch period dramas with my grandma. There's not enough room for a shower in here, the bath takes up so much space. I thought about installing one over the bath, but then I felt I was cheating on it somehow.

I climb in, careful not to drop my phone, and open my WhatsApp. The other one. The water fills up over my thighs, and covers my scars, and I breathe a long, deep sigh of relief. He is still there listed on my contacts. Josh. I can't unadd him. It just doesn't seem appropriate. I open up the last conversation. It's still there. Delivered. But unread.

Josh. Answer your phone. Don't do anything stupid. Please.

'Please,' I whisper.

His face never stood out to me. Not like it does now. He sat in my lectures and seminars with the alpha males, with Liam and Finn in their sportswear couture. Laughed with them. Lots of ending his sentences with 'mate'. He did his reading. His essays were average 2:1s. I hadn't looked into his background until that dreadful seminar when I'd asked such a thoughtless question that I'd actually left the room cringing.

I had them discussing *The Bloody Chamber* in groups. It's always a good one to get their teeth into, so to speak. The Marquis de Sade and images of pornography versus virginity. I'd flirted around the edges of the groups, with a sharp ear out for the gothic imagery, the dusky landscapes and the themes of metamorphosis.

'No it's good, honestly.' I'd cocked my head to hear more clearly a conversation behind me. 'Ever seen *An American Werewolf in London*? It's like that. But on acid.'

'Please tell me you're not basing this discussion on the film version?' I'd spun on my heel to find a set of boys, looking a bit like the wise monkeys, blinking at me.

'Did you know that Stephen Rea is in all of Neil Jordan's films?' I'd perched on the edge of the desk in front of them.

'Who is Stephen Rea?' Tom, or Finn, or Liam, or someone had said.

'He's the wolf,' Josh had said. I hadn't known his name then. It was too early in the term.

'OK. So if you're talking about the film, what do you think the major differences are?' I'd smiled at Josh. He'd been wearing a shirt and artfully distressed jeans. Sleeves rolled up. A proper jacket hanging off the back of his chair, rather than a hoody.

'Well actually, I think it's more based on the radio play,' Josh had said. 'But Angela Carter wrote the screenplay herself. So technically I'm not cheating. It's still her work.'

'Yes but you're not on a film and media degree,' I had pointed out. 'Or are you? Is this your optional module?'

'No. I'm one of yours.' Josh had shrugged and looked down.

'OK. Well, while I am impressed you've seen the film, which is actually one of my favourites, we need to bring it back to the imagery she uses in her writing.'

'Well. I think it's sexist,' one of his friends had said.

'How's that?' I'd replied.

'All the men are evil. All the women are strong and defeat them. It's like, reverse sexism. How come there's no villainous woman? Even in *Lady of the House of Love*, she's written as a heroine even though she entices men to their death.'

'OK well let's look at the historical context and political movements at the time of her writing. What was happening in the seventies? This book is actually as old as me. It came out the day I was born.'

'Ahh, it's Josh's birthday today.' The tracksuit guy had punched the top of his arm.

'Is it?' I'd smiled warmly at him and he'd smiled back and scratched the nape of his neck. 'Wow and you still came to a 10 a.m. class? I'm impressed. Did you get anything nice?'

'Nah. Not really.' He'd looked to the side. 'I didn't want anything.'

'What not even from your mum?'

'Er, no.'

'Not even a card?' I'd known I shouldn't have said anything as soon as my mouth opened but the words had just slipped out.

'I haven't seen my mum for years,' Josh had said and I'd wanted the classroom to self-destruct right there and then.

'I'm sorry. Sorry,' I'd stuttered. It had felt as though the whole room had gone silent for that exact second. 'Well. Happy Birthday. I'm sure these lads will be taking you to celebrate.'

'Hell yeah. Download tonight.' The guy on his left, Finn, I think, had grinned and looked at his friends, raising his eyebrows in an 'awkwarrrrrdddd' gesture.

'Anyway, have a think about feminism in these stories, and in particular, which role is the most prominent? Which figure repeatedly is depicted as the strongest?'

I'd moved on quickly. Later in my office I had looked Josh up on the system. Cumbria-born. Decent A-levels. Well, they'd have to be to get in here. Mild dyslexia. Extra twenty minutes in exams.

All I could think about was his mother. Where was she? How could she not have sent her son a birthday card? I'd looked him up on social media. No Facebook or Insta that I could find. Only Twitter. Mainly Leeds United-related.

For a week, those sour, terrible words had rolled around in my mouth like a bitter boiled sweet. 'Not even your mum?' What had I been thinking? I should have known better. He could probably put in a complaint. I had wanted to apologise. But Cate had said that would just make it worse, and to wipe it away. Forget about it. I couldn't. 'Not even your mum.' It became an ear worm, wriggling through my brain, my cavities, like a parasite.

How could I have been so thoughtless? So assuming. It still riles me, even now. Every time I was with him, I wanted to blurt it out. A clumsy apology. But that would have just made it worse.

Josh.

Josh.

My eyes fill with tears and I turn off the hot water tap with my big toe. My feet look pretty. Fox Glove and gel glitter on my nails. I have no idea why I bother. I can pad around barefoot as much as I want. But there's no one to see them.

They say loneliness is an epidemic.

Maybe I should try Tinder.

And then it pops up on WhatsApp.

Someone has messaged me. It's Josh's name. It can't be. It can't be him. Just the name is making me feel sick.

Do you still love the company of wolves?

I lie in the bath until I'm almost blue.

CHAPTER SIX
Simon

The suspension

'You're kidding me?' My mouth drops. It turns out the HR email was not about the promotions panel. At all.

I have been suspended. A phone call from Peter yesterday. And a summons today. I feel like I'm in some kind of nightmare.

'I know it must seem very upsetting, but the process is not designed to cause you distress.' Louise isn't smiling. She looks like she would rather be anywhere than sat in front of me right now. Is she scared of me? What's running through her head?

'You can't actually think this is true?' I spit. 'I don't get it. What exactly am I being accused of?'

'There's been an allegation,' she says again.

'Yeah and can you stop using that word please? It makes me sound like some kind of sex offender.'

'The complainant isn't accusing you of an offence,' Louise says. I hear a soft thump, thump, thump of her knee hitting the underside of the table.

'Then what am I doing here? Let's pretend it's true. Which it's not. But say it is. She must be over eighteen to even be here. So if she's a consenting adult and so am I, then what has it got to do with the university? I know it's suggested we don't get into relationships, but you can't stop people. I mean, for fuck's sake, I helped write that bloody policy.'

'It's the fact that you didn't declare it. And you continued to mark her work.'

'I have the right to know who this girl is. She might just be furious that I gave her a third or something. I mean, why am I being suspended? What's happening to her? Is she being suspended too? While you "investigate".' I make little bunny signs with my fingers and hate myself for it.

'No.' Louise takes a deep breath. 'Please calm down Simon. I appreciate this is upsetting but there's no reason to—'

'There's every reason!' I stand up so quickly that my chair topples over and I see her shrink back. This is not looking good for me.

I take a deep breath and pick up the chair. 'Sorry about that. But do you have any idea what I've got going on at home? I've got to go home and tell my wife and son that I'm being investigated for sleeping with a student?' My voice cracks and for a horrible moment I think I might cry. I tense my jaw and lift my chin.

'No. Like I said. For not declaring it.'

'Right. Well I'm sure that will go down much better, won't it? And how do you intend to prove this? She says we did. I say we didn't. I assume there's no DNA evidence?' I laugh hollowly.

'Simon, listen to me. I'm not on anyone's side. We just need to adhere to the policy and undertake some interviews. But I strongly suggest that if you have anything to say, then you just admit it now. I know it could be difficult at home but if it's discovered later that . . .'

'I. Am. Not. Lying.' I grab the desk edge so tight my fingers start to go numb. 'I want to know her name.'

'I can't tell you that at this stage. The next step will be a formal interview. You can have a representative.'

'I'll have a fucking lawyer.'

'You will obviously be on full pay. I'll be in touch over the next couple of days.'

She looks anxiously at the door. 'But I'm afraid you will have to leave campus today.'

'What about my classes? My students?' I cross my arms. 'What's happening there? If you think I'm handing over my lectures you've got another thing coming.'

'No, we can't ask you to do that. Your head of department will be making arrangements.'

I shake my head. Outside a blackbird lands on the windowsill and I stare at its orange beak for so long it no longer makes any sense.

'I've won lecturer of the year. Twice. A senate award for

learning and teaching. And this is all that people will talk about. Because of some kid with a grudge. How is this fair?'

'It's procedure Simon. You must understand we have to take this seriously.'

'If I was a woman, would I be getting suspended and marched off campus like some kind of sex offender?'

'Absolutely.'

'Then why is Jenny still in post?'

'What do you mean?'

'You want to talk about breaking procedure? How come she wasn't investigated for being the last person Josh called before he jumped? How come he was calling her? I mean, let's just say it here. It's been the elephant in the room since . . . Oh my God. That's what this is.'

'Simon . . .'

'It's her.'

'Listen . . .'

'Was it her? Jenny? Was she the one who made the complaint? Did she say I've been sleeping with students?'

'We're not at liberty to reveal the identity of the complainant until a formal statement has been made.'

'You don't need to.' I grab my jacket and start to walk while I'm still putting it on. 'I've heard enough.'

My ribcage feels tight and my breath is being squeezed out of me in little rushes, like an accordion. That horrible numbness starts flooding my legs and my thighs start to tremble. It's coming. I can't keep it down. I push open the main doors and try and gasp for air but there isn't any. I am in a vacuum and my vision begins to narrow until I'm at the wrong end of a telescope and everything has flipped in size. Big is small and small is big. Reaching out I steady myself against the wall. I don't know where I am, just that there is a wall.

Jamie is there. At the end of the telescope. I see his little chubby legs running across the edge of the pool. The seagulls caw and the sun blinds me for a second. Just a second.

I am hollow.

I feel my organs begin to shut down.

My lungs stop working.

They refuse to inflate and lie inside me, like slimy, rotten slugs.

My chest is inverting. I can feel it. I just have to let it happen. I close my eyes and I am on the waltzers at the fairground and Jamie is screaming. Then I am screaming.

The lights are too fast.

I let myself be spun round and round and Jamie is still laughing. A smile comes to my lips and I start to feel the wall again against my forehead. He is going, the laughter is fading and I screw my eyes closed and will it all to come back again so I can hear him close to my ear.

A trickle of oxygen slithers up my nose and down my throat. My palms feel the cold rough texture of the stone. He is going.

I try to hold my breath and bring him back. But the lights have slowed and the seagulls are silent.

My lungs begin to pulse and my vision stretches slowly

outwards. I turn so my back is against the wall and I slide down until my head is resting between my knees.

'Simon.' I can't look up. Louise bobs down, I can see the crown of her head and the line of her navy skirt. 'Simon. Here's some water. Would you like me to call your wife?'

I reach for the glass but my fingers fumble and the water sloshes over both of our hands.

She steadies it, and places her hand over mine. Just for a second. Then she stands a little too fast.

'No thanks.' I take a sip. 'No. It's fine. I'm leaving now.'

'I don't think you're in a fit state to drive.'

'I'm going to walk,' I say, and hold the glass up to her, like some kind of sarcastic toast. 'Thanks for this.'

I can feel her watching me. So I take another few sips. I leave the tumbler on the stone steps, brush myself down and head towards the main Student Union. It's only when I know I'm out of sight that I duck into the bar and order a pint of piss-weak student lager. What I really want is whiskey. But I can't let the students see me drinking that right now.

Louise's words ring like machine gun fire in my skull.

I'm going to be fired. It doesn't matter if I did it or not. They can't afford to take the risk. Not in this climate. I feel a burning sensation in my eyes and chest, like I've been dipped in chlorine and salt. The doctors. The treatments. The specialists.

Jamie. Jamie. Jamie.

I pull out my phone and stare at my contacts list. Trying

to make sense of it. Then I find her number and my finger hovers over the call button. I'm holding my pint glass so hard I can see the blood draining from my joints. I down the last half in two gulps.

Fucking bitch.

I slam my phone back down on the bar. I have to stay away. I've got to be careful.

And then I see her. Evie. She walks into the bar and she is shaking. That ginger girl, Bronte, with her arm around her. They don't see me to start with. I can't move. I am rooted to the spot and I will her to look over. To notice me. There is something wrong about the way she is moving. Like her knees have buckled and her spine is hunched, a puppet loose on its strings.

It's only when I feel the warmth of the blood dripping down my thumb that I feel the sting of the glass.

'Jesus.'

A kid next to me reaches over the bar and grabs a towel. The glass is so thin and cheap that it has splintered in my fist.

She has noticed me now.

'Come to the party. Coommmeee onnn.' Even Bronte was smiling. The pub was now packed and everyone was all squashed up together. Evie's thigh was pressed against mine firmly. But we were all mashed together, like a child's plasticine sculpture, all limbs and colours.

'No. I'll leave you to it I think.' I smiled and took two big gulps of my drink. It was nice not to have to rush home. Becky and Jamie

were up at the specialist hospital for a couple of days. The idea of coming home and not having to do the tube feeds and the medication, of being able to have a couple of drinks without the surging panic that Jamie would have a seizure in the night and I wouldn't be able to drive.

But then I knew that one day I would be going home to a quiet house. No sensory lamps. His chair wouldn't be in the hall. And it filled me with horror. The emptiness. I knew it could be any day. It could happen. I picked up my pint and had another gulp, and a fresh one was put in front of me by Robert. I knew I should move over to the left and let him squeeze in between me and Evie. I knew.

'Here mate.' I pulled my chair backwards instead. I don't know why, I created a little horseshoe shape. My thigh was instantly cooler. And I saw Evie's fingers go to the space where we'd been touching just moments before.

'Come on Simon.' One of the boys, Finn, Liam maybe, grinned. 'It's like, literally round the corner.'

'I think we're too old, don't you, Rob?' I leant back in my chair. 'You don't want us parent types about.'

'I'm too long in the tooth for all that carry-on.' Robert shook his head and sipped at his bitter.

'Come on. After this one, yeah?' Liam held his pint up. 'Everyone's coming.'

I beamed back.

A few more sips and I started telling my party story. I couldn't help it. I had such a captive audience.

'So, we lived in the Marsh. It was a seriously grotty area of

Liverpool. There were five of us in the house. Me, Pete, Mark, Grazy and Phil. So we'd all been out, there was this pub. The Water Witch, on the canal. It was, like a Wednesday night or something. Student night, so we'd all had a few. And we were walking home through the estate and then Phil says "What's that?". And there's this bag there. Like a cheap holdall. Navy blue. It was just wedged behind the back tyre of a car. So Phil, being Phil, just picked it up and we took it inside our house.

'So we go in, and sit on the sofa, get some tins out. And Phil just drops the bag in the corner. And to be honest, we forgot about it. We were just talking, and whatever, and then Grazy remembers, and he pulls it over and unzips it. And it was so weird. It was just full of those cardboard cylinders that you buy posh whiskey in. About ten of them. But light. Like there wasn't anything in them. So I opened one up. And guess what?'

The entire table leant in towards me and I slowed my voice down for effect.

'It was stuffed with £50 notes.'

'No way.' Finn's eyes were as wide as saucers. I didn't look at Evie but I could feel the weight of her stare.

'We checked the others, and they were all the same. All stuffed with these £50 notes.'

'Holy shit! So what did you do?' Liam said.

'Well, we pulled them all out. And underneath them all . . . right at the bottom of the bag –' I paused and looked round the table. 'There was a gun.'

'You're not being serious.' Bronte screwed her face up. 'Where would . . . I mean, why would there be a gun?'

I shrugged. 'We'd obviously stumbled into a drop-off. I told you, The Marsh was a dodgy area.'

'Shit. So what did you do?' Finn and Liam were agog.

'Well we did what anyone would do in that situation.' Another pause. 'We opened up all the canisters and threw the money about of course.'

The entire table burst out laughing and I could feel a warm glow rising in my stomach.

'Seriously. It was so un-cool. Hardly Tarantino. But we weren't daft. Whoever was watching that bag would have known we'd taken it and would've been watching our house. So we all nominated Phil to take it back.'

'Did he? What happened?' Evie asked and I allowed myself eye contact.

'He literally ran there and back and when we looked back out the window a few minutes later the bag had gone.'

'And you weren't tempted at ALL to keep even one fifty-pound note?' Robert asked, stroking his chin.

'No way. They knew where we lived.'

'It's like the start of a heist movie isn't it, where you're just shouting, "Don't do it, don't do it," at the TV,' Robert laughed. 'Right. I'm calling it a night,' he said and put down his glass.

'Ah, Rob! Can't we convince you to stay for one more?' I said and lifted up my half-empty pint.

'No, I want my dinner. Don't get into too much trouble.' We stood up and man-hugged. He smelt of leather and pipe tobacco. A bit like my dad used to. I patted his back and he leant in and whispered in my ear.

'The Marsh is in Lancaster by the way. Not Liverpool.'

'Oh. Yeah. 'Course . . . I meant . . .'

He winked. 'Have a good Christmas, Simon. Send my love to Becky and Jamie.'

'Of course. You too mate.' We shook hands and I felt a shift behind me. Coats were being flung about, drinks were being finished. People started standing and nodding and chatting and moving and I realised that, actually, I was quite drunk.

'So. Are you coming?' I turned around and Evie was stood there, wearing a black wool-type coat. She reminded me of some kind of Bourne Identity spy with her glossy hair and boots against all the hoodies and denim.

'I shouldn't.' I scratched the back of my neck.

'Si-mon, Si-mon, Si-mon.' Liam and Finn started leading the chant and suddenly I was surrounded. I looked at the boys, their fists pumping, knees loose, heads firm.

That would never be Jamie.

I would never be able to go for a pint with my son.

I would never stand at the side of a football pitch.

A graduation hall.

A wedding.

'Come on, Simon.' Evie reached out and put her hand on my arm. My skull vibrated like those shaky electric wavy wire toys that buzz when your stick touches the metal.

I should have taken it as a warning.

But I didn't.

Instead I heard it like a starting gun.

'Just for one,' I said.

The party was raw. The house was sticky and all the rooms had fire doors. Someone had thrust a strange lager and spirit concoction into my hand and I was led into a galley kitchen like some kind of zoo exhibit, as if Liam and Finn – who were beginning to look alarmingly alike – were pointing me out to all their housemates. 'Look! Look what we've got!'

I leant against the kitchen counter and ate a soggy crisp, sipping at my warm beer.

'Slippery nipple?'

'Excuse me?' I glanced down at a shot glass of something that looked like Baileys and jam.

'I'm sure it's horrendous but it might blot out the atrocity of this party. I can't believe you came.' Evie held out the drink and clinked it with her own. 'Let's throw ourselves into the festive spirit.'

'You're the one who was trying to get me to come!' I accepted the drink and knocked it back in one. It tasted like a jam tart with coffee in it and wasn't entirely unpleasant. Evie looked at me intensely and her pale skin seemed to glow in the low lights.

'I know. I didn't think you actually would though.' Evie leant against the counter opposite. 'Sorry. I should have warned you it would be hell.'

There was a shout and a squall and Finn lurched into the kitchen, with a hand over his mouth. 'Move!'

Evie and I jumped out the way as he hunched over the kitchen sink. A stream of brown vomit splattered all over the breakfast cereal bowls.

'And I think that's my exit.' I rubbed the kid's back and grabbed what looked like a clean glass, filling it with water from the tap.

'Here you go, mate.' I handed him the glass and looked at Evie. 'I think he needs putting to bed.'

Evie rolled her eyes but with a smile. Her lips plumped out and her cheeks were rosy. It occurred to me she wasn't someone who often smiled. Her teeth were tiny and almost creature-like.

'I'll do it. I should imagine his mates are in the same state.'

'I'm right now,' Finn slurred. 'Oh no hang on.' He turned and the water he'd just drunk came straight back out.

The other one, Liam, stumbled in and threw his arm around his friend's shoulders.

'S'aright mate. I'll see to you.'

'Here I'll help.' Evie went to his other side and started hooking his other arm around her. His head was lolling down to his chin and his knees were going. She buckled a little under his weight and I stepped forward.

'It's OK, Evie, I'll do it. Go on. Go back to the party. You don't need to get involved.'

She looked at me gratefully and stepped back.

Between me and Liam we man-handled Finn up the narrow staircase, one hand on the other one's back too, to keep him upright. By the time I'd got to the top of the stairs I was knackered and massively regretting my decision to come.

'I's here. Put him s'here.'

I followed them into a single bedroom with a wonky desk and pretended not to see the torn Rizla packet and sealed condom on his bedside table. Last of the optimists.

We slung Finn down on the bed and I helped get his trainers off, before having a bro-hug with Liam.

'She fancies you,' he slurred as we turned to the doorway.

'Who? What do you mean?' I pretended not to know what he was talking about.

'Evie. She fancies you. They all do.'

'Don't be daft,' I said. We ventured back out into the hallway and she was there. Standing in the doorway to the bathroom. Just watching.

'You alright?' I asked.

'Told you.'

Liam gave us both a shit-eating smirk and lurched down the stairs.

'Just checking up on you.' Evie smiled. 'You're a hero.'

'Hardly. I'm going to call it a night though I think.' I fished out my phone and opened the Uber app.

'Yeah. Me too. Bronte is off with one of Finn's cousins. Can't say there's much keeping me here.' She wiped under her eyes and her eyeliner smudged slightly. It made her green eyes widen and flare.

'Will you be OK getting home?'

I thought about offering to share my cab. Her thigh pressed against mine like in the bar.

But there were so many people around. I thought about Liam's comment and my heart began to race.

'It's only a couple of minutes from here,' she said. 'I can walk.'

'You sure?'

My phone beeped.

'My Uber's nearly here.' I held my phone up as if to prove my point.

'I'll walk out with you.' Evie grabbed her coat off the bannister. 'No point even trying to find Bronte.'

We stepped over various clusters of people sprawled on the stairs and I worried for a second it might look like Evie was leaving with me. But they were too sloppy and into each other to notice. I opened the Yale latch and the cool night air hit me hard.

'Jesus it's cold.' I zipped up my coat. I saw my Uber turn into the bottom of the road. 'You sure you're going to be OK?'

'I'm a big girl.' She turned to look at me. 'I'm glad you came tonight. Thanks for keeping me company. I don't know why I still come to these things, they're so not my speed.'

'Young girl like you? I'd have thought this was exactly your thing,' I replied.

'I don't think you know me at all.' Evie's smile was rueful, almost sad. She looked behind her, down the street and for a second, under the mist settling under the stale light from the streetlamps, I thought her eyes were brimming with tears.

But when she looked back, they were gone.

'Goodnight.' She reached up on her tiptoes and kissed me on the cheek. She smelt of honeysuckle and boiled sweets. Her cheek was warm but her hair was cold.

I turned my cheek and kissed hers back. Her hand was on my waist.

'Will you let me know you got home OK?' I asked her.

'Sure. How?' She removed her hand but I could still feel its warmth.

'Just . . . Facebook me or something.'

'You're so old,' she teased, then nodded towards the car. 'Go on, Cinderella.'

'For a change I'm home alone,' I blurted out, 'and not on a curfew.'

'Well I am.' Evie raised her eyebrows. 'My dress is about to turn into rags.'

I didn't know where to look. Or what to say. So I just made a stupid, snuffling sound.

'Goodnight Simon.' She laughed. 'Go on. Your chariot awaits.'

'I think you should let me drop you home,' I said. 'It doesn't feel right leaving you to walk alone.'

The Uber was warm and dry.

I don't even feel the pain in my palm. I know I need to get out of here. I might be on the edge, but I'm not stupid. I stride out of the bar and push open the glass double doors that lead out onto the beer garden, leaving a smear of blood on the glass that I find strangely satisfying.

Students are giving me a one-handed wave, a nod. I flash weak smiles and my brain starts to race with what I need to do next as I keep walking.

'Simon!' I look back over my shoulder and see Finn half-standing, but getting his footballer's thighs stuck in-between the table and the bench. 'Can I just . . .'

'Sorry mate,' I call back. 'I've got to be somewhere.'

I don't look back but I can only imagine the confusion on his face.

I have never said no.

I almost vomit with the irony.

By the time I get to my car my legs are shaking and I feel like it's coming again. I know I can't drive so I put my hands on the bonnet and bow my head, waiting for the panic to come. Bizarrely it doesn't and I'm just a middle-aged man, breathing heavily over the bonnet of his car. I catch my reflection in the windscreen.

My face has crumbled and my forehead is higher. I don't look like myself, but like some horrific caricature you pay £20 for from some old giffer with a Sharpie.

My stomach is solid and my throat is on fire.

I am so afraid.

I call Jason on the way home. He picks up after a couple of rings.

'Alright mate?' He sounds surprised to hear from me. It's usually Becky who rings.

'Yeah, OK, I think. You alright?' I manage to do a good job of keeping my voice steady.

'Well, you know. Kids. Football drop-offs and . . .' His voice trails off. So it fucking should.

'Anyway. Look, sorry if this puts you in an awkward position but I need some advice. Any chance you're free for a pint tomorrow?'

'Tomorrow?' Jason sounded alarmed. 'I'll have to check with the boss. Why, what kind of advice do you need, mate advice or . . .?'

I took a deep breath.

'No. I think I'm going to need a lawyer.'

'Why, what've you done?' Jason says lightly.

'Nothing, that's the point. I don't really want to go into it on the phone if that's OK?'

'Yeah, sure. Look, I'll have a word with Kath and see if I can get out. I'll drop you a message later.'

'Thanks, mate.'

He's not my mate. Not really. He's Becky's friend's husband. We do the cosy foursome dinners. Mainly at ours. Well, always at ours. It's not like we can get a babysitter.

I've been to the odd footie match with them. Once we went to see Shed Seven but I wanted to be up front and he wanted to hang at the back so we didn't really speak that much.

There's nothing wrong with him. He can be good company if you're in the mood. But we're friends because our wives want us to be and because it's more hassle not to be.

By the time I pull onto the drive I realise I have absolutely no recollection of the journey home.

I sit there for half an hour. The house is pretty soundproof. No dog to bark at me and raise the alert that someone is home. I watch each minute pass on the digital clock. I think about my lecture tomorrow. Who is giving it? What are the students going to be told? I wish I'd asked more questions.

I take in another deep breath and resolve to call HR and Peter in the morning. There's nothing I can do now. I turn my phone off, ignoring the flashing signs telling me I have messages and go inside to kiss my wife and son. It's my turn to sleep with Jamie tonight. We go to bed early and I lie on my side and watch his chest rise and fall until the squall of the sparrows brings in the first pale-blue light.

CHAPTER SEVEN
Evie

The day after

'I'm sorry, but we can't ask him to leave. There is no actual evidence saying he did this.'

Bronte's jaw fell open. 'You are actually kidding, right? Who else would it have been? He was mad about us making him clean up the rabbit. You should have seen his face.'

'Look –' the housing officer took off his glasses and rubbed the bridge of his nose – 'we need to await the outcome of the police investigation.'

'Oh, come on. They're not taking this seriously. They wouldn't even take fingerprints.'

'Well, I don't think they actually could,' Evie pointed out to Bronte. She turned to the officer. 'Look, I'm so sorry, I know this isn't your fault. Is there any kind of emergency accommodation?'

'Not for these kinds of circumstances. I'm sorry, but you're not living in a university-owned property. You'll need to speak to your landlord directly and liaise with police.'

'This is outrageous. Don't you have a duty of care?' Bronte said incredulously.

Evie locked eyes with the man behind the desk with his *Stranger Things* mug and half-eaten sandwich, and they shared a brief moment of empathy.

'How about I put you at the top of the list? All halls are full at the moment, but some are occupied by study-abroad students, who are just here for a week or two. Then we can move you over while all this gets sorted.'

'That would be great, thank you.' Evie smiled.

'In the meantime, do come straight back to us if there are any other issues, or if residents are not adhering to the student code of conduct.'

'You mean like not spreading animal entrails over her door?' Bronte folded her arms. 'Is that in the code of conduct?'

'Thanks again.' Evie hauled Bronte to her feet. 'Come on.'

They headed out into the quad and Evie shivered even though it wasn't cold.

'You know, it's probably Simon. I mean why would Harvey call me a liar? Or someone else. Someone from his Facebook appreciate page. Or even . . .'

'You're not still thinking about that post on the Common Room are you?' Bronte said. 'How many times do I need to tell you that it's just a coincidence?'

'I'm not sure,' Evie said. 'It felt so personal.'

'Well, there's a post up this morning having a go at students who are planning on crossing the picket line when the union strikes are on. I bet every person who went to class during the last strikes feels like it's a personal attack against them.

'And Simon's a lot of things but he's not stupid. He's probably shitting himself enough without doing something like that. I'm telling you, it's Harvey. I mean, what kind of person has the nickname One-Shot Harvey? A nutjob, that's who.'

'He only *said* that was his nickname,' Evie conceded as they walked in the quad. 'God Bronte, I just keep seeing his face in the union. That glass. He wasn't just angry . . . he was crazy.'

'That he's finally been caught! Two skinny lattes please.' Bronte smiled at John in his coffee wagon. He didn't smile back. 'Four quid.'

'Everyone must have realised by now. I mean, I walk into the union, he sees me. Cuts up his hand and storms out and is now mysteriously on leave. I mean. Come on.'

'I doubt anyone's put it together. Besides, who cares who knows? You're the victim. Remember?'

Evie shook her head and linked Bronte's arm. 'Not quite. But thanks hon. You've been amazing over this.'

'Maybe it wasn't your wisest move, babe. But he's the one in the position of power.'

'That's what Jenny said.'

'Exactly.'

'I think Finn fancies Jenny,' Evie said. 'He's always gazing at her and laughing every time she opens her mouth. He's constantly booking in for one-to-ones.'

'Well, I can't say I blame him. She is pretty awesome.'

'Yeah. And I bet she doesn't shag her students.'

'She doesn't need to babe, that's the difference.'

By the time they got back, Evie felt halfway normal again. The smell of disinfectant and bleach was still lingering in the hall, but even that was beginning to fade a little.

The kitchen was toasty and Marmite-scented, and her housemate Kelly was on the straight-backed sofa, very possibly the most uncomfortable sofa in the world, with her feet on the coffee table, laptop on her knees.

'Hey.' Evie flung her bag down. 'You OK?'

Kelly looked over her shoulder. 'Hi. Yeah. Harvey still hasn't come out of his room though. I mean, doesn't he need to eat?'

'God, maybe I should go and knock. Try and make peace.' Evie chewed on her lower lip. I mean, this can't go on. I don't want everyone walking around on eggshells because of me.'

'Maybe leave it a bit longer.' Kelly screwed up her nose. 'Have you guys seen this post on the Common Room?' She motioned to her screen.

'No.' Evie leant over the back of the couch. 'Whose is it?'

'Student Village Vixen.'

Evie swallowed and leant over Kelly's shoulder further.

Why is it that the victims of alleged sex offences get to keep their anonymity? But the accused get their identity sprawled all over the entire campus before they are proven guilty. One accusation can ruin someone's life. And yes, it's sexist to be saying men, but let's pull in our PC claws for a second. Only because I can't be bothered with being all delicate with the pronouns.

Let's just say a girl accuses a man on campus of a sex offence. And these days that's everything from rape to the pinch of a bum. She gets to say whatever she wants, all safe in the knowledge that from the minute the accusation is made she is protected by law with lifelong anonymity. But the man? Nope. Nada. Gets, let's say, suspended from his course. His job. All through the investigation or court case everyone knows who he is and what he has been accused of. And that shit will never EVER leave him. It will ruin his life and it doesn't matter if he's found guilty or declared innocent, the damage is done. Ladies, would you date someone once accused of rape? Even if the charges were dropped? Me neither.

I get the reasons why. The number of rapes that go unreported because of the fear of the victim, the shame that goes with it, the horror of having intimate details broadcasted to a baying court. Knickers held up in court.

It's horrendous.

But girls, if you do this for revenge, because you feel like you've done something you shouldn't, because you've cheated and want to convince yourself that it wasn't your fault, YOU do this. You drag him through the mud – and YOU are responsible for every girl too afraid to report it when she passes out at a party and her date thinks it's OK to fuck her while she is vomiting down the side of the bed. YOU are the reason women are not trusted. YOU are destroying the sisterhood.

So you made a mistake. Own it. Get your big girl pants on. You got them off quick enough.

'Fuuccccckkk.' Bronte whistled through her two top teeth. 'That's near the knuckle. Even for her.'

'I mean, seriously?' Kelly shook her head. 'That's *bold.* But, I don't know, there are some points in there I kind of agree on.'

Evie uncurled her spine and stood up straight. 'Like what?' she said casually.

Bronte gave her a sideways look.

'Well, I don't think it is fair, if I'm honest, that victims have anonymity and the accused don't.'

'Would it be different if it wasn't a sex offence?' Evie said. 'So if someone was accused of murder, should they have their identity protected until they are found guilty?'

'No. People should know. To get found guilty of murder the jury have to be convinced beyond reasonable doubt,' Kelly explained. 'That means even if you have a tiny feeling that they might not have done it, if you have one per cent of doubt, you have to find them not guilty.'

'Check out the law student,' Bronte said.

'So, you mean if every one of the jury, if all of them, are ninety-nine per cent sure the person accused is guilty, they still have to say not guilty?' Evie asked.

'Yeah. So I guess I'd want to know if my next-door neighbour is ninety-nine per cent likely to be a murderer,' Kelly said.

'Or a rapist,' Evie pointed out.

'Tricky shit, right? But say what you like about Village Vixen. She gets people talking.' Kelly closed her laptop. 'I've got netball. See you guys later.'

Evie waited until she was out in the corridor and then turned to Bronte. 'Still think it's not personal?'

'Why don't we watch some Netflix or something? It'll take your mind off it,' Bronte crooned. 'I'll make us my killer cheese toasties.'

'No. I just want to be by myself for a bit.' Bronte's puppy eyes were suffocating. Evie forced out a smile. 'I'll catch up with you later. OK?'

'Want me to cook dinner?' Bronte pushed. 'Whatever you want.'

Evie shook her head. 'Sorry Bronte, I'm getting a really bad headache. I have to lie down.' She made a move towards the door.

'Do you want my migraine tablets?' She heard Bronte start to rustle about in the cupboard but let the door slam shut.

Evie went up the two flights of stairs and paused at her door. Harvey had the smaller attic room opposite hers and there was a faint noise coming from inside. A strange squeaking. If Evie hadn't known better she would have thought it was a headboard. The prospect of him being in there making that kind of noise alone made her shudder. But she didn't move. It wasn't a squeak really. More of an eek. Like metal scraping. Then the noise stopped suddenly and Evie heard fast, heavy footsteps and she slid into her room as quickly and quietly as she could.

As her door clicked shut, she could have sworn she heard his open. Her heart began to quicken and without thinking she turned the lock on her door.

There were definitely slow footsteps now right outside her door, in the small square at the top of the stairs that joined their rooms. Evie walked backwards until the back of her knees hit the edge of her bed, and she fell ungracefully down into a half-sitting, half-sprawled position.

Then she saw her door handle move. It moved so slowly to start with that she thought her fake migraine might be real and that her vision had gone blurry. Then it carried on. All the way down. Evie stood up and grabbed her hairspray from the shelf above her head, the nearest weapon to hand. The door handle stopped at the bottom and then there was a clicking noise, not a rattle. Whoever was outside was trying not to make themselves known. A slow, gentle push. The lock stayed put and the handle began to make its way back up, just as deliberately. Evie strained to hear the footsteps. But all was quiet. So maddeningly quiet.

Evie sat there and stared for so long at the door her eyes became sore and heavy. She felt cold and tired. And she really missed her dad. The smell of his stinking terrier and tinned pilchards.

She curled up into a ball and covered herself with the crochet blanket her grandmother had told her used to be her mother's. She'd always planned to wrap Evie in it, to bring her home from the hospital. But she hadn't brought her home.

Eclampsia.

Her mum. Her features were smudged in her mind. She'd seen pictures. Laughing, a cigarette in her hand, slightly out of the shot, but the tell-tale smoke signals a giveaway. Her eyebrows weren't waxed. Her hair wasn't straightened. She was laughing, a big wide, circus smile, her left incisor crooked.

She missed her, so much, sometimes she could feel her invisible hand brushing her hair. Even though she'd only known her for a minute before a nurse snatched her off her chest. For that minute. She was loved.

She shouldn't have come here. It wasn't that she didn't feel loved, but she had no one to love back. And that was the most horrible, cold, wrenching feeling in the world.

CHAPTER EIGHT

Jenny

A week before the memorial

The programme in front of me smells divine, glossy and inky. The most comforting smell in the world. The handsome picture of Josh smiling out at me. It's my favourite. I mean, obviously. I picked it. With approval from his dad. Nothing from his mother. Nada. I have no idea if she even went to the funeral. Peter said I shouldn't go. That it was taking it too far. I was doing enough. He was worried about me. Apparently. I'd come so close to bunking off work and going anyway.

But of course, I didn't.

He truly was a beautiful young man. Eyelashes most women would kill for. Beautiful cheekbones. Those blue eyes. He is stood by a drystone wall with an ageing Jack Russell trying to get over a style. I know the dog is called Blue.

I turn the page and read the inside blurb written by our marketing team. The whole thought of that leaves a bad taste in my mouth. But why would I be surprised?

The memorial, the Joshua Tree, has been designed with the theme of connection in mind, to remind our students and faculty that we are never alone. Our Connect campaign, spear-headed by Josh's personal tutor, Dr Jenny Summers, was highly commended in the Pride of Britain awards earlier this year.

There's that god-awful picture of me holding the award. I absolutely am developing jowls.

I turn back to the cover and look at the picture once more.

Josh told me about Blue at the beginning.

I remember him sat in my office, we'd been going through the feedback from his last essay. It had been good, not quite a first but it could have been with a little more depth. We'd been picking out sections where the referencing could have been improved when his phone had rung. The home screen had flashed up on my desk, a picture of Blue slurping the camera.

'Was that your dog calling?' I had laughed as he silenced it.

'It's home,' he'd blushed. 'Sorry about that.'

'I've always wanted a dog,' I'd said. 'But I'm at work too much. I have to make do with a cat. But I'm a secret dog person really. Don't tell her.'

'I could tell,' Josh had said. 'The best people are dog people.'

At Christmas, he'd given me a card. Pushed under my office door. It was a pug with a Santa hat on. Its eyes were sad.

I feel my throat begin to roughen and I lay the programme back down on my desk. A week to go until Josh's memorial and I still haven't written my speech. I can't seem to find the words.

There's a knock at my door and I look up to see Evie.

'Hi.' She walks in and hands me a paper cup of coffee from the van in the quad. 'Extra shot,' she says with a smile.

'Oh, you angel.' I accept it gratefully. 'Let me give you some money.' I scramble for my purse in my bag.

Evie waves her hand. 'Please. It's the least I can do.'

'Oh, sweetheart.' I swivel my chair around to face her and we both make a show of taking the plastic lids off our coffee and blowing on them. Neither of us like red-hot coffee and prefer to drink it lukewarm. 'So how are things going? Have HR kept you informed?'

'Well, I'm not sure there is much to say at the moment.' Evie shrugs. 'I've been back to give an official statement. That went OK, I think. I'm just waiting to hear back. You know, I've no idea what he is going to say.'

'You should have said. I would have come with you.'

'I didn't want to put you in an awkward position any more than I already have.'

'It's not an awkward position when it's the right thing to do.'

Evie looks down at my desk. 'Well, you've got enough on.' She nods at the programme. 'I hear you're giving the main speech.'

'Well. I am sure it won't be the main one. But yes, I've been invited to say something.' I smile sadly.

'You're some kind of guardian angel on this campus.' Evie unbuttons her jacket and hangs it off the back of the chair. It's lovely. Nude, blazer style. I squint to have a look at the label.

'How I wish that was true. There's not a day that goes by when I don't think about Josh and what more I could have done to help.' I look back down at the photograph.

'Well, I didn't know him. But after everything you've done for me, I believe you did everything you could and the Connect campaign could save lives.'

'Well. I don't know about that. But it's good to get people talking.'

'He was gorgeous.' Evie leant over. 'I just can't imagine how desperate he must have felt.'

I murmur something in reply and we both make a show of blowing on our coffees again.

'How are you? Really? Have there been any more . . . incidents?' I ask.

She shakes her head. 'No, not really. I thought someone maybe tried my door handle the other night. But, I don't know, maybe it was Bronte.'

'And Harvey? That's his name, right?' She nods. 'Has he made an appearance?'

She shakes her head. 'No one has seen him for days. I hear his door go at night. I think that's the only time he goes out. Maybe he is a vampire,' she jokes weakly and then looks away for a minute.

'I didn't know he had a disabled son,' she adds, her voice low.

'Jamie. Yes,' I say. She looks up sharply.

'You knew?'

'Yes, of course. We've worked together a long time.'

'I don't know,' Evie said. 'I mean, they must rely on his salary. What if he gets fired?'

'Do you think his circumstances should make a difference?' I sit back and sip at my coffee, now it's the right temperature.

'I don't know,' she says again.

'Well. It's probably a little too late now,' I say, not unkindly, I hope.

'I know what he did was wrong, but I understand more now why he wanted to keep it a secret.'

'Did you know he was married?'

'Yes,' Evie said, not meeting my eyes. 'That's why I didn't really want anyone to know either.'

I remember it so well.

When I saw Simon and Evie in the quad in the last of the winter sleet, there was something not quite right. She was hugging her books tightly to her chest, and he was running his hands through his hair. They both looked tense.

A few days later, she came for her personal tutor appointment with swollen eyes.

She looked desperate. In a way I had seen before.

'I still don't know why I did it. Come forward, I mean,' Evie said. 'You said you've been here before. Do you mind me asking whether you'd ever thought of reporting him?'

'Whistleblowing? Of course. But that would mean a massive betrayal of confidence. Some of them knew about Jamie, or felt that they were both adults and that his life shouldn't be ruined for a mistake they'd both made. I've heard that phrase many times. Others weren't in his seminar groups or being marked by him, so technically there wasn't any protocol being breached. I felt my hands were tied. But you, you're stronger. You've had the courage to put a stop to it. Courage I really should have had sooner. I'm just as complicit in a way.'

Evie shakes her head but the words out there are true.

I know it. She knows. Simon knows it.

I won't let him get away with it, not again.

Later, after Evie has left, I pick up the picture of Josh again.

I let one tear slide down my cheek. Just one.

Then I wipe my eyes, and log into the university system. In the assignments section, Elodie's name is highlighted in red, with a sixty per cent match to another essay submitted at Warwick University. I click on the drop-down box next to it, and click resolved and watch as her name turns to black.

Do I think circumstances should make a difference?

It depends on the colour of your soul.

Josh is still looking at me when I eventually shut down my machine. I check my messages on my phone and am relieved to see there are no more from that number. It's obviously some random person who has taken over his number. Or has his phone maybe.

I try not to think about the wolves anymore.

I couldn't sleep last night. I must have, surely, at some point drifted in and out. But it felt like every second, of every minute, of every hour, he was there.

And miles to go before I sleep. I could hear him, whispering. From the lovely woods, dark and deep.

Was he there now? Was he happy?

Lots of students know about my favourite Angela Carter story. I did my PhD on her. It might not even be a student. It could be, dare I say it . . . a fan. I had a paper published not too long ago.

Or just some sick joker. That's all. I need sleep.

It's not raining for a change and the covered walkway to the quad is quiet. Lectures and seminars are over but it's too early for the Student Union. Wednesday night is student night in town so they'll all be snug in the halls of residence and the digs, eating stir fries and having pre-drink naps. I try not to look at the arts tower as I cross over the square. The smell of garlic and tomatoes drifts round the corner as the pizza takeaway starts to fire up. My stomach grumbles and it occurs to me I haven't eaten since yesterday. I pick up my pace and take the concrete steps down to the underpass. It's dark and smells of wet dog as usual. There's a bus stop at the bottom, the sprint shuttle bus that takes the students and staff into town if you can't be bothered to walk.

It's not there though, so I guess I must have just missed it. I sigh and consider walking but my heels are rubbing on the back of my foot and I already can feel the spongy, soft tissue of a burst blister. Two little circles of raw open skin that will squall when I get into my bath tonight. My feet are too soft.

Instead I go to sit on the bench and reach for my phone when I realise my bag is oddly empty. It takes me a minute to realise my purse isn't in there and I have a brief recollection of getting it out to give Evie some money for the coffee. I must not have put it back. I groan, louder than I mean to and a small clump of students glance over.

Turning around, I start back up the steps. I can live without cash until tomorrow but my train ticket is in there.

It's getting darker and I come back up into the quad to see the lilac shadows of the surrounding buildings licking the ground.

The tower stands regal and imposing, like a turret and the lower buildings a castle fortress. As I limp through the quad I feel exposed and on show. The halls of residence surround me and I feel, unreasonably, like I am being watched. The back of my heel is now burning, as if salt has been rubbed into my open skin but I am too proud to take my shoes off.

It seems a longer walk back. I only pass one person, a student carrying a pizza box that smells so divine I can almost imagine myself ripping it out of his hands.

I have to use my swipe card to access the building by the time I'm back as it is after 6 p.m. I pull off my shoe the second I'm inside and see that blood has seeped through my tights. Holding both shoes in one hand and vowing to never risk such cheap ones again, I ride up in the lift to the fifth floor and the moment I step out, I know something is wrong.

The lights turn on from the sensor as soon as I step out into the corridor but I can smell something revolting. Almost maggoty. Wrinkling my nose, I hurry towards my office, spare hand over my mouth. It's like the time Cate left those prawn shells in the bin one Friday night, and then after a scorching weekend we all came in to a stink like no other. One of the pregnant PhD students had to go home because she kept being sick in her mouth.

But this smell is wrong and almost unrecognisable. It's not food. It's more the smell when Enid brings something in and leaves it under the sofa for a few days before the stench of rot starts to seep out.

Then I realise I am right. There's something on my office door. I stop short. The smell isn't what's bothering me anymore. At first I think it's just smears, lines. But when I step back I realise that entrails are hung across my office door, blood smeared across the glass. And there, in the middle of the ooze and the grey, the strings, the yellow, dripping fluid, Josh's picture is nailed to what looks like an animal heart.

My phone buzzes and I fish for it, scrabbling in my bag, ready to call security.

But it's him.

It's Josh. I drop the phone as if it's molten.

My stomach is still retching an hour later and I am certainly no longer hungry. Security told me to go, that they would clean it up and start checking CCTV. But I couldn't leave. It was like a car crash. I couldn't not look at it.

Once the scene had been photographed, and the police had come out and poked and prodded, I stayed with the security team while they scrubbed and bleached until my door was sparkling. I feel like someone should have given me one of those tinfoil blankets like in the movies.

Student with a bad grade? They joked, before seeing the look on my face and assuring me that they would take this seriously. Nothing on the CCTV. What CCTV? The students campaigned against the spies in the sky about a decade ago and no one has been bothered to consider reinstalling anything since.

Anyone with a grudge?

I have no choice but to give them Simon's name.

I toy with the idea of showing my phone to the police, but decide it would not be wise to alert them to the fact that I have two phones. One for personal use, one for work.

I mean, I guess so do lots of people. But I'd rather give up the personal-use one. The work one . . . it's a bit more complicated.

The porter orders me a cab to the station. My feet have swollen up like pufferfish and they howl and shriek as I force them back into my shoes, white flesh oozing over the pinches of the leather.

The cab is quick but the train is slow. My head is woozy and I am reminded by the hollowness in my stomach that I still haven't eaten.

I wonder how long I can go.

It just makes no sense for it to be Simon. He would obviously be the prime suspect, so why put himself up there? Nail himself to the mast? He's stupid, but he's not an idiot.

Yes, he probably knows by now that I'm involved in a non-direct way. HR were in touch and I couldn't lie. There have been rumours. There have always been rumours. Students. Some of them love to marinate on every word that trips off your tongue. They can twist it, massage it, find whatever meaning they want. They can read so far into a glance they become intertwined in subplots and red herrings. You can't listen to the gossip. Mostly it's rumours. Mostly.

God knows it was with me.

Simon would always joke about my coven. The small group I have every year, who are allocated to me as personal tutees. He would say that I cast some kind of spell over them. That they turn into tiny fledglings tweeting 'Jenny,

Jenny, Jenny,' down the hallways, in the lecture theatres, waiting for me to drop a worm into their mouths. I'd laugh and tell him he's in no position to talk with his Facebook appreciation page.

What if the end is just the priest in your head,

What if the ground is a feather bed?

They are not mainstream lyrics.

The only person who knows how much I love that song, the slightly obscure singer, is Simon. I bought him the album. Feather Beds. And was embarrassed when he told me he didn't have a CD player anymore and asked if he could get it on iTunes?

And Josh.

Josh knew. Of course. I type back, *who is this?* And watch as the blue ticks pop up telling me my message has been read. I find it somewhat sinister and as I hobble from the train platform to the car, I am relieved there is a guard milling on the platform, then that I live in an old Georgian building, my flat nestled between two others, cosy, sandwiched. Like *The Princess and the Pea.*

The house is quiet and Enid is nowhere to be seen. Out roaming the streets, looking for 'Bad Cat', I guess. He comes back, this tomcat, now and again. She slinks in covered in scratches after he has paid a visit, then sits on the window-sill for nights at a time. Looking for him. Waiting.

Who have I upset recently? That's what they'd asked me. Same as Evie. As if we were both to blame somehow. Who have I upset? Apart from Simon, I go to great lengths to keep everyone happy. To keep everyone calm. Sometimes it exhausts me so much I can't stand it.

But there was one. Just one I couldn't keep calm.

I'd collected Ewan in my fourth year of teaching. He was sweet and long-fringed. Tattooed as they all are, trying to go against the grain and ending up like everyone else as a result. He'd played bass in a band. His best friend had been stabbed in a gang-related incident in Liverpool three years before. He had died in his arms in an alleyway. He still had nightmares. I'd read his doctor's reports on the system and then had orchestrated it so that I could be his personal tutor. He'd obviously needed someone.

He used to come for tutorials fortnightly. He'd never miss one. Then he had started to come every week. Even when there was no work to feed back on. I used to make him coffee, even though we weren't meant to use staff resources for students. Another rule I'd broken.

He'd requested me on Facebook. I'd ignored the request.

Then he had started coming in every couple of days. His dad was sofa-surfing in London. His sister had shacked up with a dealer called Whack and worked in a gentleman's club where there was a distinct lack of gentlemen.

His essays had been so perfectly constructed they'd felt lyrical.

One night I'd had too much wine at home.

And I'd clicked accept.

I mean, he was a student. A grown man. He'd just needed a friend.

There is no reply.

I watch in the dark for Enid as she pads over the rooftops, blue in the moonlight. I take a sharp knife and slice an apple straight into my mouth.

CHAPTER NINE

Simon

The denial

'I didn't do it.'

'Shit, man.' Jason sits back in his chair and stares at the frothy head of his pint. 'Listen, and don't bullshit me. I can't help you unless you are 100 per cent straight with me. Is anything she is saying true?'

'I don't know yet.' I shake my head. 'I've not heard her statement. OK, look, I admit I thought she had a bit of a crush, I was nice to her. It was flattering, OK? She was having a tough time. Getting over some kind of break-up. She came to see me, after we'd been at some party . . .'

'Wait,' Jason holds his hand up. 'You were at a party with your students?'

'Oh God. Look, everyone's an adult. It was Christmas, they begged me to go.'

Jason looks at me, his face unmoving.

The pub is quiet, unsurprisingly, for a Tuesday. The Red Lion up the road is better. Nicer seats. Craft ale. But there's a quiz on tonight. And this is not a conversation you want to have while huddles of middle-aged men in leather jackets try to show off their niche 70s acid jazz music knowledge.

The Rose was darker, grimier and still sold Mr Porky's and Scampi Fries.

'I know.' I tug at my collar. 'I know it doesn't look good.'

'Any other lecturers there?'

'No,' I admit. 'But it's not like they haven't been out with them before. I mean, Robert was in the pub with us. And I know Jenny has taken her personal tutees out for coffee before.'

'Where was she this time?'

'I don't know.' I look down at my drink.

'And this party . . . this is where she is saying it happened?' Jason rolls up his sleeves.

'I don't know. I've not been given her statement. But I mean, everyone saw us leave.'

'Together? You left together?'

'We left the house together. I got an Uber.'

'Did anyone see you get into the Uber alone? How did she get home?'

My teeth are beginning to ache. I hadn't realised how clamped and firm my jaw was. 'I dropped her off. I know it looks bad. But wouldn't it have been worse to let her walk home alone?'

'Had you been drinking?'

'It was a Christmas do, of course I had. I wasn't drunk though.' Wasn't I?

'And you went straight home?'

'Yes.'

'And can you think of any other situations where you were alone together?'

'Yeah, like I said. She came to see me after that party. She wanted some extra feedback on her case study proposal and she got a bit teary.'

'Why? Over her work?'

'No. God, they all do. The minute they sit down in your office and the door is closed, it's like one minute you're having a conversation about literature reviews and the next they are sobbing into your cheap tissue box about their break-ups and the person in their flat who never does the washing-up and eats their cereal, even though they initial every grain, and how much they miss their hamsters.'

'And that's what happened with this girl? Hamsters? Break-ups?'

I pause and think of Evie's swollen pink eyes. The twitch of her long pale fingers. Her smart black coat with the tie in the middle that made her look so elegant. Even her tears were classy.

'Not quite. She was legitimate. She transferred this year. She'd been through a bad break-up last year. Her dad is an alcoholic. It sounds like she pretty much takes care of him.

I think she was lonely. I felt sorry for her,' I say. My voice is low.

'And was the office door closed during these meetings?' Jason rubs his nose.

'It has to be. They talk about really personal stuff mate. Abuse. Sex assault. All kinds. You can't leave the door open.'

'Abuse?' Jason questions. 'And, are you trained in that? Like, those kind of problems?'

'Of course not. But like I said, you can't get a counselling appointment for weeks. We call them adults. But they aren't. They don't know how to be grown-ups. It all comes out. It's like they get a taste of freedom, of separation from their families and they see themselves as independent entities for the first time and they hate it. They pretend they don't, but they do. And they all want someone to blame.'

'What, hang on? You mean they are making false allegations?'

'No. I'm being general. What I mean is, they are scared. And they need someone to talk to. Someone who isn't their parent. And they need it now. The one-to-ones we all have, they are about five minutes on their work, fifty-five on life-coaching. No wonder we're all so stressed out.'

'How many times did she come and see you? For these one-to-ones?'

'Christ. I don't know, four . . . five times?'

'Always in your office?'

'Yes.'

'Never for a drink . . . or . . .'

'No.'

'And HR haven't told you what she's saying.'

'Not yet.'

'Strange.' Jason pauses. 'And yet they've told you her name? That's unusual.'

'What do you mean?'

'Well, at this stage, they normally just say there has been a complaint. How do you know it's her?'

I look at Jason and I realise that I am being played. He doesn't believe me.

'I don't fuck my students, Jason.' My fingernails are pressing into the fleshy part of my palm. 'No matter what the whispers are at work. I can't help it if it's me they want to come to, that it's me they want validation from.'

'And it's just you? That they come to? Not any of the others? What about the boys?'

'Yeah they come too. But no, it's not just me. They come and see Jenny a lot too. But no one is accusing her of anything, are they? Because she's a woman. That's why. If she is in her office with her door shut with a student it's because she's talking about something personal. And if I do it, it's because I'm a predator.'

Jason shakes his head slowly. 'I'm not saying you're a predator mate, I think we're all human. That's all. Like you said, she's an adult. It could have just been a bad judgement call.'

'Is that what we're calling it now?' I stare back at Jason. We both know I've got him over a barrel. 'Even if I'd wanted to, I wouldn't do that to my family.' It's a low blow and I know it.

Jason looks down: 'Well, it's amazing how fast you forget that when some twenty-something girl is groping down your jeans for your cock and you haven't had sex for six months.'

Jason's indiscreet grapple at his mate's stag do, second marriage of course, because we're that age, had stayed in Liverpool. But the guilt had made it all the way back to York. I'd promised I wouldn't tell Becky. And I haven't.

Poor bastard.

'I know. Sorry mate. I know what you mean. But it wasn't a lapse. It wasn't anything. I don't know what she's talking about. I don't even know when this was meant to have happened.' I lie smoothly.

'Listen. I can't represent you because we're mates. Plus, it's not really my field. But I can sort you out with someone. In the meantime, you've got to tell Becky.'

'No.' I shake my head and gulp down the last of my pint. 'No way, she doesn't need this.'

'Where does she think you're going every day?'

'Work.'

'And where are you? Drinking Special Brew in the bus shelter?'

'Close, writing in Costa.'

'How's the book going?'

'I'm still waiting for a bite.'

'Good luck with it all. I'm going to have to get back before bedtime.' Jason stands up and we have a bromancy back slap hug.

'Your secret's safe with me for now, but if Becky finds out you're suspended, I'm denying all knowledge, alright?'

'Sure. Thanks mate.' He pulls his leather jacket over his blue shirt and I can't help think he might fit at the Red Lion after all. Perhaps we both would. Maybe we're those guys now.

Once I'm in the car I let myself sit. I can't bring myself to turn the ignition. The car park is as flat as the sea and as dark as its depths. And I am alone.

Out of habit I click on my emails and there's a fresh one there. Winking at me.

My heart leaps into my mouth.

It's from my agent.

A publisher says they have enjoyed the manuscript and are planning on circulating it for wider feedback.

My God. This is huge. I grin ear to ear. But only for a second. Because it feels unfamiliar. Because I can't drive home, pick my wife up, swing her round and tell Jamie his dad is one step closer to being a children's author.

It's all tainted now.

I want to drive and find Evie and for a beautiful, peaceful second I think about how wonderful it would be to walk right up to her, draw back my fist and punch her straight in her haughty face and watch the blood splatter from her broken nose, her split lip.

Does that make me a bad man?

I don't even know what is good and bad anymore.

I reverse out of the car park and drive home. I take the long way, round the ring road, the lights on the road comforting and the dark blue of the sky like the velvet of my grandmother's skirts.

There are no stars tonight.

Why? It's all I can ask and I drive round and round the ring road, like we used to when Jamie was a baby and wouldn't sleep. Those sleepless, weird in-between days where time made no sense and your head would ring if there were silence.

I'd give anything to have those days back.

Haven't I had enough?

My fist comes down on the steering wheel.

The last time she came, she was different. Guarded. Held herself differently. I didn't think too much of it at the time if I'm honest. I'm not saying that to be cruel, but I didn't. I was busy. She came in, handed back a book I'd lent her because there was such a long waiting list in the library and then pretty much walked away.

I'd expected more.

I'd asked if she was OK, needed a one-to-one and she'd just shaken her head and said she was seeing Jenny.

My foot slips off the accelerator and the car starts to slow down so fast that the car behind me slams on its brakes and there is a loud blaring of a horn. I jump and hit the clutch instead and wrench the wheel back straight while I try to get my speed back up. The car overtakes me and the driver, an irate-looking woman with straggly dark hair, makes a wanking sign with her fist. Can't say I blame her.

All I need is proof. And I've got it. I know I must have it.

When I go through the front door I crank out a smile, feeling the organ grinder's monkey, and grab Becky, tell her about the email from the agent and give Jamie a big kiss. We eat tacos in the living room, Jamie has his meal through his tube, and I stroke the hair from his forehead and convince Becky to let him lie on the sofa with me. I make up a new story.

About the boy with the super powers.

The boy who blinks.

After we've settled Jamie in bed and Becky is brushing her teeth, I send an effusive reply to my agent, then log into the university system from my laptop and go to the list of essays for my last assessment. My eyes scan for Elodie Highfield. Her name isn't red anymore.

I open up the assignment. My comments and annotations are all on it. But the fact it came up as sixty per cent plagiarised has gone.

I don't sleep again. I lie watching the rise and fall of Jamie's chest and tears sting my eyes. I can't lose this.

My phone is full of messages, texts, DMs on Twitter. Students telling me to get well soon.

They'll carry on being taught, other lecturers will cover my classes. Life will go on. I think of all the times I have struggled in with the flu, that time I didn't go with Becky to Great Ormond Street because I couldn't miss graduation.

That Inspirational Lecturer of the Year award is gathering dust on my desk. I've been slid out and removed like the middle log on a Jenga tower, and nothing has come tumbling down.

'I've sorted it. Nothing to worry about.' That's what Jenny said when I asked her about Elodie's assessment. That's her role as Unfair Means Officer. To investigate when there's something fishy about an essay. Normally there's a meeting with the student and an investigation.

Sometimes it's an accident. A genuine misunderstanding of how to reference, of self-plagiarism. But there are always records. A noted mark adjustment. The red doesn't just disappear.

I download everything. It occurs to me, if this goes as far as it could, I might get locked out of the university system. So I start going through all of Jenny's plagiarism appeals. I download the entire folder and the assessments they refer to. If I can prove somehow, that she's had her fingers in the academic till, so to speak. That she's fudged the figures. Maybe I can use it to discredit her. Maybe I could use it to persuade her not to go through with this. To talk Evie out of it. It must have been her. It must have been.

My mind races through the last few weeks. How Evie started seeing Jenny more than me. How I asked about Elodie, I challenged her . . . and then this happens, out of the blue.

Then, all of a sudden, someone else comes to mind. The last person who challenged Jenny.

I swing my legs over the side of the bed. It was an appeal. We were all shocked. No one appealed about Jenny. Not ever. Her feedback was extensive, screen-casted, it put us all to shame. In fact, she'd even been asked by Peter to rein it back. Manage expectations, was what he'd said. I'd listened to her fume in the pub after work. Livid she had been told to do her job worse in case it made everyone look bad. I nodded sympathetically of course, even though it had been me who'd broached it with him. I mean, seriously? Who had the time?

It must have been three years ago. A student called Ewan. Shit, what was his last name? He'd tried to appeal his dissertation mark. Claimed she hadn't steered him in the right direction, and had, in fact, purposefully misdirected him. She had provided a dossier of evidence to the contrary, but it turned out it wasn't needed. He'd withdrawn the appeal after another student had shopped him for making vulgar jokes about Jenny in a group chat. He had graduated with dishonours.

Ewan.

Ewan Wright. He was there, in my followers. He'd posted very little since 2018. The odd football remark. Occasional retweet. Worked for a marketing firm. No surprise there.

Chewing my fingernails, I think back. The student that shopped him. Who was it? Did we ever find out? Was it anonymous? I couldn't remember. All I remember was Jenny becoming the department darling. Poor, abused Jenny. There was even an article in Hackademics about students bullying lecturers.

Jenny's so dry she must be a virgin.

That's what it said. What Ewan had said. A message to the entire cohort's WhatsApp group.

The female students came out in force and threw him so far under the bus he was pulp and tyre marks by the end of it. A new policy written on respect in learning communities. A proposed ban on sexual comments in student social media groups. At attempt at some of the lads citing freedom of speech. Shut down so fast you could hear the cracks in their necks.

I paste Elodie's essay back into Google. It's obvious.

Someone has changed the plagiarism percentage on the system. That's the only way to stop it being marked as red. And the only person who has access to that is Jenny.

But why? I know she loves her students, but she surely wouldn't be so unprofessional as to turn a blind eye to this? To make a mockery of the whole system?

Becky comes through at about 7 a.m. to let me shower before work. I'm starting to feel guilty now. But I need to fix this first. She has enough on. I can't bear the thought of her worrying about this. The curve of her face isn't as full as it used to be. The shadows under her eyes are greenish and purple. She's lost weight again, but it doesn't suit her. Her figure is becoming all angled and her hips are too thin. I look at her, feeding Jamie, holding the tube in the right place and for a second my heart wants to shatter into a million pieces.

I shower, kiss my family goodbye and head towards

campus. I need to show this to HR, to Peter. I try calling on my way in to let them know that I'm coming. I'm not stupid. I know just turning up like some kind of unhinged lunatic will not go in my favour.

No one answers as per usual, so I leave a voicemail and pull over into a Costa, deciding I should give them a chance to call me back.

The girl behind the counter smiles at me and looks back twice while she crushes the beans. I can't imagine why. I accidentally see my reflection in the mirror behind the till and I look old. I have stubble, not even sexy designer Clooney stubble, I just look unwashed. My eyes are grey. My skin is sallow. The girl must only be about twenty. She looks at me again and I smile back politely. She blushes and looks down. It's cute. Then, for a horrible moment I think it's because she's a student. She recognises me. She knows. I still have no idea what they've been told. My smile falters and I step away from the counter.

I stare down at the floor while I hear the spit and hiss of the machine then, without meeting the girl's eyes, I take my offered cup, nod a thanks and sit as far from her as possible, tucked away in a corner.

My heart is drumming just that little bit too fast as I open my emails on my phone.

There's another one from my agent. I open it and my smile breaks out so fast and hard my cheeks could split. Another publisher is making positive noises. Fresh voice, high concept.

I quickly forward it over and text Becky.

She replies fast even though I know it's meds time.

I'm so proud of you – Jamie too

And it makes me want to hang my head in shame.

Nevertheless, I email my agent back. I think I'm getting another reply when an email pops in from Jason.

Have you told her yet?

Bastard. I swipe it fast so it deletes before Becky sees it. She knows the password and even if she wasn't checking up on my accounts, sometimes they go straight to the iPad.

I learnt that once the hard way.

PS Any news from HR? They need to give you an interview date. They can't leave you hanging. Do you want me to get my mate to drop them a line? He'll do it for free.

Stop fucking emailing, I want to shout.

I check my phone to see if I had any missed calls and had accidentally put my phone on silent, but there's nothing. I sigh, half buzzing, half stressed.

The girl from behind the counter comes over and wipes the table down next to me. I can see she has something on a tray, and her eyes dart over to me, back and forth like a lizard's tongue.

I stiffen as she stands up, takes a deep breath and turns to me.

'Hey, um, this is going out of date today – wondered if you'd like it? It'll just get chucked otherwise.' I look down and see she is offering a slice of very fresh, gooey-looking Rocky Road.

I meet her eyes and smile.

'I'd love it. Thank you.'

She walks away and I notice she swings her hips a little. I smile and check my emails again.

Suddenly I am absolutely starving.

Louise from HR doesn't call me back so I decide to try my luck and I drive over anyway. I can't just sit there. No one on security bats an eyelid when I pull into the car park. I don't know what I was expecting. To be manhandled back into my car? Maybe I have over-reacted to all of this. Maybe it's just some procedural thing and I'll be back at work in time for Josh's memorial. Nevertheless, I put my head down and weave through the throngs of students, not making eye contact, deliberately making myself small. It seems further than usual to HR but I breathe a sigh of relief when I get there, almost like I've been given a get-out-of-jail-free card. I go to the reception and smile a little bit breathlessly at the girl.

'Is Louise in please?' I ask and give her my full name, watching carefully to see if she recognises it. She doesn't appear to.

I pace up and down until Louise comes out of a frosted glass door to the left-hand side of the desk.

'Simon?' She looks concerned. 'Did we have an appointment?'

'No. I couldn't get you on the phone. It's urgent.'

She looks uncomfortable for a second and I realise I have made a major faux pas.

'Sorry, it's just, I'd not heard anything from you and I have some new information.'

'I think it would be better if we schedule in a formal meeting.' I am given a thin-lipped smile.

'Fine. When?'

'We will be in touch.' She nods. 'As soon as possible.'

'No.' I shake my head. 'I'm sorry, that's not good enough. It's been nearly two weeks and I've heard nothing. I'm going out of my mind here. Surely I have rights?'

Louise looks at the girl who is typing away and pretending not to be listening.

I hope she's sworn some kind of confidentiality oath.

'OK. Pop through. I've got five minutes.'

I follow her like some guilty schoolboy. This squat creature of a woman. My shoulders have never felt lower.

She ushers me past the private, more discreet meeting room into what is essentially a glass box in an open-plan office and it takes me all I have left not to roll my eyes. I am on display.

'Simon.' She sits and gestures for me to do the same. I consider staying standing to give me some leverage but realise that's not what is needed in this situation. So I bend both knees.

'You really shouldn't be here. While you're on suspension the terms of your full pay are that you remain off-campus.'

I bite my tongue. 'Louise. I have reason to believe I'm being stitched up.'

She looks at me and her brows raise but there's a flicker at the corners of her mouth. For a second I think she's trying not to laugh and I feel my insides roughen like sandpaper. I have to stay calm.

'Just listen. Jenny Summers, in my department.' Her eyelids flicker and then it's clear. I always knew she was involved. Two-faced bitch.

'About a month ago, I brought up a plagiarism concern to her. In her official role. A student she's extra close to, Elodie Highfield. It was more than sixty per cent plagiarised. These things aren't accidents. Not at that level. Anyway, I was expecting to be told the outcome of the investigation, but when I asked, she just told me she'd sorted it.'

'Right.' Louise's face was poker.

'I ended up going into the office to see what they knew. But she'd never recorded anything with them. There'd been no meeting set up. Nothing official.'

'Well it sounds like something the head of department should be dealing with, or the student experience manager. But I'm not sure of the relevance here?' Louise's voice was kind, but she was sounding the ends of her words crisply. I knew I didn't have long.

'I think one of the office girls mentioned it to Jen. That I'd been asking. Chasing it up. I think she went and changed it. Overrode it. Made it look like a system error.'

'And why would she do that?'

'Because Elodie Highfield has a mother with early onset dementia. She is her sole carer. She has a learning support plan. She is one of Jen's little . . .' I stop myself just in time. 'Protégés. Personal tutees. She has unnaturally close relationships with them. I think she got Evie to report me, to make sure I didn't report her. To rake my name through the mud so to speak.'

'These are incredibly serious allegations Simon.'

'And the ones made against me aren't?'

A sigh. She doesn't say anything and I can't read her at all.

I stand up. 'I want a meeting. An official one. And I'm bringing a lawyer. These allegations are unfounded and a deliberate attempt to defame me.'

Louise takes a deep breath. 'We are still taking statements.'

'I don't care.' I jump in. 'You can take mine. Before the end of the week. And unless you have any proof, apart from the word of an unstable undergraduate student, I want to be reinstated immediately.'

Louise looks at me. At first I think she is intimidated. Impressed even.

I turn and walk out before I am proved otherwise.

On the way to the car park I don't bother to hunch over. I have nothing to hide. I grab a coffee at the union and wander about in the quad, feeling the sun on my back and feeling the buzz from the swarm of students. There's a shadow from the arts tower and I move to the side so I am not in it. Pasted in the bookstore window there's Josh's smiling face on the poster for his memorial. And in the reflection, I see her. Evie. Getting a drink from John's cart. I dart to the side and peer from around the pillar pasted from ceiling to ground with brightly coloured flyers, adverts for house shares, RAG, society bar crawls, film night. It's exhausting just looking at it all.

I see her scowl at her ringing phone and shove it down deeper in her pocket, before taking the cup and making her way towards the library. I can't help it. I follow her, staying well back.

Every part of me wants to run up to her, to grab her by the shoulders and shake her. Demand to know what she thinks she is playing at.

I've never wanted her to see me more.

But I stand back, one foot in the shadow of the tower.

She struggles to get her student ID card out one-handed from her purse, so she puts down her coffee on the wall to the underpass while she fumbles with her bag.

I move a little closer.

She holds her card between her teeth, puts her purse back in her handbag and picks her coffee up again.

See me.

For a second I think she might but she turns her head and I swear loudly, as I am knocked out of the way by a tall young man who is running backwards to catch a ball.

‘Shit, sorry man.’ He lays a hand on my shoulder and the human touch makes me want to cry.

‘It’s cool.’ I smile and look back to where Evie stood a second ago.

She has gone. I wait a moment to make sure she isn’t going to magically reappear like some kind of Polaroid. I turn, and realise I have absolutely nowhere to go.

CHAPTER TEN

Evie

The day before the memorial

'You want to go to the quiz this week?' Liam looked at the floor quickly, and shuffled his feet about. The library wasn't exactly quiet. It couldn't be with the constant click, click, click of keyboards, but his voice still felt like it was echoing off the glass walls.

'Yeah, sure. Are we all going?'

'Um, I dunno . . .' Liam trailed off and looked down the aisle. There weren't many books left. Not really. Most of them were now e-books. But Evie liked the hard copies still. Feeling the weight of them in her arms. It made her feel more productive, proactive somehow.

'Or we could just go for a drink tonight?' Liam smiled and he looked lovely. His eyes crinkled and his cheekbones rose sharply. She wanted to ruffle his hair.

'Yeah, I guess so. I mean, I hate being in the house right now.'

Liam scratched the back of his head. It was the third time since he'd come up to her. Evie wondered if he had nits.

'Thanks. You know how to make a guy feel great.'

'Oh, I didn't mean it like that.' Evie slapped his chest, a move that was a little girly and uncomfortable for her but she hadn't meant to offend him. It was true though. The house felt oppressive and even though Harvey had a water-tight alibi as he'd been signed in at the shooting club, when that *thing* had been spread all over her door, she still didn't like sleeping with him opposite. Liam had offered to switch rooms with her. Bless him. But she hadn't wanted to make a fuss.

Little Liam, who looked like a designer car twoccer in his variety of skinny joggers and shiny hoodies.

'Anyway, so maybe tonight?' Liam sniffed and Evie got a sudden worry this invitation was only being extended to her.

'Totally, let's see what the others feel like. I mean, it's the memorial tomorrow, right?' She smiled warmly and made her studying excuses. He walked off and Evie saw him drop the books he had just collected in the return bin.

Bronte was cooking moussaka when Evie got back in and Kelly was flicking through a magazine at the rickety kitchen table. The thought of the moussaka made her stomach turn. Her weird yogurt sauce thing always curdled and it was like eating rubber-flavoured aubergine.

'Babe, I've made double.' Bronte grinned. Her hair was tied up with a pair of knickers again. At first Evie had thought it cute and quirky but now it just seemed a bit try-hard. What's wrong with a bobble?

'Oh. That's lovely of you but I'm not that hungry.' Evie grimaced. 'I had a really late lunch.'

'Oh, no problem, I'll plate you some up and you can eat it later,' Bronte said. 'What we doing tonight? Netflix or quiz?'

Evie gulped. 'Actually, Liam wants to go out.'

'Oh, fine then,' Bronte said. 'When did you see Liam?' she asked casually.

'Commons,' Evie said and rested her elbows on the counter. 'He was, well, never mind.' She opened the fridge then remembered she had said she wasn't hungry and shut it again.

Kelly looked up, her brown shiny bob swinging against her pointy chin. Evie thought she looked like a goblin sometimes. In the nicest possible way. Curled ears and bright eyes.

'Oh he finally did it then?' she said.

'Did what?' Evie hoisted herself up onto the counter.

Kelly glanced at Bronte then back down at her magazine. 'Doesn't matter.'

'No, what do you mean?' Bronte looked back over her shoulder. 'Another man falling for the luscious charms of Evie?'

Evie shot her a confused look, then realised she was probably being over-sensitive.

The front door went with a bang and Finn sauntered in, his record bag slung across his body.

'What's up, bitches?'

'You know you can't call us that.' Bronte pointed her spatula at him.

'I only do it to wind you up.' Finn threw his arm round her and opened his mouth. 'Gimme,' he said.

Bronte spooned some of the sauce into his mouth and Evie watched his eyelid twitch.

'Nice.' He nodded. Evie looked away and smiled.

'Anyway, are you blind or summat?' Finn took a slug from his posh water bottle and winked at Evie.

'What?' Evie crinkled her brow.

'You cock-blocked my boy!'

'Erm, I don't think it's cock-blocking when the cock is aimed at you. I think that's actually just saying no,' Kelly pointed out.

'Are we talking about Liam again?' Evie bit her lip.

'Again? So, come on. Do you like him or not? He likes you.' Finn pulled a chair out and sat down noisily.

'Finn. He's great, you know he is. We all adore Liam but I'm in no place to start dating.'

'Can't you just fuck him?' Kelly said, chin in hand.

'Kelly!' Evie laughed.

'Such vulgar words from such a sweet mouth,' Bronte said.

'I'm kidding,' Kelly said. 'Besides, no one wants that level of awks around here. Don't shit on your doorstep and all that.'

'I'm not planning on shitting anywhere.'

'Ah. Come on. Can't you throw him a bone?' Finn said. 'He has shit luck with women and he really likes you. Just, you know. Give him an ego boost.'

'You want me to sleep with someone to make them feel better about themselves?'

'Hand job?'

'Finn!' Bronte threw a dish towel at him. 'Leave it. This is the last thing she needs right now.'

'Actually, I disagree. I know you reckon you're still on the rebound but you've got to break that streak soon. Might as well do it with someone who is a good guy.'

'Come on, Finn.' Evie jumped down.

'I mean. One drink. That's all.' Finn looked at the others. 'We could all bow out tonight last minute, right?'

'Oh that's not going to look obvious at all.' Kelly rolled her eyes.

'Anyone seen Harvey?' Finn asked.

'Nope,' Kelly said. 'You think he's got his mother's dead body in his room? Careful if you're going in the shower Evie.'

'I can't believe we can't just kick him out.' Bronte shook her head.

'Maybe it really wasn't him,' Evie said quietly.

'Well who else was it?' Kelly said. 'Who else shoots rabbits like some kind of deranged *The Hills Have Eyes* crazy.'

'Ooo we should watch that tonight,' Bronte said.

'I just can't comprehend anyone we know would do

something like that. Anyway, they said it was too big to be a rabbit. More like a pig.'

'Well, the locks have been changed now at least,' Bronte said. 'If it happens again, we know it's got to be him. No one else has the keys.' She opened the oven door and slid in the moussaka.

'I can't believe the police thought it was some kind of joke,' Kelly said. 'I mean, who is that sick? And anyway, what have you lied about?'

'Nothing,' Bronte said sharply. 'Evie is as open as they come.'

Evie gave her a thin-lipped smile.

'God. I'm really not sure about tonight. I don't think I have the energy.'

'You don't have to come,' Bronte said. 'I mean, I think you should, but if you can't face it I'll stay in with you. But, I don't know. What with tomorrow . . . maybe we could all use a drink.'

'No, I'll come.' Evie gathered her hair up in a ponytail. 'I'll maybe have a hot bath first though.'

But an hour later, even after she'd slapped on some mascara and a fresh top, the energy still wasn't there. A hot bath in digs was hardly travertine tiles, thick white candles and bubbles. It was an avocado tub with blackened sealant, wet salmon towels on the floor and mould on the ceiling. Even the last of her Christmas bubble bath had done little to set the mood.

Evie dreamed of living alone. A flat of her own where she

could cook what she wanted and curl up on the sofa without having someone's feet shoved in her lap and be forced to watch *Love Island*. She wanted to be able to make a cup of tea without having to make six, and carry them through with her knuckles burning against the mugs. A place where she could leave her milk and it would still be there the next day. Where her keys were her own. Where, if she felt like it, she could lock the doors for an entire weekend.

Staring at herself in the mirror she could barely paint on her smile. Bronte had been in with a glass of something. She'd tried to bring it to her in the bath. But Evie had pretended she couldn't hear the knock. Taking a sip, she closed her eyes and tried to picture herself in the pub. The loud laughter, the shouting into people's ears to have a conversation. Having to stand up all night, listening to awful music and watch as the world kept turning. Just. Kept. Turning. But she was standing still, like the fair workers in the middle of the Speedway ride with their cigarettes in their sleeves and hearts in their fists. Finn nudging her. The lost, hopeful look in Liam's eyes. Bronte standing so close to her she couldn't breathe. The sheer effort of forming words.

Harvey wasn't home. She could tell. His door was closed but there was no light under the door. No shuffles. No movement. The house felt paused.

Blowing out her cheeks, she went down both flights of stairs, the eyes of Josh swivelling as she walked past. She moved quicker.

'Here she is,' Bronte sing-songed as Evie went into the kitchen and put her glass in the sink. 'Feel better?'

'Have you noticed how much washing Finn does?' Kelly was peering into the machine. 'I mean, he must put on a load a day. How much must that be costing us? Should I say something?'

Evie stared back at her blankly. 'Sorry, what?'

'You OK, hon?' Bronte paused, adjusting her boobs inside her top.

'God, I'm so sorry. I'm not feeling that well,' Evie said. 'I'm not sure I can come out.'

'Babes! I'll stay in with you,' Bronte said. One boob remained at mid lift.

'No. Honestly. My head is killing me. I might just go to bed.'

'Well. I don't like leaving you alone.' Bronte crossed her arms. Evie noticed she had taken extra care on her eye flicks.

'Seriously. Please go. You look gorgeous. I think I'm just going to take some tablets and go to bed.'

'Who's going to bed?' Finn jumped down the last stair and appeared at the door like a spring. 'Evie? Do you need company, because . . .'

'Shut up!' Liam appeared behind him and thumped him on the arm. Finn grabbed him in a headlock and they looked embarrassingly like a pair of tweenage brothers fighting over the Xbox.

'Sorry, guys.' Evie deliberately made her voice weaker.

'I think I've got a migraine coming on. I just need to lie down in the dark.'

Finn opened his mouth and Liam immediately slapped his hand over it.

'Come on,' he said without meeting her eye. 'Let's just go.'

Evie looked at Bronte. 'Honestly, I really just want to go to bed.'

'Just for one?' Bronte pleaded.

'For Christ's sake.' Kelly grabbed her fake leather jacket off the back of the chair. 'Are you incapable of being apart for even an hour?'

Evie didn't dare look at the wounded stare she was sure would be in Bronte's eyes. 'Have a good time, guys.' She turned and filled up her glass with water. 'Sorry to be such a downer.'

Then without dragging it out, she headed back up the stairs, locked her bedroom door and fell into a deep, empty, cavernous sleep.

When she woke up, it was pitch black and she had no idea whether it was three in the morning or ten at night. Sitting up groggily, Evie reached for her phone. But when she waved it in front of her face, the screen was black. There were no other clocks in her room, so she pulled back her duvet and tapped her lamp. The room filled with shadows and, cocking her head, she could hear no noise. She plugged in her phone, then unlocked her door and opened it slowly. The house felt as much of a shell as it had before. No breathing, creaking of steps, clinking of mugs. It seemed there was only a very small proportion of the day when someone wasn't pottering around.

The hall light was out. Had she turned it off? She couldn't remember.

Looking behind her, her phone still hadn't come to life, so she flicked on the switch and watched the brash lighting spool into the off-green, thinning carpet.

Treading carefully in case it was, in fact, an ungodly hour, Evie made her way down the stairs, listening out for signs of life from Bronte's room. A light was coming from under the kitchen door, and a sizzle and spit, as if someone were frying. She could smell fat but no flavour.

'What time is it?' Evie asked as she blearily opened the door, expecting to see one of the boys with an open packet of cut-price bacon in one hand and a spatula in the other.

But it was neither. Instead a tall, gangly shape was hunched over the hob. He didn't turn around and for a moment Evie nearly ran straight back up the stairs.

The white plastic clock with its red hands read 10.33 p.m. and she realised everyone must still be out. And she was alone in the spindly, crumbling house with Harvey.

'Hi,' she said carefully to his turned back. 'I . . . I didn't realise you were in.'

'Didn't think you lot were in either.' Harvey sniffed but didn't turn around.

'We're not. I mean, they're at the pub. But I'm sure they will be back soon,' Evie added in a rush and Harvey shook his head.

Evie looked back up the stairs as her stomach growled loudly. She hadn't eaten since breakfast and even the thought of Bronte's moussaka wasn't repulsive. She didn't exactly want to stay in the vicinity of Harvey, but what else could she do? She couldn't avoid him forever and, anyway, the police were positive he hadn't been the one responsible.

She took a step further in.

'What are you making?'

A sigh. Then a pause so long she didn't think he was going to bother answering her. Could she blame him?

'Pancakes.' He eventually replied, with a bit of a snort at the end.

'Pancakes? Really?' Evie edged towards the fridge.

'Yeah, why?'

'Don't know. I only really eat them on pancake day.'

There was silence from Harvey. Evie opened the fridge and wondered if making a sandwich and getting out of there would be the quickest and least excruciating option.

Bronte's moussaka was there, plated up, even with a side salad, all wrapped in clingfilm with a Post-it note on it telling her how long to heat it up for and at what temperature. Evie pulled it out and sighed a bit too loudly. She would either have to get on and eat it, or at least pretend she had, otherwise she'd get the eyes.

Peeling back the wrapper she gave it a sniff, rubber and cottage cheese, and then opened the pedal pin and slid the whole lot in.

Harvey glanced at what she was doing, but said nothing.

Evie buttered her bread in silence and watched as Harvey poured a yellow liquid into the pan and swirled it around expertly.

'You look like you know what you're doing there,' Evie said and tried to catch his eye for a smile but his baseball cap was pulled low.

'My little sister loves them,' he said by way of explanation.

'Aww how old is she?' Evie prompted, and slapped a depressed-looking slice of ham onto her bread.

'Why are you talking to me?' Harvey's voice was deadpan but firm. 'Don't you think I'm some kind of psycho.'

Awkward. Awkward. 'I'm sorry about that,' Evie said. 'I think we all just over-reacted. I was scared. You know . . . the rabbit.'

'It wasn't a rabbit. It was a pig.'

Evie decided not to press him on how he knew that.

'I'm sorry. I really am.'

'I'm surprised they've left you alone. Precious princess and all that.'

Evie bristled. 'I said I am sorry and I meant it. You don't have to like me, but can we please be civil?'

'I don't know you. I have no idea if I like you or not.'

'We've been living together since September,' Evie pointed out.

'And this is the first time you've said more than two words to me. And only because you feel guilty,' Harvey said, then stood back and in one deft move from his wrist, flipped his pancake over.

Evie stayed quiet and cut her sandwich in half. The only sound in the kitchen was the sizzle of the pancake and the ticking of the clock. The counter tops were sticky and the washing-up was mounting in the sink under the harsh fluorescent lighting.

Harvey slid the pancake onto a plate and, to Evie's surprise, handed it straight to her.

'You can't eat that. It's got mould on it.'

'What?' Evie looked down. 'Oh shit.' He was right. There were little dots of furry blue on the crust. She retched in her mouth. 'Oh, God.' She opened the bin again and tipped it straight in. 'Oh, God. I can't . . .' She made a gagging sound again. 'Sorry, I've got a thing about mould.'

'Good job you didn't eat it then.' Harvey poured more of the pancake mixture into the pan.

'Are you sure about this?' Evie held up the plate. 'That's . . . Harvey that's really kind. Thank you.'

He shrugged and Evie sat down gratefully, sprinkling some tea-stained, clumpy sugar over the top.

'She's fourteen,' Harvey said, while Evie was mid-mouthful.

'Your sister?' Evie held her hand over her mouth to reply.

'Yeah.'

'Are you close?'

'Yeah.'

'So . . . tell me why they call you One-Shot Harvey?' Evie smiled. 'This is delicious by the way.'

'*They* don't. Whoever *they* are. Liam called me it once. On the Xbox. I've got good aim.'

Harvey flipped his pancake onto his plate, and then sat down at the table. They both chewed in silence, until a sudden clatter and yowl of a cat in the backyard made them jump.

'What was that?' Evie dropped her fork with a clatter.

'Just someone coming home pissed.' Harvey shrugged.

'No, no, it came from our back garden,' Evie said, her eyes on the black window that overlooked the garden, which was precisely one metre square of grass, and then cracked flags with dandelions and other weeds crawling between stones. She cocked her head, not taking her eyes off the window. 'Listen,' she whispered.

There was a scrape, and another rustle, near the back door. Harvey heard it too and turned in his chair. With the lights on in the kitchen, they couldn't see anything outside apart from their own reflections. And Evie realised whoever was outside could see straight in. Her heart began to race.

'Why would anyone be in the yard?' she hissed.

Harvey got up and leant over the sink, cupped his hands and peered out between them. 'I can't see anyone.'

A loud peal made Evie scream, and jump up from her chair.

'Jesus Christ,' Harvey said, clutching his chest. 'You gave me a heart attack.'

'Who's at the door?' Evie said. 'I'm scared. Please, Harvey, you go.'

'What are you scared of?' he scoffed. Evie tailed behind him, hating herself for playing the submissive damsel.

She watched from the hallway as Harvey went into the

living room and opened the front door onto the empty, dark street.

'There's no one here.' He shrugged and stepped onto the road of terraces and cars so tightly parked they looked like paper chains.

'Are you sure?' Evie followed him into the living room.

'Positive,' he said, looking both ways. 'It'll just be kids playing knock-a-door-run.'

'There are no kids on this street,' Evie said quietly.

Harvey came back in, closed the door and locked it, just as a loud hammering started up from the kitchen door.

Evie screamed again. Harvey pushed past her and made straight for the back.

'Wait, wait.' Evie ran behind him. 'Please don't leave me on my own.'

Harvey fumbled with the lock then yanked open the door. Evie, half expecting to see a man in a doll mask, or someone brandishing yet more butchery, ducked behind him. But there was nothing there except the moonlight shining onto their overflowing bins and a feral-looking ginger cat perched on what remained of their rotting shed.

'Seriously. It'll be some . . .' Harvey trailed off as he spotted something on the doorstep. 'What's this?'

'Oh, Jesus what now?' Evie backed away. 'What is it?'

Harvey stooped down and picked up a shallow black cardboard box emblazoned with love hearts. The kind you might find in Clintons around Valentine's Day.

'It's got your name on,' Harvey said.

'I don't want it,' Evie whispered. Harvey locked the door and put the box on the table.

They both stood looking at it.

'Maybe you've got a secret admirer?' Harvey said.

'I doubt it.' Evie pushed the box towards him.

'Do you want me to open it?'

'Yes please.' Evie stood back. 'I can't handle any more body parts.'

'You sure?' Harvey asked.

Evie screwed her eyes shut. 'Please just do it. Tell me what it is.'

There was a moment's silence, and she heard the lid being lifted. But no gasps or noises of disgust.

'What is it?' She looked through her splayed fingers.

'A photo.' Harvey frowned.

'A photo?' Evie let her hands fall and moved closer to him. 'Of what?'

'It's of you, I think. Is that you?' Evie took the picture from him with trembling fingers. She was about fourteen, fifteen, with a group of friends, all in school uniform, their arms around each other, grinning.

'It's me,' she said softly. Her hair was blonder then, her hips narrower, eyebrows thicker.

'Wait. There's something else.' Harvey plucked out a small black envelope from the box and pulled out a gift tag.

'What does it say?' Evie's heart was hammering so hard she could hear the blood pounding in her ears.

'It says . . . You're not who you say you are.'

CHAPTER ELEVEN

Jenny

The memorial

I look at myself in the mirror, but despite trawling through every website possible trying to find the perfect outfit, and facing the trauma of going to the post office to return it all, I still don't feel right. I can't look glamorous. I can't look scruffy. I can't look too clinical. In the end I settle on an old favourite. A silky dress with a vintage print, and brown leather peep toes. Wedges made it look too christening-like. I put a navy military-style fitted jacket over the top and it works. The neckline is low without being too revealing and the skirt falls just below my knee. The lines are all smooth, my hair is straight and not fussy, my make-up is eyes but no lips.

I feel sick. There have been no messages now for nearly a week. I have almost managed to convince myself it's one of his friends just playing some kind of horrible prank. Like I said. They're still just children really. Maybe they found my number on his phone. Although, I did of course tell him to put it under a fake name. But maybe I'm in his favourites or something. I have no idea. But I can't let myself crumple now. Not today.

My speech is on my iPad but I have already memorised it. I can't look down. Not at any point. It's unprofessional and this needs to look as if it is coming from the heart. Everyone will be there. I feel a tear begin to swell and I pinch the flesh on my ribcage until it's unbearable. I only let go when I don't think I'm about to cry anymore. There will be a bruise there tomorrow.

I don't eat breakfast as I can't risk the bloat, and then drive to the station. No teaching today. Wednesdays are usually my working from home day, as most universities avoid scheduling classes in the afternoons due to sport. But not today.

The train ride is painfully slow and I try to sit as still as I possibly can so that I don't crease.

There's a man sat three rows in front. He's facing me because I'm on one of those trains where the seats change direction halfway through the carriage. His face is hung and his bile blonde hair looks salty and itchy.

I keep looking until he becomes aware and looks back at me. His eyes are grey and sad and his coat is cheap. I suspect he may have a faint odour to him but I'm not close enough. I wonder who makes him smile. What kind of home he has. I worry about him for no real reason for the rest of the twenty-minute ride. He looks up once, twice. I try and smile both times, to make a connection but he resists. Eventually he gets off at the stop before mine. I watch him walk off the platform towards a tired-looking housing estate. I think he has a limp. But then again, I could just be imagining it.

I am calmer by the time we arrive and I buy a skinny latte at the station for the walk. The sun has blessed us and although there's a chill in the air, there will be no rain for Josh.

Campus is busy. But I shouldn't imagine it's all for us. I head over to the Peace Garden. It's not really a garden at all. It has a poorly maintained water feature that all the third years put washing up liquid in at the Graduation Ball, as if no one has ever done that before, and leave for the porters to clean up. There are smooth and shiny treacle-coloured stone walls in a square around it, and various planters, made of the same stone. Fresh herbs and flowers are stuffed around them, and there is a honeysuckle bush to one side that mixes with the lavender and doesn't smell quite right. A few benches and patches of grass that look like a card shark has spread them out like a pack of cards. You can see the arts tower from here, but it doesn't cast a shadow.

The sculpture has already been installed and a tall box is over it to keep it veiled. Nearer midday, we'll remove that and cover it in a sheet for a more dramatic flourish when the time comes. It's beautiful. Welded locally by a metal sculptor, interwoven with polished wooden leaves with tiny pegs on. The idea is you put a prayer, a good thought, or a kind idea, on the leaves of the tree. The Joshua Tree.

It's quiet still. Just a tech guy fixing up a microphone to a lectern that I don't need.

'Hi.' I smile at the guy in his university fleece. 'How's it going? Are we all set?' I nod at the lectern.

'Yeah fine. Are you one of the speakers?' he asks. He has lovely brown eyes, like a cocker spaniel. His name tag says Ahmeel.

'Yes. I'm last I think.'

'You must be important,' Ahmeel says, winding up a cord.

'Hardly,' I reply. 'Do we need to do a sound test or anything?'

Ahmeel taps the mic a couple of times. 'There. Done.'

'Oh. The glamour.' He laughs and I walk up towards my office to check for mascara smudges and run through my speech one more time.

Josh's dad will be arriving soon and I know he wanted to speak to me beforehand. The thought makes me feel sick.

I nod hellos at my students and take the lift so I can avoid any more contact.

Peter is in the hallway frowning at the copier when I reach my floor,

'Do you need a hand?'

'Ah Jenny. Just the woman.'

I peer over his shoulder and read the error code.

'Oh it's just a jammed bit of paper,' I say, opening the lid.

I see it straight away, yank it out and the machine comes back to life.

'I don't know what we would do without you,' Peter says in relief.

And to think they still earn a third more than we do.

Cate bobs her head round my office door while I'm taking off my jacket.

'Hi. You look lovely.'

'Thanks.' I smile. 'Need to make an effort really.'

'How are you feeling? Are you nervous?'

'No,' I lie gently. 'It's only five minutes. And it's not like we're not used to public speaking.'

'I know . . . this seems more personal though.'

'What do you mean?' I ask, perhaps more sharply than intended.

'It's a really important moment for his family. That's all. It's not like a lecture where no one's really listening anyway.'

'Thanks.'

'This is more . . . intimate.'

'Well. That's made me feel a whole lot better, thanks Cate.'

'I'm so sorry. I didn't mean . . .'

'It's fine.' My cheeks are aching from the pain of keeping the grin in place. 'Anyway,' I sigh. 'I just need to do these emails and then we can walk down together if you like?'

''Course. Knock when you're ready.'

She disappears and I log on. While I wait for my desktop to spring to life, I think about that night. How can I not?

I'd been at the pub. The Graduate. I didn't make a rule of drinking with students. After all, I'm not Simon. But it was the end of the term and the sun was shining. I had nowhere else to go. Everyone else had gone too, and someone had the idea of calling it a summer social, to get out of the dodgy 'should I go to the pub with my students' ethical horror. We'd even sprung for a little marquee at the back and one glass of Pimm's each that was downed within fifteen minutes of us arriving. And that had just been the staff.

Josh had been there with his friends. Liam. Finn. Tommy. Bronte. A few others. He had stood on the sidelines, his shirt all crisp. He wouldn't have looked out of place with a glass of prosecco in his hand rather than a pint.

I turned away because I had to.

Simon had put a glass of red in my hand and held court. One by one each lecturer had peeled off, one anecdote at a time, until the staff had sat in little clumps and the students had piled like hamsters over the extended beer table.

'This is a bit of an anti-social summer social don't you think?'

'What are you talking about?' Simon had grinned. 'It's been brilliant.'

Of course he'd thought it had. I'd taken my glass over to the grown-ups and joined in the din. I'd glanced up once or twice. Yes, at Josh. But that's not unusual for me. Some people have hobbies. I have people. I collect them. Put them in my pocket. Some I put back. Others I cling to. But I never, ever throw anyone away.

My foster mum, one of them, always said it was my super power. I could look at a person and tell you their name, their story, their pet and their dream within minutes. It didn't matter if it wasn't real.

Few people are.

Then, Josh had looked back up at me. We'd held a gaze for a few seconds and then he'd smiled. A slow smile. I'd refused to look away. That wouldn't look good.

So I'd smiled back.

When my eyes had returned to the table, Simon was watching.

I check my make-up again in the mirror and shake out my hair. The idea was that it would be a candlelight vigil but it's not getting dark until later now. Everyone is hoping for a pleasant dusk instead. The pictures won't be as good if you can't see the flicker and the flames.

The garden is much busier now, the Student Union president and his cronies are all there, as well as the head of central welfare and guidance. I can see Josh's friends, Bronte, Finn, Liam. Evie isn't here, but then she never knew him, so I guess there's no reason for her to come. Maybe she should have come for Bronte. She is a nice girl, Evie. A little naive. I'd even say a little self-involved. Not in a selfish way. Just in an introverted way. She's one of those people that floats in their little bubbles without really understanding others. Not understanding that their presence does soothe and their words can be the balm for the soreness of anxiety and low self-esteem. Take Bronte. She comes across as the extrovert. The one who gets invited to all the parties, who drags Evie along no doubt. Who chatters in seminars, who laughs the loudest. But around Evie she is like a mistreated puppy waiting for its owner to throw a scrap of bacon onto the kitchen floor. I know why. It's not because she adores Evie. It's because she needs to be adored back. She needs it to thrive, like a sunflower turning its face to the rays.

She'll come good in the end.

Elodie is there, hiding like a little wallflower. I didn't think she knew Josh that well, although they were both in my small group. I stand and watch from the stone arched window as they gather in twos and threes. I see Josh's dad in his good suit, and his girlfriend, I think it is, in a Boden dress. I swallow hard and think again of his name flashing on my screen. The phone call the next morning. The way I'd hugged and held my seminar group that afternoon, as we'd all cried together.

The pain for them. It's so real. You can call them snowflakes. Generation Z or Y. It doesn't make anything they are going through any less real.

Yes we didn't shudder and break at the slightest breeze in our branches. Our roots were strong and our boughs were bendy. We would sway but always be grounded. But we'd grown up in a time where our value wasn't score-boarded under the watchful eye of a social empire that capitalises on the hunger for self-worth.

May the odds be ever in your favour, indeed.

I head down to the gathering and, for the first time in days, I feel the lack of Simon. He would have flanked me. He would of course have charmed the parents, told bittersweet anecdotes, fist-bumped and gently patted backs. He would have emotionally vampired the entire event. But he would have been next to me.

I want to scream.

Evie. Evie. Evie. What a mess.

I head for Elodie and give her a warm smile and her little eyes light up. They are cornflower blue and her best feature, because they twinkle brighter than Venus when it passed over. She looks like a doll with her button nose. I heard Finn ask once if she had Down's Syndrome. I'd torn a strip off him until I'd realised from his blushes that he was genuinely asking and not trying to be mean. She does have a child-like quality to her, which is a surprise given she's had little childhood herself.

Or perhaps that's exactly why.

'Hello darling.' I give her shoulders a squeeze. 'How are you doing?'

'Wow, you look beautiful,' Elodie says, her pink smile revealing little pointed teeth.

'Oh thank you.' I wave my hand away. 'I don't feel it though.'

Elodie points to the cameras. 'I didn't realise this was going to be such a big thing.'

'Well, Josh wasn't, isn't, the only one. The numbers across the country are dreadful and rising. It's not just about him anymore.'

'Your campaign is going to change that, right?' Elodie looks up earnestly.

'Well, no, probably not. But if we can do more here, at this university, well, from small beginnings . . . it's all got to start somewhere.'

I feel a tap on my shoulder and I turn around to see our Communications Director, Hayley, stood with a cameraman, with the ITV logo on the side.

'Hi Jenny, all ready? Do you need anything?' Hayley asks. 'These guys here are from ITV, and BBC Radio York are almost here. Did you want a few words with Jenny now? Or after?' She looks at the young woman stood behind with notepad and an iPhone ready to record.

'Actually, now would be great,' the woman says.

I crank up my smile. 'Sure.'

'Shall we . . .' I follow her to the side of the garden where there is a little part of the wall still free and we sit, legs crossed towards each other.

'I'm Sam. I just wanted to get a few comments from you about Josh and the inspirations behind the Connect campaign. Is that OK?'

'Of course.' It's all there and polished.

'You were Josh's personal tutor. Is that right?'

'Yes, that's right. And I taught him for three first-year modules.'

'And what is the role of a personal tutor?'

'It's a little like a pastoral role. Every student is allocated a member of staff to talk to mainly about academic progression and any issues they are having with their studies. They're also someone they can go and ask what they think are stupid questions, about policies, procedures, etc.'

'But it's not a counselling role?'

'No. It's not.'

'And do you find students tend to use it like that? I see you contributed to an article in the *Times Higher Education* Supplement two years ago where you were quoted as saying mental health support for students is grossly under-funded.'

'Yes.' I nod. 'I do believe the level of need is something that academic staff can't deal with, not only because of the sheer volume of students needing help, but also because we are not trained as counsellors.'

'So if a student came to you needing mental health support, you would have to turn them away?'

I pause. 'No, I would never turn anyone away who was distressed or needed to talk.'

'But you don't think it is your place to do that?' she presses.

'I am an academic, not a counsellor. But more than either of those things, I am a human.'

'And did Josh try to talk to you? About the way he was feeling? Before he jumped?'

'I don't really think that's appropriate. Do you?' I try to stand up, my knees shaking. Hayley was raising her eyebrows at me and pointing at her watch.

'Did he tell you that he was going to try and commit suicide?'

I stand up.

'The amount of pressure you must be under is phenomenal. I mean, surely that's one of the reasons you started this campaign? Lecturers like you can't be held responsible for the actions of their students, can they?'

'I didn't realise anyone was holding me responsible.' I turn away and march towards Hayley. 'Don't bring her near me again. She's fishing. Bit bloody sensationalist for ITV.'

'Oh no. She's not ITV. She's a freelancer. Valid press card.'

'You're kidding me, Hayley? She's got a full-on agenda.' I glance behind me and she is furiously jabbing at her phone, surely twisting all my words into some kind of pitch to the red tops.

'OK. Don't worry about her now. I'll deal with it. Just come and say hello to Josh's dad and we will get going.' I nod, smooth down my skirt and follow her over to Josh's dad, Ben. I am also introduced to his girlfriend, Camilla. Milla, she tells me and kisses me on both cheeks. Her skin feels like velvet, and I have to say, I admire her guts. Being here. She'd only just got together with Ben before Josh died. I'm surprised she doesn't blame herself.

'What you've done, for Josh, for the other students, thank

you so much.' Ben pumps my hand and I feel my teeth rattle.

'I know I keep saying it, but I'm so sorry.' I reach out for their hands and we end up holding them all together in the middle of our little circle. For an instant I want to shout 'annnnnnnnd break'. We are all squeezing too tight.

'I . . . we know,' says Milla, looking at Ben nervously, 'how much he admired you, Jennifer.' I feel like telling her to fuck off. What's with the 'we know'? You're weren't Josh's mother. His family.

I shake my head swiftly and part my lips.

'He really looked up to you. Couldn't stop talking about you. It must have been a little . . . overwhelming,' Ben added.

'I was just humbled that he had so much respect for my teaching methods. My research. Honestly. It was never uncomfortable.'

'Jennifer.' Ben let go of my hands and I feel the blood begin to course back into my crooked fingers. 'Thank you. Please just accept it.'

'And thank you,' I replied. 'For raising such a wonderful young man.'

I stand with Milla as Ben makes his speech at the lectern. It's short. Predictable. I wish I could have taken a look at it first. Made some edits. The wellbeing centre go next and I barely listen while they talk about the campaign, the support available that we all know isn't available, through no fault of their own. The gardens are full of students, faculty and parents.

Grief is a great leveller.

'It's time.' Hayley appears again in my ear and ushers me to the front.

I bring my iPad to life just in case, and step forward to the lectern and take a deep breath.

'Josh once told me, that spring was his favourite season. The smell of his dad's roast lamb. The softening of the skies. New life everywhere you look. I remember thinking how unusual it was for a young man to have an affinity with such a delicate season. I take some peace, some kind of comfort, that when Josh left this world, there was indeed new life all around him. New starts. A time for change. Too long have we ignored the rise of suicide in males. Too long have we grieved without purpose, too long have we wept silent tears. It is time to take care of each other, to not look the other way, to not cross the street when you see somebody in pain.'

I talk about the success we have had from getting our MP to lobby in parliament. I talk about the power of words. I am applauded in the hollows. At the end, just before I pull down the cloth and reveal the Joshua Tree, I think I see him. His brown hair, his neat shirt. Stood at the back of the throng, as usual. Arms folded, leaning against the pillar adorned with gaudy posters and angry advertising. Eyes on me.

I freeze for a second and wait for him to disappear as he does most days, then I realise it's not a ghost at all.

'So today,' I continue, my voice strong, 'I ask you to join me in unveiling Joshua's Tree. A place to come when you feel alone. A place to write a note of support for someone who needs to hear it. A place you will always find a friend.'

I pull down the cloth and everyone raises their mobiles to film. I saw Finn's arm round Bronte, she is wiping away tears.

It's not Josh stood there at the back. Smiling.

It's Simon.

'Jenny.' Elodie is waiting for me when I come down off the lectern. 'I need to ask you something.'

'Sweetheart, not now,' I say, my eyes forward as I move towards him. I can't believe he has come, has had the sheer nerve to show his face. I look round for Hayley but she probably doesn't even know. Josh's dad is hugging his friends, Bronte's face is earnest and Finn is squeezing her shoulders. Liam is stood to the side looking down. My eyes darken and I turn back to Simon. He is still there, leaning against the pillar in his suit and tie.

I don't know what to think and for a moment I want to hug him. He looks like a lost little boy. Everything starts swimming and I reach out to steady myself as my knees become weak. It's Ahmeel, the tech guy. I grab his shoulder and take a deep breath.

'You OK?'

'Yes,' I gasp. 'Sorry, it's the heels.'

'You were amazing up there. You feeling a bit overwhelmed?' he asks, his face kind. I look into his eyes and wonder who he really is.

No one is ever what they seem.

Not even me.

When I look back, Simon has gone.

I can see Hayley hovering, craning her neck to find me. On the other side of the garden, Elodie is looking nervous and biting her fingernails to the quick. I've told her off for that before.

Sighing, I head over to her, and she gives me an anxious little smile.

'What's wrong darling? Sorry about that. I had to . . . Doesn't matter.' I smile. 'What did you want to talk about?'

'Maybe not here,' she says, drawing her cardigan over her bird-like frame.

'OK. Well I have some things to finish up now, then I can meet you in my office in about half an hour? Forty-five minutes, maybe?' I am beginning to get slightly impatient. It's becoming almost daily. The cups of tea. The soothing. The constant drafts of my essays and now ones for other modules. And it's not like I don't want to help. I do. But after a while these essays are becoming mine. And I wonder if I did the right thing after all. I only wanted to help. But maybe I've just made the situation worse.

Of course she bought that essay. Stupid, stupid mistake. But Elodie isn't one of those spoilt, entitled kids who coasted through their A-levels with private tutors, or with a natural affinity with academia. Those kids don't impress me at all. My foster mother once told me, when I came home with yet another A, that being smart, that's not because of something you have done. It's a gift that you're given. When the As come easy, you don't deserve praise for being good at something that you haven't worked for. Be kind. Be a good friend. Be a good person. That's what deserves praise. Or the C you get in Maths when you have struggled with Ds all your life.

Elodie must have worked her little, eczema-ridden fingers to the bone to get the grades to get in here. It's a shame the UCAS system doesn't test tenacity, resilience, or an actual desire to think for yourself.

She was exhausted before freshers' week had even started. She doesn't live on campus. She can't afford it and she has a full-time job looking after her mother. An actual full-time job. Yet she's never missed a single lecture. I've changed her seminar timetable under the radar to make sure she gets home in time to stop her mum going walkabout. I see her eyes growing heavy in classes, her little elfin head asleep on the desk in the library after being up all night with a woman who claws and screams at her and sees nothing but demons.

She's never missed a deadline, always done the reading. She wants to get out of here so badly. To have a job that isn't wiping her mother's shit off the bathroom wall. To be able to pay for a carer so that she can attempt to have some kind of life.

So yes. I changed the essay. I removed the red.

And I'd do it again.

Don't get me wrong, I know I'd be fired if anyone reported

me. I have turned a blind eye to the biggest academic sin there is.

The sheer gall that Simon thinks, after what he has done, he can throw me under the bus. That he could question my ethics.

I've known. I've always known. What he does. What he did. What he's doing. Right now.

I see people in a way other people don't.

It used to be that I felt sorry for him for needing that kind of validation. That escape from what I can only imagine must be a living hell, where your child cannot reach up his arms to cuddle you back. He will never hear Jamie say I love you. Never kick a football with him. Every year he watches hundreds of students graduate, in the cap and gown that Jamie will never wear.

Sometimes good people do bad things.

Or do bad people do good things?

I'm not sure I know the difference anymore.

For the next half hour I continue my performance and give the quotes I know they want. I look at the tree and I know I should feel pride that I've made a difference. But I know deep down that a hashtag and a few posters won't change anything. A beautiful sculpture will be here – but only to remind people that they are not alone in the dark, with the despairing thoughts that chew and splinter the bones of them and spit them out like gristle. They'll know that others feel it too. That it creeps over everyone. Depression is not a black dog. It's a pack of hounds.

And I have no idea how that is supposed to make anyone feel better.

Josh looked at me once, on a really bad day, when he was too wrung out to even cry, he said the woods were lovely, dark and deep.

I knew what he meant.

I promised him better days, sunshine and air.

I lied.

CHAPTER TWELVE

Simon

When I wake up I put on my suit, kiss Becky on her cold cheek and drive round the block.

IT pick up on the second ring, unusual for them.

'Hi. It's Simon in the English department.'

'Alright mate.'

There is a pause. I am sure this is a pause. Has my account been suspended? Surely not, because I can still access my email.

'Hi. Yeah. So. I'm just tracking down an issue with a student on the plagiarism checker. A couple of weeks ago there was an assignment that was highlighted as a red flag. Anyway, I'm just getting the report together for the student meeting and it's gone. I just wonder if you could have a look and see what's happened?'

'Yeah can do. Email over the student ID and assessment code and I'll give you a ring back.'

'OK, thanks. I'm working from home today. Let me give you my mobile number.'

I reel it off and hang up. It's too early for the memorial. So I drive back to the Costa and get in the queue, half hoping to see that girl again. She's not on shift it would appear, so I order myself an espresso to make myself look cultured and check my emails again.

There's one from HR. I have a meeting on Friday. I forward it to my lawyer and take a deep breath. In a strange way it makes me feel relieved. It gives me a deadline. Just another two more days. I can do this.

I drink my coffee and stare blankly at the font of the newspaper, watching the letters crawl and collide with each other when my phone buzzes.

It's my Twitter and there, in my DMs, is a message. From Ewan Wright.

I jab at it eagerly. The one I had sent had been innocuous. I couldn't just start blabbering. I had asked how he was, said his name had come up on LinkedIn, all that kind of bullshit.

He said he was pleased to hear from me. 'Course he was. I bet he'd rather he never heard from any of us at that uni again. No. He wasn't pleased. But he was certainly curious.

I'd asked if I could pick his brains about something. People like it when you say that. It makes them think you have something worth picking at.

He sent his mobile number and there's no time like the present, so I go to dial it and then think better of it. I don't want to look desperate. I need to keep at least some shred of self-respect.

I leave him hanging on 'read' and order another coffee. I drink it fast before it goes powdery and feel it in my rib-cage, in my breath.

I used to be able to drink three cups of coffee before bedtime and still sleep for eight hours as soon as my head hit the pillow. That's exhaustion. But lately I feel jittery if I have anything stronger than a cup of tea.

Jenny will be speaking at the memorial and I cannot look like a car crash. She needs to know she isn't going to break me. I need to send her a warning. She needs to feel fear.

She needs to know that I know exactly what she's playing at. She needs to know she hasn't broken me. That I am not afraid.

It's Elodie who spots me first.

She locks her eyes on me and I shrivel back. She used to worship me. Beg like a puppy for a compliment. Even an acknowledgment from me would make her quiver. But now there's disgust in her eyes. I can't turn away. I stare back, and try to lift my chin, and when that fails, my eyebrows. That's when I realise my face has sagged under the weight of humiliation. Actual weight. I can't lift anything at all.

Then the worst thing happens. I can take the disgust. The revulsion. It's the pity I can't take. And that's the expression I see on her face now. That pathetic creature who thought a degree would actually buy her out of the hell hole she's living in. That it would actually be some kind of golden ticket. That each letter she types on a battered keyboard while watching over her mother sleeping might be a step towards something better.

She is me.

I have no idea who I have become.

It's enough to make me run.

I spoke to the lawyer last night. He said my best option is to admit that I had slept with her and to put the fact I hadn't reported it down to a case of bad judgement. Her work could be remarked. I probably wouldn't get fired. A written warning perhaps. In a he-said-she-said, I have no chance.

Fuck. That.

She came on to me. That's how I knew it was her. The others aren't so brazen off their Insta. They might send thirsty messages that they laugh off as a joke, pictures that would make their dads turn to the bottle. But it's not often they drag me into a toilet cubicle and offer their throat like a lamb to a wolf.

It had been a month or so since that house party. She'd started ending her emails with an x. I was using emojis. I should have realised then that I'd taken it too far.

Staff–student social. That's what Jenny had called it. I mean, how come no one is pinning her up as breaking ethical boundaries? Surely if drinking with students is that bad, why host these cringeworthy mixer events. They only come for the free booze. Albeit just the one. All within the proper boundaries. Jenny had said.

Evie had been there. Jenny had been upset that night. Of course she hadn't let on. But I could tell. She was quiet. Usually she is reserved, but very dry, witty. Her conversations are nuanced, like exquisite symphonies. She never wastes a single word. Everyone has a purpose. She is succinct and sharp. There is something really quite beautiful about it. But that night she'd been totally off her game. She wasn't weaving everyone into the conversation the way she normally does. She wasn't unassumingly the linchpin of the entire debate. Oh I might be the loudest, perhaps even the funniest, but I'm not normally the webcaster. Not even close.

I sat next to her and brought her in, in the way you're taught to coax a contribution out of the most reluctant student. She'd even seemed grateful. Something I'd never seen from her before. I hadn't really noticed just how quickly I'd been drinking. I'd arranged to stay at a colleague's that night so I wouldn't come home drunk and stinking and wake up Becky and Jamie.

It had been a bad day. More rejections from agents. I'd joined in a fast-moving round and was feeling no pain. I'd even been bought a couple from the students which Jenny had tutted at. But surely that was better than the other way round, I'd pointed out.

Evie had kept glancing up at me. She was sat with Bronte, Finn and Liam and a few others. Her hair was up, with a few loose glossy tendrils framing her face, crisp dark-blue jeans and a black, one-shouldered top. She'd seemed so out of place with the hoodies and the DMs. The unicorn hair and the piercings. You could almost see her thinking, Oh it's all so droll.

For a minute she'd reminded me of Josh.

And that's when I'd known what was wrong with Jenny. This time last year, Josh had been here.

I'd put my hand under the table and given her hand a squeeze. I'd meant nothing by it. Nothing at all but a gesture of sympathy. Or support. But she'd snatched it away as if I'd poured acid on it. So fast that she'd banged the underside of the table and everyone had looked up.

'Ouch,' she'd muttered while squirming away from me. 'Sorry, I was trying to cross my legs and misjudged.'

Everyone had gone back to their business and I'd bent my head a little and leant in towards her.

'Sorry,' I'd whispered. 'I didn't mean to startle you. Just seeing if you're OK. You look down.'

Her jaw had stiffened and she hadn't replied. I'd moved back to my sitting position and re-joined the conversation, feeling embarrassed. She'd crossed her legs away from me and struck up a conversation with Peter.

The beer had broken my seal and a few minutes later I'd excused myself. In the bathroom I'd looked at myself in the mirror. I was old. My jowls sagged. My eyes were bloodshot. And I could smell a faint whiff of stale deodorant and plaque. I was a joke in a blue suit, an ageing, sad lecturer. I took my phone out to see if Becky had sent me a nice message or a picture of Jamie. Nothing. Just two more email alerts. Two more rejections.

I'd washed my hands and gone out into the corridor and there she was. Evie. She stood in the little square section where the toilets were, looking at the doors, like Alice in the rabbit hole.

'Are you lost? I think that's the one you want.' I'd smiled and nodded towards the ladies.

'Massive queue,' she'd said with a little grimace. 'I thought I might be cheeky and look for the disabled one.'

'You look lovely this evening,' I'd replied. I wasn't trying to be creepy. It had just come out. She did. Her skin was tight and her eyes were bright. She'd looked back at me but she hadn't said anything. So I didn't either. We'd stood there, her hand on the door handle.

She'd swallowed.

'So do you,' she'd said quietly. I'd expected her to blush, drop her eyes to the floor maybe. But she hadn't. She'd just kept staring, as if she had made her mind up about something. As if she was on a debate stand and had just delivered a killer line to her opponent.

'Hardly,' I'd quipped, and almost looked down at the floor myself. 'I've just looked in the mirror. I'm wrecked. And old.' I hadn't meant that last bit to come out.

'Not to me.'

Right then I'd thought about Becky. Her back to me. The freckles on her shoulder. The empty side of the bed. The emails. Jenny pulling her hand away. I hadn't realised it before. But she was the closest thing I had to a best friend. I had never felt so tragic and alone.

Then Evie had leant forward and with one hand, a move I have only ever seen in movies, had grabbed my jacket collar and pulled me into the disabled toilet.

Now, stood, leaning against the pillar, seeing Jenny there, under the dusky lights surrounding the Joshua Tree, she looks like an angel. The whiteness of her skin, the darkness of her hair. Like Snow White or Briar Rose. She is so pale you can almost see the blue of her veins when she turns her cheek.

I won't leave until I make sure she has looked in the whites of my eyes because, My God, I looked into hers.

I don't have to wait long. She feels the weight of my stare.

Her eyes meet mine while she is talking, and for a second she stumbles over her words. No one would notice but me.

It's like she has seen a ghost.

I wait to see the look in her eyes and then I stride away into the undulating students until I have been engulfed. There was fear. Pure fear. I am right.

Let her report me. No one can prove I've been here. Somehow, I know she won't though. I walk back to the car and my hands are shaking.

I've been imagining coming here for days. I've been consumed by it. I'd lain awake last night next to Jamie and listened to his breathing, the tick-tock of the machine. The lights had changed on the ceiling, lavender and blues, inks and swirls of black. Tiny pin pricks had flickered on one by one into the constellations and each one had burned my eyelids like a freight train heading towards me at full speed.

This book won't be published if there is any smidge whatsoever of reputational damage. I can't lose this now. Not when I am so close. Jenny's setting me up. She knows it. I know it. Evie knows it.

The only way to bring her down is to prove what she did

about that essay. HR will question her but that's all. She'll deny it. They have bigger fish to fry. I need more.

I reach the car and take a deep, long breath. Was that enough? Perhaps I needed to be more obvious. More direct.

It's only when the safety lights flicker on down the pathways leading into the quad that I realise I have been sitting here for hours.

She campaigned for those too, I remember.

I don't know whether I have waited here intentionally. I'd like to think not. But when I see Jenny crossing the car park I flick off my lights and wait until she's traversed the tarmac and is heading for the main road. Quietly, I open the car door and shuffle out of the seat. I don't quite know why, but I follow her onto the main drag. She'll be heading to the train station of course. She's not one for after-work drinks normally. Even on a day like today. My throat clenches and my nails bed into my palms. I hang back a little, ensuring at least three people are between us. She is swinging her hips with a lilt I don't like. She looks too confident for someone who should at the very least have had a call, an email even, from HR. I get that she would have had to keep up appearances at the memorial. But this is the way I have often seen her. Chin raised and hair shaken back in the day, scurrying like an exhausted mouse on the way home.

But not today. She is walking that touch slower than usual, as if she is quite literally stopping to smell the flowers. I don't like this.

I speed up a little as she makes a left along the cobbled

path. This isn't the way she usually goes. The road is narrow. It's one of the tourist attractions of the city, crooked and uneven. It houses gift shops, olde worlde-type affairs selling Harry Potter knock-offs and Game of Thrones memorabilia. It also sports designer spa-at-home-type places where you have to hand over £50 for some bubble bath at Christmas.

It's at one of these places that Jenny pauses outside, then goes in. I'm surprised. She doesn't look the type to spend her money on such frivolous things.

Saying that, her skin is always glowing and smooth so maybe I'm wrong. The shop is small so I don't follow her in. Instead I skulk under the overhang of one of the restored Tudor buildings. I can see the curve of her cheek through the glass-fronted wall as she chats to the glossy blonde woman behind the counter. She hands over her card and takes her bag, chocolate brown with cream rope handles and thick ribbon. I step back into the dusky shadows as she comes out, checks her phone and then heads back the way she came. My heart stops for a second as she walks right past me. But she has no reason to look in the shadows. I step out and follow her again. Closer this time. Weaving in and out of the lessening throng. They are beginning to spill over into pubs and beer gardens, which consist of benches and heaters outside. Jenny carries on, stumbles once with her heels on the cobbles, and I see her left ankle go completely over. It must have hurt but she carries on without even breaking her pace and with only a hint of a limp.

I don't know what I'm doing here. I know she won't be going anywhere other than to the train. But I am compelled.

The station clock is lit and beautiful. It casts a yellow moon-like glow over the entrance as she walks through it, like some kind of spotlight. I would have stopped there. But the way she falters, pauses and looks around her, it makes me take a few steps closer.

She walks slowly to the centre of the station and stands in full light, in full centre stage. As if she is waiting for someone.

For a horrible moment I think it's me. I think it's me she is waiting for and I shrink against the nearest stone pillar, even though I have no reason to be afraid of her.

I watch as she shifts her weight almost imperceptibly and her knees bend and straighten in tiny butterfly movements. Her feet are hurting, I can tell. The Big Board above says there's a train due to Harrogate in ten minutes. She would normally get herself a drink. A diet coke when she thinks no one is looking. But she doesn't. She just stands there. It's strange. Even when her train is called she just stands there and watches it pull in and out, people buzzing around her like flies.

Eventually, she turns in a slow circle, and I duck behind an arch to avoid her eyes sweeping across the station, the platforms.

I peer back around the archway, she is walking away now. A little less of a swing to her hips than usual. Her head is down.

I turn and walk back through the streets towards the university. It seems so much longer on the way back. All of a sudden, I begin to pine for my son. It hits me hard, a bowling ball to my gut. I want to be the one to tuck him in. So I start walking quicker. I want to be at home, away from all of this, in the living room, watching a movie, reading to Jamie. The luxury of fantasising about a book deal. Hot food in my tummy. I break out into a jog.

The campus is much quieter now and I jump over the low wall that takes me across the football field and to the back of the car park. It only cuts off maybe a minute but every second feels worth it.

My head is spinning with everything. I see Jamie running across the side of the swimming pool. His little legs a blur and his chubby arms flailing. *I don't need any help daddy.*

He was there. He was right there. And then he wasn't. I didn't see him fall, not amongst the sea of legs. I didn't hear the splash of his chubby, seal-like little body hit the water.

It was only when I got closer, I saw the blood on the tiles. The way it collected round the rivets and ran, mercury through a puzzle, a maze. There were so many limbs, kicking and shrieking, I screamed. Not shouted. I have never heard a man make the high-pitched, almost animal sound that came from my mouth. No. Not from my mouth, from inside my soul.

His little body was blue when they pulled him out. He'd been knocked unconscious as soon as his temple hit the cruel rough, sharp edge of the Spanish pool. His skin was wet and rubbery and I couldn't get hold of him properly. He kept slipping through my fingers like a seal. I watched strangers that spoke in different tongues breathe life back into his tiny lungs when I couldn't. His eyes opened. But I couldn't see him there.

Becky's laugh. Evie's lips.

And him.

My lungs close like a Venus flytrap.

I stop running and bend over, hands on my knees and try to gulp oxygen down into my body. But I can still hear footsteps. Faster and faster, or is it the blood pounding in my ears?

With the head between my knees I can see someone approaching, upside down. I try and stand and turn but I'm so dizzy the ground tilts. Then all of a sudden the footsteps are close, and stop right next to me.

'I'm OK' I start . . . holding a hand up, embarrassed. But instead of a voice, a reassuring hand on my shoulder, I feel a feel a blow to the back of my head. A blinding pain. And then the wet grass soaking through the knees of my suit.

The sky has burned out.

CHAPTER THIRTEEN

Evie

The day of the memorial

Evie woke up feeling stiff and sticky.

There was no blind on her skylight and the sun was rudely nudging her eyes open.

There was a sour, sweaty smell and Evie could feel her hair curling with the dampness at the nape of her neck. Her bladder was bursting, her head was throbbing and she was so thirsty she was tempted for a second to swig from the stale contents of her hot water bottle.

She rubbed her eyes and tried to piece together the rest of the night.

There was some kind of whiskey. Was it whiskey? Something that Harvey had pulled out from underneath his bed. For her nerves, apparently. They'd sat in the kitchen, drinking shot after shot, more or less in silence. The pancake mixture had curdled on the side. When the others fell back in at gone 2 a.m., Harvey hadn't even bothered with excuses and had disappeared.

'What? Oh my God? I thought you were ill? You were drinking with Harvey?!' Bronte had squealed.

'It's . . . we've had a weird night.' Evie's eyes had flown in panic to the table. But the box had vanished. Harvey must have silently, thoughtfully taken it. No questions asked.

'Well it was probably kids,' Liam had said, while picking the bits of mould off the bread and shoving it in the toaster. But he'd cast an anxious look out the window. 'What's this?' he'd pointed at the measuring jug.

'Harvey made us pancakes.' Evie's voice had been muted.

'It looks like spunk.' Finn had stuck his head over Liam's shoulder. 'He so spunked in that.'

'Oh my God, you didn't eat it did you?' Bronte had gasped.

'Oh fuck off,' Evie had said. She'd pay for that today.

Now, she gathered her hair up into a ponytail and wiped the smeared eyeliner off the top of her cheeks, before she ventured downstairs to find Liam eating a fried egg sandwich. The smell made her stomach turn.

'Hungover?' Evie asked, flicking on the kettle.

'Yeah I'm not feeling too clever,' Liam yawned. 'You OK? So what went on last night then?'

'Oh God. It was weird. I came down just after ten and Harvey was in. We were just making something to eat . . .'

'Harvey *cooked* for you?' Liam wiped a smear of yolk off his top lip and Evie looked away.

'I told you last night. How drunk were you? He was just making . . . Oh never mind, the point is that we heard something in the yard. Like a bang. You know, like when you open the gate too hard and it hits the green bin? And while we were looking, the doorbell went. So we answered it and there was no one there. And then someone knocked at the back door.'

'And then what?'

'Well. There was no one there either.'

Liam looked at her expectantly. 'So what happened next?'

'Well . . .' Evie paused. 'Nothing . . . That was it.'

'Oh. OK. We used to do that shit all the time until some old bastard's pit bull chased us down the street and Johnno pissed himself. Like, actually pissed himself.' Liam grinned nostalgically. 'Good times.'

'There's no kids who live round here,' Evie said again.

'So . . . were you really scared?' Liam asked.

'Yeah, I was. I mean, with that horrible thing on my door. It feels like I'm being targeted.'

'What, because of that complaint?'

'What? What do you mean?' Evie fired back.

Liam dropped the rest of his sandwich on his plate. 'Erm, nothing. I don't know.'

'Did Bronte tell you something?'

'What?' he said. She could almost see the cogs whirring in his brain, when his phone buzzed. He grabbed it that little bit too fast and shoved it in his hoody.

Evie felt the bile in her stomach start to rise again.

'What did Bronte say?'

Liam sighed. 'Well. You know. You were a bit off last night. And she told us that, you know, you've been having a really hard time. Something to do with a lecturer.'

'Great. Thanks. Thanks a lot Bronte.' Evie kicked the chair in front of her.

Liam's phone buzzed again.

'Are you going to answer that?' Evie snapped. 'It's getting on my nerves.'

'Nah. It's just Finn winding me up.'

Evie narrowed her eyes.

'So did you shag them then?' Liam said, then laughed as if it was some kind of joke.

'It's none of your business,' Evie said coldly, and snatched up her mug. As she did, Liam's phone buzzed again and he fished it out of his jumper to try and silence it. But Evie was faster.

The video on the screen was from Pornhub. It showed a thirty-something large-breasted woman dressed in a school uniform on her knees servicing an unattractive man in a lecturer's gown.

Her entire body went cold, then hot again. She started to shake. The kitchen door opened and Finn came in, balancing two mugs in one hand. She threw Liam's phone at him so hard it whacked his forehead with an almighty crack and he dropped both coffees, yelping.

'Ah fuck. FUCK. What did you do that for?' He screwed his eyes up and pressed his hands to his head.

'Do you think it's OK to talk about me like that? You complete and utter bastard.'

'What are you even on about?' Finn stared at the smashed mugs. 'You can clean that up.'

'How could you make fun of me like this?' She picked up the phone and held it up. 'It's just vile.'

'Sorry, listen Evie, it's just banter,' Liam said. 'It's just lads. It doesn't mean anything.'

'Yes, it does,' Evie said.

'Look. I'm sorry. Obviously you weren't meant to see that,' Finn said. 'Ow. Fuck, I'm getting a bump.' He peered at himself in the mirror.

'I can't believe you. Both of you.'

'What's going on?' Bronte staggered in, her kimono skew-whiff.

'Oh don't you dare play that card with me. You *told* them?' Evie shouted.

'GUYS,' Bronte said.

But Evie didn't wait to hear. She pushed past Bronte and ran up the stairs two at a time. She slammed her bedroom door, whacked on the lock and threw herself back into her bed, a horrible bursting sensation behind her ribs.

She could hear Bronte knocking on her door, pleading, but she pulled the duvet over her head. Now everyone would know.

She buried her face in her pillow, and breathed in Hugo Boss.

*

After a couple of hours of pretending to research her linguistics case study, she made sure there was no more knocking and whimpering and slunk moodily down the stairs. She clicked the kettle on for the cup of tea she still hadn't had, flung open the cupboard door, grabbed her least favourite mug because her Penguin *Room of One's Own* mug was STILL in the sink, crusting over with rusty-looking dregs of tomato soup that some TWAT had borrowed without asking and then left to fester. Like it meant nothing. Like they could just use it, and leave it like that.

Evie grabbed the kettle too hard and scalding water slopped over her hand. She screamed and dropped it, and felt another burn on her thigh as it fell on its side and more hot water seeped into her jeans.

The pain was excruciating and, without thinking, she pulled down her jeans to her knees. The skin was bright red and angry so she ran the cold tap hard and, holding her burnt hand under it, started splashing water onto her leg. This time she couldn't stop the tears, and didn't hear the quiet click of the hallway door open. It was only when she felt the sweet relief of something ice cold being applied to her leg that she looked up. Harvey was there, holding a packet of frozen peas to her burnt skin, and he gestured for her to take it.

'What are you doing?' She looked down, mortified that her knickers were on display and began to hike her jeans back up.

'Here.' Harvey pulled out a roll of clingfilm from the

drawer. 'Wrap your hand in this.' He looked away as he handed it over and pretended not to see her wriggling to cover her bum.

'I dropped the kettle,' Evie explained.

Harvey sniffed and took a step back. 'That's going to blister if you don't keep something cold on it.'

Evie nodded, and gave up trying to pull her jeans up over the frozen peas.

'Thanks,' she said without meeting his eyes.

Harvey turned to go, then Evie stopped him.

'Harvey . . .' Evie snapped. 'Thanks. For . . . well. Thanks.'

'It's OK,' Harvey said.

When she went back up to her room, the box was there, lying on her bed.

Evie picked up the photo and looked at the girl with the blonde highlights. The girl she used to be.

You're not who you say you are.

Is anyone?

The park was colder than she'd imagined and the sun was satisfyingly pale. Evie was glad for her hoody. It made her feel less obvious, more like every other anonymous student. It was the vigil tonight. The house would be empty. Except for Harvey. The thought of that strangely comforted her. How the tables had turned.

She bought a coffee from a van and sat on the bench to watch the ducks and felt relieved she hadn't brought her phone with her so she wouldn't have to deal with Bronte.

She'd forgive her. She'd have to. She didn't have anyone else. It would be a very lonely next eighteen months without her. But that didn't mean to say she couldn't be angry with her for a while.

That would put the kibosh on Liam's crush, she imagined. The boys thought she was some kind of grade-grabbing slut, the exact girl that Village Vixen ripped to shreds.

A mallard broke ranks and skated across the pond, quacking, agitated by some mysterious duck hierarchy. Evie looked up to see a man stood in the shallow trees opposite. For a moment she thought he was part of the branches that stretched and stroked each other and he seemed to have a slight sway, as if he were moving with them. Camouflaged in the browns and greens.

Evie looked deeper and then around her quickly. The park wasn't empty. Toddlers ran on fat little legs, exhausted-looking mums and the odd dad chasing after them, grabbing their arms when they raced towards the water edge. The creak of the swings and the thump, thump, thump as they softly landed in the wood chips at the bottom of the snake slide.

She looked back. He was still there. His face was shrouded by the fresh blooms of the bushes. He was wearing a beanie, pulled down low.

Evie's eyes searched for a dog, a spaniel or something that would give him a reason to be lurking, woven into the copse and moving with the breeze.

But nothing.

He was looking directly at her.

Then he raised his arm and hoisted a rifle onto his shoulder. Evie froze. It was pointing right at her. She opened her mouth to scream but there was no air in her lungs.

She felt it before she saw it. A sharp pain on her breast, on her heart.

Death didn't hurt as much as she'd thought it would. She waited for the agony to come, the blood to froth from her mouth, the sky to quiver and the sweet darkness to come.

She would be with him again.

Her clawing hands flew at her soaking chest but her breath still came.

And instead of blood, her hands, her heart, her ribs were covered in blue paint.

She didn't know whether to laugh or cry. It came out as both. A stranger, a runner, was there suddenly. He bent down in front of her and asked her what had happened, if she was OK. She tried to point at the woods, to find the words.

But the man had disappeared and the spindles of the thicket were empty.

CHAPTER FOURTEEN

Jenny

The day after the memorial

I close my office door and put a mug of sugary tea down in front of Evie. Her eyes are puffy and swollen and her friend Bronte is hovering outside like a parent at the pre-school gates. If we are much longer I expect I'll see her nose pushed up against the glass.

She is being very un-Evie like today, her knees pulled up to her chest, her hair in an odd shape.

'Here you go.'

'Thanks, Jenny.' Evie takes a sip of tea and lets out a gentle sigh. 'I'm so sorry you've been caught up in all of this.'

'It's not your fault, Evie.'

'It is. It feels like such a massive mess.'

'OK. Have you spoken to the police again?'

'No, not since it happened. I mean, he was there and then, he'd just vanished.'

'Sweetheart, I really don't think it could have been Simon.' I see Evie's hands shaking as she sets down her mug on the table in the office.

'Well, he's the only one with a reason to do this. Or maybe he got one of his students to do it. Everyone knows now. I'm sure they do. It's probably one of his bloody groupies.'

'Well. Boys are strange creatures. They have a pack mentality. Simon is many things. But he isn't unstable, or stupid. I'm sure he would be mortified if he knew these things were happening to you. You told me a boy had asked you out and that you'd said no? Could it be . . . a bit of jealousy,' I question.

'Liam? God. No. He's . . . harmless. A PIG. But harmless.'

'OK let's speak to HR again and make sure Simon understands what is going on here. We can also get in touch with student support. Are you sure you don't want to take a leave of absence? We can obviously sort out extensions . . .'

'No. I'm not letting them win. No way.' Evie's chin is raised and her eyes spark. I like it.

'Right. I'll set it up.' For a second I want to lean in to Evie, smell the stale shampoo on her head, cradle her soft cheek in my hand. Breathe her in.

She is so vulnerable, like a fragile fledgling fallen from the nest. This isn't the girl who first strode into my seminar, all swinging hair and heeled boots. She is crumbling like butter being rubbed into sugar. 'We'll fix this OK? I'll fix this.'

'Thanks, Jenny.' She gives me a wan smile.

'In the meantime, take care of yourself.' I pause. 'Or let that one take care of you at least.' I nod in the direction of the glass. 'She's dying to. Let her.'

Evie laughed softly. 'She's atoning.'

'Don't be too hard on her. I know you feel she betrayed your trust but it's hard being the supporter. Sometimes they need support too.'

I watch as she gathers up her bag and coat and when she stands, I can't help myself. I open out my arms and she presses into me and for a moment I'm back there. Josh in my arms. His tears on my shoulder. Time stands still, and I don't even care that Bronte is scrabbling at the door like a clumsy mouse on steroids. For a second I don't care that the world could see us and I am breaking all the rules.

She sniffles and breaks my embrace before I do. Her lips are plump and her skin is milky and flushed.

'Thanks Jenny.'

'It's OK.' I smile back. 'I'll crack on now with some calls. Stay strong. Be brave. And don't let the bastards grind you down.'

'I won't.' She hooks her bag over her shoulder and leaves, Bronte leaping on her like a puppy as soon as the door opens.

I stand there for a while. I can still smell her. No perfume. Just the essence of her.

It's happening again.

I go to my desk and pull out the memorial programme.

I trace my fingers over his picture. I'm too involved. I know I am. But I can't let Evie go down the same path. I just can't.

Without getting permission from the powers that be, I pick up the phone and call the student support office.

There's an email in my inbox from Peter, and another from HR. I knew they'd be coming for me. I know what Simon will have said.

Lovely Ahmeel though. There shouldn't be an issue with any paper trail now.

I tap my biro against my teeth and stare straight ahead. I wonder where Evie's mother is. I know she isn't around. She mentioned it before. It's just her and her dad.

I have to deal with this. I reapply my lipstick and open Peter's email first. Then the one from HR. I have to attend a meeting to give a statement about Simon. That I already knew. But there's nothing in there regarding a disciplinary. Which means that's what Peter needs to see me about. They clearly don't want the hassle which is good news.

I straighten my blouse with the V&A print, and head down the corridor. Peter is in his office, he summons me to enter when I knock. I smile brightly and shuffle the deck of cards in my head.

'Ah, Jenny.' He motions for me to sit down. I do so demurely, but with calm confidence. I must hold my nerve.

'Jenny as you know there's been a little bit of trouble with Simon.' I nod.

'Now, during an interview he has made an allegation. Regarding your role as plagiarism officer.'

I nod again, and give him a smile. 'Ah yes. I may know what this is in reference to.'

'Elodie Highfield. Can you walk me through that case? It is alleged that Elodie's essay for ENG217 was highlighted as more than sixty per cent plagiarised. Can you talk me through how you have handled this?'

'Absolutely. Simon brought this to my attention. As protocol states, I had a formal meeting with Elodie. My investigations concluded she had indeed used unfair means, insofar as she hadn't referenced properly. The material had not been Harvard-referenced in the style we would have expected, and larger than normal chunks had been used from certain journals. It was a case of poor academic judgement rather than deliberate plagiarism. For that reason, and due to her mitigating circumstances, submitted retrospectively in regards to her being her mother's carer, I have deemed this essay as non-assessed, allowing her to be able to resit uncapped.'

'And the plagiarism mark? That has been removed from her record?'

'Yes. Due to the reasons I have just mentioned,' I said firmly. 'I know Simon, well, I suspect he was unhappy with my decision. I believe he thinks my work for mental health has made me . . . soft.'

'Can I see the essay, Jenny?' Peter sat back.

'Yes of course. It's on the system.' My heart does a somersault.

Peter leans towards his machine and begins clicking and dragging, making annoyed, huffing noises.

'I miss printed-out essays. They're so much easier.'

'Me too.' I lie. 'More satisfying.'

'That's exactly right.' Peter smiles at me over his glasses.

I breathe out slowly.

'Ah, here it is.' He begins to skim-read Elodie's essay. Actually, my essay. Her real essay is floating around in some kind of deleted cloud somewhere. According to Ahmeel.

'Ah yes, I see what you mean here . . . naivety isn't an excuse though for unfair means. Although certainly less punishable than deliberate plagiarism.'

'Absolutely. Immediate exclusion from the course, if memory serves me right.'

'Yes. Not required here. Did you minute the meeting?'

'Of course.'

'And who was present?'

'Well. Unfortunately just me and Elodie. I know it's good practice to have a second member of staff, but you know what it's like with the increased workload. No one has a second to breathe. Is there any news on the new lecturer position? It would make all the difference, so some of this protocol doesn't slip through the cracks.'

'Yes, yes.' Peter blusters. 'OK, I'll feed back to HR. Nothing untoward here. As you were. Can I have the minutes of the meeting?'

'I've already filed them.' I smile sweetly. 'Take care Peter.'

There's something wrong. I can feel it the minute I open my office door. There's a smell of rain even though my window is shut and something smells odd. Tangy and metallic. I look round until I can put my finger on it. I take two sweeps of my room before I see that my handbag isn't hung over the back of my chair as usual. It is upright on the little two-person table in the middle of the room. It almost looks jaunty. I furrow my brow, trying to remember if I had actually moved it. There's something poking out of the top. I take a deep breath and take a step towards it. As I get closer I realise it's the memorial programme poking out of the top. I pull it out of my bag and realise what the smell is. Josh's face is covered in blood. I drop it in disgust. From the stain and the odour, I am pretty sure it is blood, but I don't want to get any nearer to inspect it. There's a smear on my palm and down my wrist. I open my door and am about to call out into the corridor, then something stops me.

Someone knows. I look down at my palm. I have blood on my hands.

It's not a joke.

The same person, the person with Josh's phone, they messaged me after the memorial and forced me to stand under that clock at the station for an hour. Wait for me there.

Were they watching me? Laughing? Toying. I looked for

you. I did what you wanted. There was some part of me, some tiny part that looked out in the sea of commuters and looked for his face. Alive. Dead. At this moment, I would believe either.

I dash to the ladies and see with relief that all the stalls are empty, then turn the faucet on full blast in the middle sink. I wash and wash my hands. But I can still smell the blood. The water in the sink is running too fast and splashing out onto my skirt and I grab the edge until my knuckles bleed white. Turning off the tap I take one deep breath, then another. And another. My lungs feel as though they are humming. After a while I look in the mirror. My make-up hasn't smudged. My lip liner is intact. I am drawn, like a child with a fine-line felt tip.

I pull back my shoulders and walk out again into the world. I need to get rid of my phone. My other phone.

I didn't buy it for Josh.

I'd bought it for Ewan.

Policies had changed. All of a sudden, we weren't allowed to reply to students after 6 p.m. or on weekends. We were banned from social media contact. The university was battening down the hatches and it was fast becoming them and us.

It was about the time the fees began to hike, and while the students had wanted more, more, more, we'd been told less, less, less. Be professional. Don't get involved.

I remember being told, when I was in the care system, to

always tell a trusted adult if you were scared. If something was wrong. Such as a teacher. Always a teacher. Like they were some kind of priest. Obligated. Oath-sworn.

I tried to talk to a teacher once.

It's a different type of teaching in higher education. All of a sudden it has stopped being a trusted relationship. Now it's about power.

And it's the power you have over them, apparently. No one talks about the power that they have over you.

When I clicked accept on Ewan's request, it was so harmless.

Nothing sinister. Nothing dangerous, or inappropriate. We talked about feedback on work, or what we were watching on television. I was younger then.

I started to scroll through his photos. His comments. He was sweet and self-deprecating. He didn't live on campus but at home with his mother, who wrote cake of the week recipes for *Woman's Weekly*. And he was older. Technically a mature student at twenty-two.

I got another phone. Another WhatsApp. Just in case I was disciplined for replying to students out of hours. A number that wasn't on my work record. You couldn't be too careful. It's ridiculous that I had to resort to a burner phone to do my job properly. I gave all my small group the number. Their needs couldn't be squeezed into 9 to 5 p.m.

Emergency essay help. CV advice. I never put my name on it.

Ewan liked talking to me. He told me things he said he

couldn't tell his girlfriend. He talked to me about his black dog. Nick Drake. The way that he sometimes couldn't get out of bed because he was so afraid of the ceiling giving way and the sky shrinking and shrinking until it became so small it was a pinprick.

He'd drunk and snorted away his first-year loans and given up his campus halls' place to concentrate on what he had come to university to do in the first place. He'd wanted a better life. He hadn't wanted to be a barman forever. He was moved by Hardy. *The Mayor of Casterbridge*. His dissertation proposal was exceptional.

And then it all went wrong.

Because Ewan became very angry.

I made him very angry.

I shut my office and stare at the bag. The memorial programme is still there, where I'd dropped it with a splatter. Opening my cabinet door, I grab the cleaning spray I keep there, because the cleaners always do such a terrible job, and start wiping the table down. I grab an empty carrier from my collection and swipe the programme into it, then pausing to fish out my purse and keys, I swipe my handbag and its entire contents into it too, and tie a tight knot.

Then I shut down my machine, lock up my office and stride out to the bins. I throw everything into the main one.

Josh's blood is *not* on my hands.

When I think back to that night, it was the silence in the void that was the worst. I couldn't bring myself to look over the edge. The night was a blackened dome and the drumming of the rain was bouncing off the steel of the roof like machine guns.

The only screams I heard were the ones inside my own head. I didn't wait for them. I don't even know if there were any. I clattered and stumbled down the back stairs and I ran and ran until I reached the sparse copse that bordered that section of the campus and I fell to my knees. Mud soaking through my trousers, oozing into my finger nails. I squeezed the earth and my eyes found the moon and I stayed there for what could have been minutes, could have been hours. Waiting to feel the beat of the ground and the blood in the sky.

I wanted to strip naked and howl at the moon.

But when the sirens came, I crawled out of the undergrowth and walked calmly to my car.

My burner phone was lighting up like a Christmas tree on the passenger seat.

So I took a deep breath and opened the messages from my students. The grief, the pain, the shock. It spilled out from the screen and engulfed me.

It was time to do my job.

CHAPTER FIFTEEN
Simon

A week after the memorial

'This is a joke, right?' Becky is rigid. Her eyes are the widest I have seen them in years.

From the look of the police officer sat opposite me three hours earlier, it is not a joke.

'Becky . . .'

'What, you've been pretending to go to work? You've been charged with harassment? What the fuck?'

'Becky, none of it is true. I swear, I absolutely swear.'

Becky turns away from me and I can see her shoulder blades through her worn-down T-shirt. Her hair is up in the scruffy way that I love and the kitchen smells of hyacinths and rosemary she has picked from the garden.

I am an intrusion.

'Becky. This student. She has a crush. Had a crush. There

was an incident, a few months ago, when we were all at that department drinks thing. She tried to kiss me. For a moment . . . I admit. Becky.' I reach out and grab her shoulders but she won't turn. 'I was tempted. Just for a second. It's not you. It's not your fault. None of it is your fault. Things . . . I felt so alone.' My voice cracks and I hate myself for it. 'But I pushed her away. I pushed her away and I walked away.'

'And you expect me to believe that?' Becky wrenches free of my grasp and whirls around. 'God, how stupid do you think I am? No, scratch that. How stupid am I Simon? How stupid am I? How many? How many girls?'

'Becky, I swear to you. I swear on Jamie's life.'

She raises her hand so fast it's a blur. I don't realise that she hit me until the hotness begins to throb on the side of my face.

'Don't you ever, EVER, use Jamie's life as something to swear on. Don't you think his life is precarious enough?'

'I'm sorry . . . FUCK. WHY IS THIS HAPPENING TO ME?' I kick the cupboard but Becky doesn't even flinch.

'Don't you mean to us?' Becky says softly. 'It's always about you. Your job. Your book. Your guilt. I wasn't there either. I didn't . . . I'm his mother and I didn't get to him either.'

'Becky . . .' I reach out to her but she backs away. She actually backs away from me as if she is scared of me.

'I can't do it anymore Simon. I can't keep soothing you. I can't keep telling you it's not your fault.'

I feel the blood drain from my face. 'You think it is . . . you think it's my fault?'

'Something has to be.' Her jaw is clenched and her eyes are wild. 'I mean . . . why? Why are you being accused of this if you didn't do it? Why would you be getting phone calls from the POLICE? Do you know . . . what it would mean if you got charged with harassment? You'd be fired? How would we cope? How would we . . .' Her voice gurgled in her throat. 'How could this . . .'

'Becky . . .' There are tears in my eyes and I see her at the patio doors, the embers of the June sun glow from behind her and for a second I think she looks like an angel.

'Look me in the eyes,' she says. 'Look me in the eyes and right now, swear you didn't do these things.'

I step towards her and without hesitation I hold my palms out to her. 'I swear I did not do these things. Someone is setting me up Becky. Someone is trying to frame me. And I don't know why.'

'Is that what you told the police?'

'Yes. Of course. And I think I know who it is.'

Becky rubs the bridge of her nose. 'I need to bath Jamie. I can't cope with all of this.'

'I'll bath Jamie,' I say. 'You pour yourself a drink. Relax. And then I'll come back, once Jamie is settled. We can talk.'

She just stares at me but I walk forward and cup her beautiful face in my hands. 'You and me. Against the world.'

'It always used to be,' she says sadly.

When I come back she is sitting, nursing a glass of red.

The downstairs bathroom, the one we had adapted, is steamy and there is condensation on the windows. I never remember to turn the fan on. Jamie lies there, not meeting my eyes as I wash him down. He is changing. Beginning to grow hairs. He is growing up. Except he isn't. He isn't growing towards anything. He is stuck. Sometimes I see so much pain in his eyes I can't stand it. We were out for a drive and the noises of the Sunday League were drifting through the open window. Dads shouting from the side-lines, kids in their multi-coloured strips, missing goals. Shouting. Heads on the back of their hands, frustration. I would sell my soul to the devil for Jamie to miss a goal. To be able to give him a pep talk in the car. About getting back up again. About trying again. Jamie will never have the chance to make mistakes.

How lucky they all are.

That night his eyes were quiet. He didn't blink much and I knew what he was thinking about.

Sometimes I have thought about it.

I have.

Only because I love him so much that I can't bear to see him in this kind of pain.

He is fresh now and clean, in pyjamas, like a toddler, watching TV. His window to the world.

Becky's fingers scrape round the rim of her glass and she doesn't meet my eyes as I sit down next to her and pour myself a glass.

'I think Jenny is trying to set me up,' I say calmly. 'I called her out on a plagiarism thing and I think . . . well I think she might have convinced this Evie to put in a complaint. To discredit me.'

'Jenny?' Becky spat out. 'Why on earth would she go to those kind of lengths? That's just ridiculous. And why would the girl go along with something like that?'

'You've no idea.' I lean forward and try and take her hand but she pulls it away. 'You've no idea the power she has over her students.'

'Isn't that what's being said about you?' She can't meet my eyes.

'No, just listen. It's like they'll do anything for her. There was this student, a few years ago, Ewan. He was one of Jenny's pets. You know, he came from a troubled background and she was constantly giving him one-to-ones. Then all of a sudden, something happened. I don't know what. But something. He stopped coming to see her, even put a complaint in – about her supervision not being up to scratch. Then he gets into some kind of social media row and he's out.'

'So?'

'So it was another student who shopped him. For some sexist comments he had made. What if this is just what Jenny does? Gets her disciples to do her dirty work for her? A couple of days ago someone hit me on the back of the head. I didn't say anything because I didn't want you to worry. I think she knows I am on to her. I think she sent someone after me.'

I look at Becky but her face is blank. I could have just told her we were having fish for tea. It's like a mask.

'Becky, please say something.' This time I grab her hands and as I squeeze them a tear falls down her cheek. It's the most exquisitely painful thing I've ever seen and it slices through me like a knife.

'I want you to leave for a few days,' she whispers.

'NO.' I try and squeeze harder but she yelps like a puppy in pain and I drop her hands as if they have burned me. 'Becky, I haven't done anything. You have to believe me.'

'You've lied to me. Isn't that enough?'

'Becky . . .'

'No.' She stands and takes her wine to the Belfast sink, tossing the contents against the white ceramic. It stays there for a few seconds, bright red, like blood on snow, before it starts to fade. 'I need some space.'

I bury my head in my hands and my voice is muffled. 'But what about Jamie? You can't cope alone.' I feel as if my heart is breaking, actually coming apart in huge, fleshy chunks.

'What do you think I've been doing?' Becky hissed back.

'But what are we going to tell him?' I can feel my heart begin to crumble.

'That's not my problem.' Becky shakes her head. 'Book into a hotel or something. If you actually care as much as you say you do, then that's what I want. You have to give me some space.'

I nod mutely and stand up.

The milk is still out so I grab it to return it to the fridge, something I never do apparently. As I open it I see an expensive-looking bottle of champagne on the shelf.

'What's this for?' I hold it up. 'Who bought us this?'

Becky is stood with her back to me.

'I bought it. For you.'

'What why?'

She turns and I can see a sliver of sympathy in her grey eyes. Just for a second.

'Your agent called on the landline while you were at the station. She didn't want to leave a message on your voicemail.'

'What . . . and . . .?' My eyes widen and Becky's eye steel.

'You've had an offer. A three-book deal.'

The milk slides out of my hands and spills all over the floor. I can't speak.

'Congratulations,' she says, then turns and walks into the living room, closing the door behind her.

This is not how I thought this moment would be.

I should be popping that champagne, throwing my arms round Jamie and Becky. We should be ordering in a curry from the fancy Indian. We should be leaping up and down, holding hands and Jamie blinking well done, I love you.

Not packing a few shirts and a spare pair of jeans into a weekend bag. I don't know how long I'm going to be away for so in the end, I reluctantly pull the suitcase down from the top of the wardrobe. It's covered in a greasy film of dust. We haven't been away for so long. The last holiday we took was in France. We drove, to make it easier for Jamie. Becky slept the whole way so Jamie and I listened to Jeff Wayne's *The War of the Worlds*, the French countryside spinning past us, like a carousel.

I could tell he was hanging on every word, every track. He was sat up front, with me, I have learnt to read his emotions simply by the brightness of his eyes or the crackle in the air. When it finished, and the Martians had all died from the flu, we started again.

We watched the movie when we got back. The Tom Cruise version. But there was no crackle in the air.

I transfer my clothes into the suitcase, add my wash stuff, MacBook and charger. When I get downstairs, Becky is busy sorting out Jamie's bed. I stand in the doorway, and my throat clenches and I can't bring myself to say goodbye. I just can't.

In the hospital, after the accident, a doctor told me it was unlikely that Jamie would wake up. He told me to hold his hand and say goodbye. But I wouldn't. I wouldn't say goodbye. That was admitting something. It was giving up. I refused. Becky was sobbing over his little chest being forced up and down by machines. The shadows in the dimmed ward licked at the edges of the bed like demons.

I wasn't there when his eyelids opened. I was getting Becky a coffee from the machine, and when I heard the sobs I thought that was it. I thought he was dead.

The coffee scalded my forearm as it fell to the floor, and I ran back into the room. She was kissing his face all over, holding his hands. But they were limp.

'What's wrong with him?' she asked the doctors. 'Does he not have any strength?'

His lips, dry and cracked, didn't move.

His whole body was frozen, not even a twitch.

'What's the matter? He's awake? He's awake right?' Becky looked at the consultant.

It was the darkest moment of my life.

Until now.

But I'm still not saying goodbye.

I leave my suitcase out of sight and go in, kiss him goodnight. Becky is pulling back the duvet on her bed.

I thought it was your turn tonight? blinks Jamie.

'Got to work mate,' I say, and stroke his head. 'I'll see you in the morning.'

Becky glares at me but he will. Even if I have to FaceTime him. There's no way I won't be there when he wakes up.

I will not give up now.

It's raining outside but I can't even appreciate the poetic justice. It's not that sort of rain. It's thin and pathetic and barely graduated from mist. Yet I still wipe my face when I get into the driver's seat. I sit there for a while. I don't want Jamie to hear the rev of the engine.

The police officer was the one who convinced me. Tell your wife. He had kind eyes and a cup full of empathy.

'I didn't do it though. I haven't done anything.' My hands were twisted into claws and I'm sure my eyes were fox-like and wild.

'In which case, son, there's no reason not to tell her is there?'

Son. I'm forty bloody three.

It wasn't like it was on TV. Not that I expected it to be all *The Fall* or even *Broadchurch*. Definitely more *The Bill*. On a budget. No one-way mirror or even a cup of bastard coffee.

Just a small cramped room, me, the copper and his leaky biro.

'Am I being charged? Do I need a lawyer?'

'No, you're not being charged, and you're welcome to call a lawyer.'

I think of Jason and cringe. It's not going to look good for me.

'It's just a chat. At this stage.'

'Well whoever has been vandalising doors could well be the same person who attacked me last week. On the sports field. I'm a bloody victim here not a perpetrator.'

'You were attacked? By who?' The police man paused. There was a dark-blue ink stain on his bottom right lip.

'I don't know by who,' I said exasperatedly. 'If I did I would have reported it.'

'So why didn't you?'

'What? Report it? What was the point? I thought it was a hard-up student. A mugger. Someone hit me from behind on the back of my head. I must have blacked out for a minute or two. That's all.'

'Did they take anything?'

'No,' I admit. 'That was the weird thing. My phone

was still in my top pocket and my wallet was in my bag. Everything accounted for.'

'Can I have a look at your phone?' He held out his hand.

'Why do you need my phone?'

'Why don't you want me to have a look at it?'

'I don't give a shit, I just want to know why?'

'Because it's quicker than trawling through your phone records. But we will just do that if we have to.'

'Knock yourself out.' I unlock it with my thumb print and slide it across the desk.

The police officer picks it up. 'I just want to check your call log.'

'Why?'

'Because one of the complainants says she was texted by an unknown number last week. Someone who made some very disturbing threats to her.'

'And why would that be me?' I challenge and sit back in my chair. I have nothing to hide.

'Because, Mr Davidson, the threats were warning this particular young woman that unless she dropped her complaint against you, things would not turn out well for her. So, you see, we have a motive there.'

'What the hell? You think I'm going to go around scaring kids like something from a bad horror movie?'

'You made a call last Thursday, Mr Davidson. At 6.08 p.m. Who was that to?'

'I can't remember, I make loads of calls all the time, what does it say?'

'The number isn't in your contacts.' He holds it up.

'What? I have no idea. Jesus. Can you remember who you called last week?'

'The thing is Mr Davidson . . .'

'Dr, if you don't mind.'

'Apologies. The thing is I do know this number. This number belongs to the complainant.'

I hesitate. 'Wait . . . what? I've never called Evie.'

'I didn't tell you her name.'

'Yes I know but obviously she is the only one who has a complaint in against me.'

'Well I checked that too. Apparently there was another complaint made against you today.'

'*What?*'

'Maybe it's time you get some legal advice.'

In the rear-view mirror I watch as the lights are dimmed. There's an ageing tabby limping across the front garden wall, making that awful hacking death rattle sound in its spindly throat it is so fond of. I think it's called George. It looks so desperate, so scraggy, half bald, with a squint in one eye. When we first moved here I thought it was a stray in trouble and tried to coax the poor beggar into a cardboard box with a blanket and some milk, ready to take it to the nearest rescue centre, or failing that, the vets to put it out of its misery. The miserable creature was a paw away from its fate when the neighbours, Keith and Julie, came running out demanding to know why I was bundling their precious pet into a cardboard box. It was awkward. We've always eyed each other suspiciously after that. And not just the neighbours. George is the harbinger of doom. He's always lurking whenever something bad happens. He was there on my doorstep like the bloody dead moggy from *Pet Sematary* when I got my final rejection on my last book.

My book.

For a second I feel there could be a smile buried deep within and I go to fish into my pocket for my phone. But I can't bring myself to look at my emails. I don't want the moment to be like this. Sat in my drive, leaving my son. My wife. For a lie.

For a moment I think the tears are about to come but they don't seem to want to budge. It's as if all the moisture in my body has solidified into some kind of jagged iceberg inside my stomach.

I'm putting my phone on the dashboard when my home screen awakens with my notifications, and there, on LinkedIn, is a message from Ewan Wright.

CHAPTER SIXTEEN

Evie

Evie turned on her bed to face hideous wallpaper, smelling the stale sourness of her pillow and her own tacky breath.

The police at least had taken the paintball incident seriously. She'd had to go through the details of that night in excruciating detail. She had also recounted to the male police officer what she had told HR. They'd pressed her. Had she been drinking? Had she said yes? As if somehow it would be easier for everyone if she hadn't consented. If she had been out of her head. That was too far, an accusation too strong. Can you imagine what Village Vixen would have had to say about that?

She'd told them about the box. But not about the note.

The night of the memorial had almost been a relief. The text, from Simon's phone.

I'm going to fucking kill you.

An actual threat. It had been enough to kick everyone into action.

They were all interviewed. Kelly didn't come back to the house much anymore. She stayed at a friend's most of the time and went home at weekends.

The atmosphere in the house was twitchy and static. Almost like the radio had been turned off too fast and there was a slight buzz and hum in the air.

She could have been imagining it but it felt like everyone was avoiding her. Whispers in the kitchen. Hisses in the hall.

The boys were shamefaced. Cups of tea were made for her, but they didn't seem to like to be around her too much. In case whatever it was was catching. Or perhaps it was the wild look in her eyes.

She stopped going to lectures. She'd felt as if every glance were boring into her, as if she were about to see ravens perched on the edges of buildings. Walking into the lecture theatres felt as if she were walking onto a stage, naked, a spotlight on her in front of a baying crowd.

Girls looked at her that little bit too long. Boys looked away immediately.

Yesterday Harvey had knocked on her door, a gentle rap with his long, smooth, vampire-like fingers.

'Wasn't sure if you'd seen this?' he'd said and handed her the student paper.

Seconds later she'd slammed it down so hard in front of Liam that the entire kitchen table shook and Bronte's coffee spilled over the edges.

'What. The. Fuck?'

'Don't worry, I didn't mention your name,' Liam said, eyes all innocent. 'It's supporting you.'

'Where? Where is it supporting me? How?'

'A lecturer has been suspended over allegations of misconduct. I don't give any details that would identify you and, you know, I'm a reporter. I'm holding power to account . . .'

'You wouldn't even know about it if it wasn't for me. You have stuff in here about the student being "*subject to a reign of terror after she filed her complaint*".'

'Sweetheart, I think he's just trying to help,' Bronte said.

Harvey snorted.

'Don't you start,' Bronte spat. 'A paintball gun? You're the only one into guns round here. You're always creeping after Evie these days.'

'You better not be accusing me of anything you stupid bitch.'

'Harvey!' Evie shouted.

'Don't you threaten me!' Bronte reached over and pushed his shoulder.

'When did I threaten you?' Harvey threw his arms up to hold her off, his lumberjack shirt was wrinkled and Evie noticed brown, dirty smears under one arm pit. Grease maybe?

'It was implied.' Bronte folded her arms over her chest. 'You may think you can stalk other girls, but you won't get away with that with me.'

Harvey looked at Evie then stormed upstairs. His door slammed and Evie closed her eyes.

'Bronte. Please. I can't do with everyone arguing.'

'You started it,' Liam muttered, then pushed his chair back with an ugly scrape, stood up too fast and knocked his head on the fire extinguisher. 'Ahh fuck.' He rubbed his head, then stormed back out into the hall. This time they'd both jumped as the fire door slammed shut.

'God. My nerves.' She'd put her hand to her chest. 'My nerves. What do I sound like? Some kind of Victorian madwoman demanding smelling salts.'

'Honey . . . Actually . . . there's more.' Bronte held up her phone apologetically and Evie snatched it out of her hands.

It was Village Vixen.

And she was howling for blood.

A little birdy tells me a lecturer from the English department has been suspended on allegations of misconduct, aka shagging a student.

And according to inside sources, another girl has come forward now too.

So here's my question.

Neither of these girls are making allegations of coercion or assault. This is not a Harvey Weinstein situation. What gives them the right to point fingers and potentially ruin lives for an act they not only consented to, but engaged in willingly?

It used to be that women were chastised for sleeping with

authority figures. If a secretary was shagging her boss she did it to, excuse the expression, get ahead.

It's always the woman's fault. The homewrecker. The siren.

But now, it's flipped. The reclamation of sexual power in women is a wonderful thing. But are we striving for equality here? Because if so, you can't play that card and then run shrinking back from it, because you feel guilty. Or you wake up with a bit of regret.

Or, dare I say it, a lower mark than you expected.

If you don't want to be a victim, don't play one. Or maybe they do?

There is so much out there now on power, consent, gaslighting, manipulation, it's started to make sex feel seedy again.

I have no idea who this second girl who has come forward is.

But the first one? I know exactly who you are.

And it's not the first time you've lied . . . is it?

Evie had started to tremble.

'There's no way she knows it's you.' Bronte shook her head. 'It's just filling column inches.'

'Did . . . could Liam have?'

'He doesn't know who she is. I've asked him before. Anyway, of course they don't know. I mean, all that cryptic bullshit. You're the most honest person I know.' Bronte gave her arm a squeeze. 'You're going to have to chuck it in the fuck-it bucket. I mean, look at all this support.' Scrolling down the comments, Evie looked over her shoulder.

He's a lecturer, he is in a position of trust, he was abusing it.

OMG you realise this is nothing but slut-shaming.

Village Vixen, only have one thing to say – bring back fox-hunting.

But there had also been comments so vicious and vile that they had skinned her to the bone.

She'd lost almost half a stone in a week.

Evie stared at the wall now, she looked at the photos she had hung up in some kind of pretence that she had a vivid life, that she belonged. The one of her and Bronte that she had printed and framed for her birthday, in a club, all eye liner flicks and jeans and a nice top.

They both had such wide smiles but even now Evie could see it didn't reach her eyes.

There was a hum from her desk and she turned over, reaching for her phone, expecting it to be Bronte asking her what kind of sandwich she wanted from the van on the way back from her lecture.

But the name that flashed up was dad.

Evie felt her eyes swell again. She couldn't face it. She couldn't explain. He'd be so angry. So disappointed.

She let the phone drop softly onto the bed and turned away again. The last few days, weeks, the year had been horrific. It was only now she was really seeing the people who cared. Harvey, a boy she had laughed about so callously in the kitchen, behind his back. Bronte, a friend who she had been so dismissive of, even irritated by, simply because she wanted to be around her so much.

She thought she didn't have anyone to love, but it had

been staring her in the face the whole time. And what exactly had she given back? *I don't deserve them*, she thought as she swung her legs over the side of the bed.

Enough of this. Dragging herself to the mirror she took a good look. She looked like a wraith, with blue shadows under her eyes, her veins like spider webs creeping underneath translucent skin. No wonder people were staring at her, she looked like a creature from a Japanese horror film.

Running the shower she massaged the soft shampoo into her head, feeling all the tiny muscles groan and relax.

Maybe she would offer to go to the SU with them, buy them a drink. It was time to sort herself out. The toothpaste felt sharp as it cut through the mush in her mouth. She spat it out and felt purged.

Not much longer now.

Then she could put all of this behind her, like a lucid nightmare. Finally, she would be able to move on.

Once she was dressed in her jeans and a crisp white T-shirt she felt almost human again, human enough for mascara and bit of lip gloss. Not quite eyeshadow yet. That would be taking it too far.

Opening the door, she saw Harvey, sat in his doorway flicking through a guns and ammo magazine.

'Harvey, you don't need to keep watch you know.' Evie smiled. 'I'm fine at home.'

'I'm not. I'm reading.' Harvey sniffed. 'Where are you going? You're all . . .' He motioned up and down her.

'Dressed? Human.'

'Something like that.'

'Well, I thought I might try and leave the flat. Before sunlight causes me to burst into flames,' Evie cracked ruefully.

'Lecture?'

'No. I wondered if you and Bronte fancied a drink. My treat.'

'A drink?' Harvey's eyebrows shot up.

'Don't look surprised. I figured I really owe you. After that awful accusation, and then, everything you've done. You've really showed up, and you barely know me.'

'Forget it.' Harvey looked down at his feet.

'Shall we get Bronte then? She should be back by now.' Evie looked down at her smart watch. 'Oh hang on. There's a message.'

Evie pulled out her phone and swiped to unlock. 'It's Kelly. Bronte . . . what?' Evie looked up at Harvey in surprise. 'She's at the police station. Why would Bronte be at the police station?'

But Harvey didn't look surprised at all.

'What?' Evie said down the phone. 'I don't understand. What do you mean?'

'Just what I said. We are interviewing a suspect. She has more or less confessed. So it's now a conversation about the charge.'

'But I don't get it. Why is *Bronte* there? Did she see something?'

There was a sad-sounding pause. 'I'm sorry Evie, Bronte *is* the suspect.'

'What? What did she do?'

'The entrails at the very least. We checked the CCTV in your local butchers. The paintball . . .'

'Was *Bronte*?'

'No. A friend of hers. He is the one who . . . came forward. Tommy Haffenden. He said it was meant to be a joke, that Bronte told him it was some kind of game you were both playing.'

'Tommy . . . Tommy who used to live *here*? And the door? The text?'

'Now that I can tell you DID come from Simon's phone.'

'*What*?'

'I know, it's a lot to take in.'

'Did . . . did she say why?' Evie reached out and grabbed onto the handrail of the stairs as she felt her legs start to sway.

'Not yet.' The officer sounded exhausted. She could imagine that this was far down his list of priorities. 'Obviously, we won't let her come back to the house, we can talk about restraining orders.'

The words bounced around Evie's skull and ricocheted like tiny, tugging nips and pinches, pulling her brain every which way. Restraining order? Bronte?

Her friend who followed her around, licked her shadow, cooked her dinner.

Realising the officer had stopped talking and there was a

long and flaccid silence on the line, Evie let her arm hang down limply at her side.

She sank to the top step and rested her head against the wall.

She had come here, so determined, so convinced it had been the right thing to do. Now, her world felt grey.

She had nothing. No one. The only person she had left, the only person she could really trust, who could look out for her, wasn't there.

Evie sat for so long, just staring down the hallways, waiting for the tears that never arrived, she barely noticed Harvey when he sat down beside her.

'Kelly's back. She's come to pack a bag for Bronte. She's going home for a while. So, you know, you don't need to see her or anything.'

She nodded, ever so slightly.

'I always thought she was a bitch, not gonna lie.'

She could be. Evie knew that. She'd treated Harvey terribly.

'Why?' Evie opened her mouth and the word crumbled out, cracked and dry.

'Just the feeling I got. Dunno. Sly eyes.'

'I mean.' Evie tried to swallow but her throat felt clogged with sand. 'Why would she do it? I thought we were friends? She didn't believe me all along . . . she . . . I just don't understand.'

'Maybe she was jealous?'

'Of what?'

'This Simon guy? Maybe she liked him.'

Evie just shook her head. 'Were the boys in on it too?'

'I don't think so.' Harvey shrugged.

The sky outside the window at the bottom of the hall grew darker and after a while a few shards of rain sliced across the glass. They watched them in silence.

Evie thought of her dad in the Lakes. Sat in the hideous green armchair. Drinking his cheap whiskey, thinking about her, about the little girl he would take conkering and to the park on a Sunday. The way his eyes had started to become more opaque, haunted by the ghosts that thrust their tongues into his ears late at night.

She thought of last year, the pain. The never-ending crying. The way she'd felt as if someone had drawn her up on the gallows and left her to drain out. She'd been an empty sack. She'd had nothing left.

The rain carried on coming and after a while she let her head loll down onto Harvey's shoulder. He smelt of grease and smoke.

But at least it felt real.

The kitchen was empty when she went downstairs, she had made sure she heard the click of the front door. Had Kelly known too? Had she been in on it? Was the whole friendship a lie after all – and she'd never ditched Kelly. Not really. Were they all? Harvey? Kelly? Finn? Liam? All laughing at her while she stood and screamed.

The kitchen was barren. The washing-up still hadn't been

done and there was a foul smell emanating from the bin. Something fishy.

Harvey had gone to a lecture. She had made him. She wasn't going to feel responsible for him failing too. And now she was alone, the house seemed both huge and tiny, like she was Alice down the rabbit hole and everything was pulsating, growing and shrinking around her. She couldn't be here. Grabbing a jacket and her keys she left and ran out into the rain. It was getting heavier and she didn't have a hood or an umbrella. She had no idea where to go. Up ahead she saw two boys, one lanky and one broad. They were walking up the street from the bus stop, laughing, holding folders and bags over their heads to shelter from the rain. It was Liam and Finn. They were coming towards her. Evie couldn't move. Her chest began to feel like it was caving in and their eyes looked hollowed out, their cheeks sunken, like *The Scream* painting. The rain was sticking her hair against her forehead but she couldn't even raise an arm to wipe it away.

The boys were getting closer. Evie took one step back.

They were holding something. One of them had something in his hands. A knife. It glinted in the reflection of the rain and they began to move forward, like hyenas, shoulders high and hunched, hackles and spines raised. They came towards her snarling, drooling and Evie opened her mouth and screamed.

'Hey, hey you OK?' One of the boys held up his hands and grabbed his friend's arm to pull him back. 'Mate, careful.'

Evie's breath rattled and spat. They were not hyenas.

They were not even Liam and Finn. And the knife . . . a metal water canister. She began to shake violently.

'It's OK, what's happened?' The boy pulled down his hood. 'Are you hurt? Did someone hurt you?'

The rain began to thrash and hammer on the gutters and the grates.

'No.' Evie was so quiet she almost mouthed it. 'I'm sorry. I'm OK.'

'Can we call someone?' The other boy, shorter, tattoos poking out from under his sleeve, fished in his back pocket for his phone.

'There is no one,' Evie said. And that minute she knew how true it was. And finally, all the tears came.

The boys had panicked of course. Tried to take her home, but she couldn't stay in there alone. She'd apologised clumsily, left them staring at her bewildered as she staggered off down the street onto the main road. Worried they would come after her, try to get her home, she watched as the lights of the uni sprint bus came up the hill, painting the rain a golden yellow.

And there she found herself sat at the back of the bus, the storm unyielding, and she was staring at an advert on the back of the seat in front of her for the Connect campaign. Jenny's campaign.

Half an hour later she was towel-drying her hair and sipping sweet tea. Jenny's office was warm, and smelt of bay and rosemary. Evie's jacket was hung over the radiator and her shirt was clinging to her back.

The tick-tocking of the clock was melodic and smooth and made her eyelids feel heavy. She felt like she could sleep for years.

'Darling. I know it's so bleak for you. It must feel so horrible.'

Evie nodded.

'Tell me what you think your options might be now, going forward.' Jenny crossed one leg over the other, her shoe almost dangling off her big toe. Evie stared at it.

'I don't know. I'm so behind. I can't focus. I can't concentrate. I'm so humiliated. I don't want to go out. I can't face lectures.'

'Oh, Evie. You need to hold on to the fact you tried to do a good thing. And, well, I'm not sure I should be telling you this. But as a result of your complaint, another girl has come forward.'

'What?' Evie's head shot up sharply.

'Absolutely. I can't tell you her name. To be honest I shouldn't really have told you at all but I can't bear to see you in this kind of pain.' Jenny leant forward. 'What you've done, is sparked this girl, maybe even more girls, to come forward. It's incredibly brave and you must hang on to that.'

Evie looked blankly at Jenny, as if she couldn't quite believe what she was hearing. 'But . . .'

'I know it's hard to hear. I expect he made you feel special, the only one?'

'Not quite,' Evie said flatly.

'The point is you've lifted the lid on something. Something major. Don't lose your nerve now.'

'Don't.' Evie's face started to crumble. 'I can't handle it.'

Jenny pushed her chair back and stood, looking out of the window. The minster bells were ringing and the rain was still drumming against the glass. The sky was low and ominous and thunder rang like the kraken.

The lights in the office weren't on and the clouds appeared to be rolling in. Jenny turned and half her face was in shadow.

'Sometimes you have to make sacrifices, Evie.'

She reached out and stroked the top of her head. 'As women, we all have to make them. Especially when it's for a cause. It's not fair. It's not right. But that's the way it is. Good things come from dark places, the darkest places.'

'I didn't think it would all come to this. This *hatred* for me. I don't understand it. I can't understand any of it. Why people care so much, hate me so much for it. I made a big mistake and I'm sorry. But . . . his was bigger. So much bigger. Right?'

Jenny stayed there, her hand still softly grazing the crown of her head.

'We all make mistakes, Evie.'

'What, what do you mean?'

'I mean, nobody is perfect. Nothing is black and white. It's not about the mistakes we make. It's what we do afterwards that counts.'

Evie nodded dumbly and sipped at her tea. It was

lukewarm, and she wondered for a second how long she'd been sat, listening to the ticking of the clock.

'I keep thinking . . . about his wife and son.'

Jenny didn't say anything and the clock continued to tick. The sky continued to roll.

'Maybe I should have thought about them at the time,' Evie said eventually and looked out the window. 'I've made such a mess. I don't know where to go from here.'

'Well. You can stay in your room, be a victim and shrivel away. Or you can hold your head up high. You work out who to trust. You create an inner circle. You work out what actually matters.' Jenny sat back down and reached for her coffee.

'It's the looks . . .'

'Believe me, people are far too interested in themselves to be thinking about you. Besides, there's 75,000 students on this campus. Only a handful actually know anything. Or think they know. Don't give them the satisfaction.'

'And this other girl? Is she . . . what year . . .?'

'I'm sorry, I really can't betray her trust,' Jenny said. 'But I am sure, once this comes out, you'll find you're no longer on the receiving end. It's not looking good for him at all.'

'And what happens next?'

'I don't know the exact protocol. But you need to move on. You've made your statement. Leave it in their hands now.'

'Jenny . . . what is she saying?'

'Very much the same as you, that he treated her as his

pet and gave extra one-to-ones. That he sent her some . . . social media direct messages.' Jenny looked uncomfortable and swivelled her eyes away.

They both sipped their drinks. Evie's eyes ran over all the certificates on her wall. The glass gleamed in the dark shadows.

Best pastoral support. Best teaching innovation. Outstanding leadership in student voice.

Student voice. That's all they talked about, heard about, Evie thought. The importance of student voice. Bronte once joked they were consulted so much they should get half the lecturers' salary for doing their jobs for them.

'I can't believe Bronte could do this. Why would she hate me so much?' Evie's eyes began to fill with more tears.

'Well, I can't give you a straight answer. But most things, in my experience, are born from old-fashioned jealousy.'

'Jealousy of what?' A tear escaped and Evie impatiently brushed it away. She'd had enough and the skin on her cheeks was thinning and sore.

'Evie. Look in the mirror. Then look deeper. You're beautiful inside and out. Perhaps she had a crush. On Simon? Or . . . Liam? I often saw them together last year. I actually thought at one point they were an item,' Jenny said.

'Bronte and *Liam*?'

'I couldn't say for sure. It was around the time . . . well. It was a difficult time. After Josh, I think everyone in that circle fell apart. These things can either make or break a relationship. A friendship. When tragedy strikes, getting through it is just the beginning. The aftermath, the sweeping up the tatters. That's the quiet, empty kind of pain that not everyone could handle.'

Evie watched the eyes of her lecturer not darken exactly but flash, like a torch in a storm tunnel.

'Were you close to Josh, Jenny? Sorry I know I shouldn't ask that. But, everything you've done since. The campaign. The memorial. What you do for your students.'

Jenny let out a small sigh and smiled ruefully. 'Yes, I was close to Josh. Closer than I should have been. Oh, not like that. It's very hard Evie. Knowing where to draw the line sometimes. Like the line is some kind of infallible immoveable object.'

'Did he ever tell you . . . did you suspect . . . that he was . . . so . . . far gone?'

Jenny's voice was a whisper. 'Yes, I suspected. I wanted to tell someone. His parents. His friends. But I couldn't.'

'Why?'

Jenny just shook her head. 'In my position . . . I had made some mistakes before. Getting too involved. I'm ashamed to say I don't think I handled it well . . .'

'Is that why? All the work you do? It's what you do afterwards that counts?'

Jenny looked out the window and tried to answer but something gobbled up her words. Something almost fairy tale-like, and sinister, like a crone's withered hand grasping at her throat. All she could do was let out a choked sound.

But that seemed to be enough.

CHAPTER SEVENTEEN

Jenny

A week before the hearing

I am cold.

This is unusual for me. I am normally a warm person. Simon once joked it's all that pent-up fiery frustration in me. At least, I think he was joking.

I am not warm now.

The train is busy and I can smell the exhaustion from the other bog-eyed commuters. We look as if we are on the way to the gallows. I can't stop thinking of Evie.

Her name is whistling through the trees that we hurtle past, I hear it in the hiss of the doors, the rattle of the windows. It's some kind of message to me. I want to help her so much it hurts.

My knees are shaking and my teeth, while not chattering, are vibrating on a delicate hum. My bones are cold.

I keep remembering him.

We were walking, with coffee. He was outside John's van when I grabbed my morning latte. His eyes were so lazy they were practically dropping.

We walked up the spine of the campus towards the English department together and his usual piney, rosemary scent had vanished. He smelt of washing that had been left in the machine too long.

He hadn't been to bed yet, he told me. He couldn't sleep. His head was wracked with howling dogs, the screeching of bad things. No, he wasn't coming to class. He couldn't concentrate on anything. The only reason he was out of his room was because he thought the walls might close in.

No, he didn't want to see his friends. They didn't understand. He didn't want to fake it, drink, make merry. He had begun to loathe them but he didn't know why.

'Their laughs are demonic.' That's what he said. They taunted him.

He had been depressed before.

But not like this.

I begged him to let me call his parents, a friend from home, to reach out to anyone. But he wouldn't let me.

When we got to the lecture theatre he looked at me with such empty, glassy eyes. I tried to touch his arm, to make sure he was warm, his blood pumping. He felt like dead meat. A slab of sinewy muscles and flesh.

Then he turned and walked away.

I watched him go, eaten by the hive of students buzzing around him.

That night, I did something stupid. I got his number from his student file and I powered back up my other phone. I hadn't used it for a long time. Not since back when I thought he had needed someone. Needed me.

And I messaged Josh.

It wasn't that I was trying to be secretive. But I knew the kind of trouble I would get in with the pencil pushers and the policy makers if I called him or emailed him. We are not here to be their counsellors. We are not here to fix them.

I knew there was a three-month waiting list.

In three months, there would be nothing left of him.

Talk to me, I said.

Perhaps it was because I reminded him of someone. Of the mother who never even sent a birthday card. Perhaps it was the tell-a-teacher myth. Perhaps it was the fact I reached out at the right time.

But he did.

It wouldn't be another Ewan situation. It wasn't like that.

Josh would never push me up against my desk, his eyes greedy, his hands heavy.

And horribly, intrusively, Josh is gone. And all I see now is Ewan's unshaven face.

I screwed my eyes shut to block him out but he's still there, hissing, wheezing his nicotine-stained breath down my neck.

'You want this. You want it as much as I do.' He smelt of

frozen oven-cooked food and his T-shirt of cheap washing powder.

I didn't want it. Perhaps, late at night, maybe once I'd thought that I did. I would think about him. I won't lie. I'd imagine what it would be like to be wanted, desired like that. The soft fuzz of his cheek, the tense upper arms, the bright tattoos on his forearms cradling the soft, untouched skin of my lower back.

The wrongness of it all.

The breaking of the rules. Cat-lady Jenny. Teacher of the year. She would surprise them all. She was more. She wasn't just needed. She was wanted.

I tried to think like that, of myself in third person, as he covered my mouth with his, but all I could taste was revulsion and I pushed him off me.

'What the hell do you think you're doing?' I hissed and straightened myself up. That was when my office door was still wooden, and heavy. I'd asked for them to be changed to glass doors after that. Safety for students and staff. Another one of Jenny's little campaigns.

'What?' he wiped the corner of his mouth where a bit of spittle had formed and my stomach flipped in horror.

'I . . . what did you, why did you think was going to happen?' I stammered.

'What? Why did I think you wanted that? Maybe because you've been messaging me, for like, weeks.'

'But . . .' I shook my head. It was true. There was no way

I could deny it. Oh God. Had he saved it all? Did he have proof?

'Fuck's sake . . .' He stood back. His dark hair was hanging in his eyes and he flicked his head to move it out the way.

'Ewan. I'm so sorry. I didn't mean to give you the wrong impression.'

His jaw was stiff and his eyes defiant.

'You totally gave me the vibes that you liked me.'

'I want to support you. I know how hard it is for you and . . .'

'Ah, fuck off. I don't need your pity,' he spat.

An icy fist closed round my heart. I wasn't in control here. I wasn't in control at all. He wouldn't let me. I felt real fear run through the blood in my veins.

He looked at me, down at me. He was so tall. This young man, barely out of a sixth form blazer. Thinking he knew the rules when he wasn't even sure what the game was.

I stood as tall as I possibly could and swung my hair behind my shoulders.

'I think you had better leave Ewan,' I said firmly.

I had seeds I needed to plant.

Josh. He was nothing like Ewan. He sat outside my office door with his re-useable coffee cup. He held the door. He called me first, when he got the placement he had wanted. He adored me.

Or so I had thought.

The train pulls into the station and I stand up. My knuckles are white from clutching my handbag too tightly.

I hadn't even noticed the crimson half-moons my nails had made in the fleshy part of my palms.

I step off onto the platform and start to walk towards the car park. I don't know why but I become even colder. It is not dark yet. It's still that dreamy kind of dusky. It hasn't been a sunny day, so no ashes of warmth are still flickering. Most people have gone towards the main entrance where there's a taxi rank. The car park is towards the back of the station, accessed over a walkway, and there's only a couple in front of me and a young girl behind me who appear to be heading that way.

And yet I can feel eyes on me. I feel as if my movements, my walk, my gait, is being studied from afar. I pause and turn. A young girl with dip-dyed blue hair looks at me quizzically and I smile quickly, my eyes over her shoulder. There is no one there. No one behind us. My eyes sweep the platform underneath. It's busy but not packed. Not many people from Harrogate tend to use the commuter trains after 7 p.m.

I turn back and carry on walking. I'm tired, and I can't remember the last time I ate something hot. My heels ring on the metal steps down to the car park.

My car is at the end, the nearest place to the departure platform, the furthest spot from the steps. The blue-haired girl scuttles off through the alleyway, onto the back road and the couple are already climbing into their shiny grey Kia Sportage, probably stopping at the M&S Foodhall on their way home to have amazing sex, I think, not even bitterly.

As I walk towards my car the feeling comes back. Again,

I stop and turn, but all I can see is the couple reversing out of their space. I glance at the alley but it looks clear. Fishing in my bag, I grab my car keys and look up towards my car. And that's when I realised. There wasn't anybody behind me. There is someone in front of me.

'What are you doing here?' I clench the keys in my fist and feel the metal bite.

Simon is leaning against my car, against the driver's door. He doesn't look good. His cheeks are sunken and his hair is lank. He looks unwashed and crumpled, as if he has been sleeping in his designer shirt and jeans.

'Looking for you,' he says. There's an emptiness to his voice that I recognise. I take a small step towards him.

'You've come a long way for that,' I say and try not to look as nervous as I feel.

'Safer here I thought.' Simon doesn't make an effort to move out of the way.

'Safer? What do you mean?' I try and laugh as if I have no idea what he is talking about. The car park is almost empty. A beat-up red Ford Focus and a blue hatchback are all that are left. The train to Leeds has pulled out of the station now and most of the passengers who got off here have dispersed. The two platforms stretch ahead, a crumpled *Metro*, a crushed coffee cup.

The breeze has picked up and I realise I am now actually shivering.

'You're cold,' Simon says. 'Shall we go somewhere and talk?'

'What do you want, Simon?' I say and nod towards my car. 'You could have just rung me.'

'You wouldn't have picked up,' he says and he's right. We both know it. I struggle to meet his eyes.

'Did you do it?' I ask. I don't know why. I know the answer.

'Does it matter?' he says. He isn't blinking.

'Probably not,' I reply honestly.

We are at stalemate.

'Why did you do it Jenny?' Simon's voice is dark and rolling, like a boulder down a tunnel.

'Do what?' The words are just falling from my lips.

'You know what. Evie. Now Elodie. Fucking *Elodie*?'

'So it's acceptable to fuck Evie but not Elodie?' I can't help myself.

'Was it worth it?'

'Was what worth it?'

'Destroying my life. Convincing that little coven of yours to turn on me. Make false allegations. Make me out to be a predator. Just because I was on to you with that forged essay. Does your precious reputation mean that much?'

Simon's eyes start to blaze and I realise I am not nervous. I am frightened. I am frightened of the man that stands before me, with his five o'clock shadow and his salty, sour smell. He has the eyes of a desperate man.

And I hate him for it.

'You don't understand. You don't understand what that poor girl has been through,' I hiss. 'OK, Elodie made a mistake. She was sorry. Really sorry. Does that mean she should be punished and have all her chances taken away from her?'

'What the fuck? Are you listening to yourself? That's exactly what you've done to me.' Simon thumps the car bonnet and I step back.

'So you admit it then? Finally?' I say. He glares at me and shakes his head and turns, his palms facing down on the bonnet, his shoulders hunched. For a second I think his shirt is going to split open and his skin will turn green and for some reason I stifle a laugh.

'Do you think this is funny?' Simon turns his head slowly over his shoulder. 'I have lost my wife. My son. Possibly my job. I . . . I had a book deal. That's all going to vanish. It's all going to disappear.'

'Well maybe you should have thought of that before . . .'

'I didn't DO IT.' He shouts and turns so fast that I jump. 'You know. You KNOW. You set me up.'

Shaking my head, I step back. 'I didn't do anything apart from offer those poor girls support.'

'Poor girls? You mean like poor Ewan Wright?'

Simon walks towards me and I freeze, my legs are solid and my spine feels fused. I can't move.

'I know, Jenny.' Simon is close now he just whispers. 'I know what you did to him. He told me.'

'What? That he tried to have it off with me in my office and I pushed him away? Fine! I admit it. I made a mistake too. I didn't realise my intentions would be so skewed in the mind of a boy who I thought was a man. OK? I misjudged it. I absolutely DID NOT have sex with him.'

'Just like I didn't have sex with Evie. Or Elodie.' Simon thumps his chest. 'Why? Jenny, why? It must have been you. You must have told them to do it. WHY?' He is so close now, I can smell the plaque from his un-brushed teeth. The stale body odour from his shirt. I wonder where he is sleeping. His car perhaps.

'I TOLD you. Evie was distraught,' I cry. 'She came to me in floods of tears. Said she couldn't cope with the guilt, the rejection. That you . . . you fucked her up against the wall in some pub toilet.' I wrinkle my nose in disgust. 'Then you pretty much walked out before she'd even had a chance to clean herself up.' My voice is rising higher and louder. Simon looks around but I don't care. My arms fly up and I push him hard in the shoulder. 'And then you ignored her. Wouldn't meet her eye in seminars or return her calls.'

'She never called me! That's not what happened . . .'

'You used her. YOU USED HER. YOU FUCKING BASTARD.' The tears are coming now and I feel it. I feel the pain for Evie writhing in my gut. I can't help myself. I reach out and push him again. 'You're a fucking bully Simon. Calling her, threatening her? And what about what you've been doing to me? Pretending to be Josh? Trying to scare me?'

'I have no idea what you're talking about.' Simon yells back and I see a conductor hurrying across the metal bridge.

'YOU'RE LYING. HOW do you have his phone? What

else did you keep?' My voice is wavering and verging on hysterical.

Simon grabs me by the top of my arms and I start to twist and wriggle. 'I didn't do it. You know me Jenny. You know me. I would never do anything to risk losing Jamie.'

'I thought I knew you.' I really am crying now. 'I thought you were my friend.'

'And I thought you were mine.' Simon's voice cracks.

'Miss. Is everything OK here? Sir, please step away.' A broad Yorkshire accent drifts towards us from the edge of the car park. We both turn to see a portly conductor coming towards us, reaching for his walkie-talkie.

Simon immediately lets go of my shoulders and steps back.

'Sorry. Everything's fine. I'm leaving,' he shouts back.

The conductor pauses in his path and looks at me. I nod weakly. 'It's fine. Everything is fine.'

He nods and releases his hand from his belt but doesn't retreat. I look back at Simon and he looks as if he could melt on the floor into a puddle of clothes. The Wicked Witch of the West.

'Please. Please Jenny. I won't say anything about Elodie's essay. About Ewan. About anything. Just get them to withdraw the complaint. I'm begging you.'

'Why do you think they'd listen to me?' I ask quietly.

'Everyone listens to you. Your word is God,' Simons says. 'And I know, deep down that whatever fucked-up game you're playing, you have a heart.'

He turns and strides towards the blue hatchback and I just watch him go.

Do I? Have a heart? Sometimes I am not sure it's still beating.

I watch as he does a three-point turn one-handed in that arrogant way men do and watch his tail lights come on as he drives away. I wonder where he is going and then I remember he doesn't know where I live. No one does.

If anything ever happened to me, no one would know. People make a charitable donation now rather than sending Christmas cards. Or at least they say they do. Cate would call my phone for a while if I went missing. But she wouldn't know which door to come and knock on to see if my pale, swollen, bloated white body was bobbing in the bath tub in an ocean of red. I could be there for days. Weeks. Even Enid would just fuck off out of the cat flap and live on mice and puddle water.

I do not really exist to anyone. Outside their lattes and wines. Outside my office door.

The conductor heads over. 'You alright love?'

'Yes. Fine. Sorry. Just, bit of an argument with a friend.' I hold up my keys. 'I'm off. Thanks for checking up on me.'

'Some friend by the looks of it.' He raises his eyebrows and I nod as if in agreement.

He was one once.

He listened. He listened not in the way so many men do when you can tell they are listening to wait for a pause in the conversation so they can jump in and with an anecdote that involves them. He asked me questions. He knew my cat's name. My mother. I'd had a few drinks. It was the night Josh caught me looking at him in the beer garden and I'd thrown Simon's hand off me. I hadn't meant to, truth be told. It was a reflex action. I don't like being touched. I never have. My foster mother stopped trying to cuddle me when I was eight years old. She went on a course, I think. Showed affection in other ways. I think that's what she was trying to do anyway. The piano lessons. The baking. The strange pulled-back gummy smile. Doughnuts after sports day. Soft powdered sugar on cakes.

I don't remember too much of it. Before.

I told Simon that. I told him that and he never tried to touch me again.

Brought me coffees without being asked.

Put my birthday in his phone and bought me expensive bubble bath from the place I love but can never justify. I don't even know how he knew.

Soft, powdered sugar on cakes.

And then he betrayed me.

And then . . . he was just like all the others.

I get into my car and slam the door too hard. I have no idea if I am hot or cold anymore but I drive home fast. Too fast. By the time I park outside my door my heart is pounding and I am trembling so violently I can feel the rattle of my bones.

Enid's there when I get in. Her eyes are defiant and

ungrateful and I feel the hackles on my neck start to buck and writhe.

Her spine bends at the sight of me. She can tell. She knows. She lets out a silent hiss, her mouth flexes and her ears flatten and before I know what I am doing I reach out and kick her so hard she slides across the kitchen floor. Quick as lightning she rolls over and leaps onto the counter and over to the table and I reach out and try and grab her. She pauses and my shoulders hunch. My fingers scrabble and search for something, anything. They close around something glassy, smooth. I grab it and before I even check what it is I hurl it at Enid's head. She darts and it strikes her in the flank. She yowls and falls to one side but still makes it to the cat flap. This time I chase her, sobbing, begging for forgiveness again. My hand closes around her tail and she turns and slices down my forearm with silvery metal claws. I scream and snatch my arm back and she is gone. Nothing except the slow thwack, thwack, thwack of the cat flap ringing back and forth in her wake.

I lower myself onto the floor by the cat flap and look at the four angry welts on my skin. Little bubbles of blood are blossoming like buds.

'I'm sorry.' I start to cry but the tears are dry. Instead my face stretches and contorts and my skin feels so tight it might split.

After a couple of hours I have licked my arm raw and I now lie, curled in a ball, by the cat flap waiting for Enid to come back.

Down in the darkest corner of my mind something is poking and pulling, niggling and piggling its fingers into the wound. I'm worried she won't come back.

Perhaps she doesn't need me.

Perhaps she never did.

Perhaps she is out in the cold, watching the lights of the cars and the hum and crash of the commuters coming home on the main road.

Watching the door. Waiting for me to go to bed so she can sneak back in. Sneak back in behind my back. Eat the food I pay for. Drink the blood she has drawn.

Take, take, take.

I didn't mean to hurt her. It was just a little reminder. A little reminder that she is not the one in control.

She'll come back. She always does.

CHAPTER EIGHTEEN

Simon

I know it was stupid. I couldn't help it. But it doesn't matter now. Everything is unravelling so fast and all I can see is Jamie and Becky and the books whirling around me like Dorothy's house in the cyclone. It is as if the world is a hurricane and I am the eye of the storm. A sense of calmness has come over me. It is as if nothing matters now. It doesn't matter what I do. Or don't do. I have no control. There are no consequences now. Because nothing I do, nothing I say, has any bearing.

I saw Ewan yesterday.

Normally I'd be embarrassed. I'm not actually sleeping in my car although it looks like it. I can't even stretch to a Premier Inn. No, it's airbnb and it's just a room in a flat belonging to a man called Carlos who has a designer moustache and eats an alarming amount of corned beef in a can. I'd joke about it but nothing is that funny anymore.

We share his bathroom. It is avocado green. I don't spend much time in there.

I haven't shaved in a week and I'm running out of fresh shirts. Everything is crumpled and I haven't slept. I feel like I'm in a nineties Brit Pop song, staring at the Artex ceiling, the damp in the far right corner.

I have made so many mistakes.

Gazing at the condensation running down the window, Jamie's little head pops into my mind. The poppy bruise. His glassy eyes. Like a doll. Drip. Drip. Drip.

The smell of Becky's shoulders.

The softness of her. The way I see how Jamie used to be in her smile. In her laugh.

There are so many different kinds of love.

Ewan picked the bar. It's definitely a bar and not a pub. One of these ridiculous apothecary-type affairs where it takes twenty minutes to mix your drink in a jam jar while adding random household objects to make it cooler.

I order a whisky sour then almost send it back because it doesn't have a rusty nail in it.

Ewan is late of course. If I had any credibility left I would have been late too. Instead I was early. I was on my third whisky sour by the time he arrived and hoped he would take himself to the bar as I was bankrupting myself and facing another week in a room that you wouldn't even pick to hang yourself in.

He arrives in a shirt rolled up strategically to show the hint of his ink. His hair is smarter these days, his shave cleaner. He also looks to have grown a foot and widened a metre.

'Ewan.' I stand up and offer my hand out to shake, hoping he doesn't attempt a fist bump or anything crass. His grip is weak, I am pleased to note, but his slap on the back of my shoulder is very manly. He smells expensive. But not too expensive. A smell that says I have spent a lot of my monthly budget on smelling this good, because it's important to me to smell this good. I can't help but inhale a little. I do not smell good. I smell of roll-on deodorant from the garage.

'Wow, Simon, can I get you a drink mate?' He looks down at my glass.

'No, no, I'll get them.' I stand and pat the breast pocket of my jacket, as if to prove I have money in there.

'I insist.' Ewan motions to my empty glass. 'What you drinking?'

'I'll have a pint, err, Guinness please mate.' It'll last longer. I tell myself I'll let him have this one. He probably feels great, buying his old lecturer a pint. I feel a bit of relief though too. I'm not sure he's going to stick around for a second drink.

When he comes back we banter for a bit. Talk about his graduating class. Who he is still in touch with. He shrugs off any detailed questions and after a while I get the impression the last few months at uni weren't the best days of his life.

I'm about two thirds down when I bite the bullet.

'So, Ewan. The, the thing I wanted to talk to you about.'

'Yep.' His back stiffens slightly. 'What is it? The messages. That social media stuff?'

'How did you guess?'

'Well. It's been everywhere hasn't it? Other unis. What do you want to know? 'Cause I've not changed my story. I never posted *any* of that shit. Someone set me up.'

'Yeah, I remember at the time . . . I remember you saying you hadn't done it.'

'It didn't do me much good.' Ewan swills the remains of his pint about but I don't get up to offer another. Not yet.

'Did anything happen? I mean, nothing actually formal happened, did it?'

'I got a bollocking and my appeal got thrown out.'

'The appeal? About . . .?'

'My dissertation. It didn't even reach the panel. I was pretty much discredited.'

'Discredited,' I repeat. My mouth is sour. 'You got your 2:1 though right? You graduated.'

'Yeah. With pretty much all the girls on campus hating me and all the lads too scared to back me. Not publicly anyway.'

'Who do you think did it?' I can barely breathe.

'Well. Someone who wasn't happy with me I guess. I . . . I dunno. Someone must have got hold of my phone when I was drunk. No one believed me though.'

'And who was it? That reported you? Do you remember?'

'Nah. I just got told there had been a complaint. Then all these screenshots got shoved in front of me. I hadn't got a leg to stand on, but they'd all been deleted off my phone. So they couldn't prove it either. It didn't put me in a great position for the appeal.' Ewan scratched the back of his head. 'Why? What's going on?'

I think about the text to Evie's phone. The proof they allege they have on Elodie's.

I pause. Sip my drink. Then look him directly in the eyes.

'I'm being set up.'

Ewan looks back at me and shakes his head. 'Fuck man. What's the sitch?'

'Jenny.' Ewan's eyelid flinches. 'It appears to be my round,' I say and go to the bar. I pay on a credit card.

Now Ewan really starts to spill and it becomes clear he is still not over what went down. I bite back smiles, smirks, and the bitter taste in my mouth sweetens as he tells me about their late-night chats on snapchat.

Did he screenshot them? 'Course not. Why would he even think he might need them? It started with an inside joke, he said. The movie *Brief Encounter* and how Jenny would sometimes walk with Ewan to the station. He didn't live on campus. Couldn't be trusted, he joked. The truth was he couldn't afford the halls. His loan was going towards helping out his dad who had been laid off.

'I started hanging around after my last lecture in case she was walking that way too. I liked talking to her. Her voice was soothing. She had something to say. We sometimes had a coffee from the stand if we both missed a train. Not going to lie, sometimes I would miss it on purpose, if she was late. Just to talk to her a little bit longer.'

'And then . . . what happened after that?' I ask.

That's when he messaged her. For the first time. Found her on Facebook.

'I thought I was being daring and bold. It was just a clip from YouTube from the movie. It was late and I'd had a few beers with my dad. I thought it was cute. I was mortified though. She didn't reply. She didn't even mention it.'

'Did she watch it?'

'Well it turns out no. I apologised. When I next saw her. Said I was sorry if it wasn't appropriate. She laughed and said she never used Facebook. And then she gave me her number, man. Just, handed it over like it was nothing. In case you need me. That's what she said.

'I didn't know what it meant, you know? I mean, I know she's not a teacher. Not like school. But *still*. So I sent her the clip again and this time I got two blue ticks. She replied straight away. Something about it being easy to lie when you're trusted.'

'Holy shit. Wait, what? What does that mean?'

'I know right? I was full on pumped. I thought she was giving me a message. You know, that we could get away with something. Because everyone trusts her. I couldn't believe my luck. I mean, I thought she was hot. Older woman. You know. Anyway, I googled it and it turned out to be a quote from the film.'

'But still . . . it's a sexy-sounding message,' I point out.

'RIGHT?'

Ewan says he didn't know what to think. What to say. Blood pumped through him and he felt nervous. It was ridiculous really. This was hardly his first rodeo. But there was something thrilling, something challenging. A prize to be won, a goal to be gained. And even more than that, he wanted her. He wanted her to want him.

And yet . . .

It continued like that. The second guessing. The, he hoped – God he hoped – mind games.

'And then that scene in her office.' Ewan shakes his head and looks down. 'Cringe man. Ultimate cringe. I wouldn't have minded if I could have laughed it off with mates. Called her a cocktease and gone home and had a wank.

'It was the humiliation. I had told her things, things I had never opened up to anyone about. Stuff from when I was little. We even watched *Brief Encounter* together on FaceTime one night when I couldn't sleep and I was having bad dreams again. Look. I even kept the message. The last message.' He held up his phone and I read it.

'What's that? Another *Brief Encounter* quote?'

'Yeah. And then, you know, after all of this, she rejected me. But it wasn't just that. She was *surprised.* Not biting her lower lip, whispering *I can't, I'm so sorry, but I can't.* You know, like I thought she might be. There was nothing in it. NOTHING there for her. I was nothing to her. Just another student. That's why I got so angry. I know, I know. It was childish and pathetic.

'But I never breathed a word to my mates. To others on the course. I knew that's what she was afraid of. No matter what, it's a bit dodgy isn't it? That's why I thought there was something there. Why would she risk getting herself into trouble for nothing? When I walked away, she ran after me and grabbed my arm and said, "I think it's better that no one knows about what happened here".'

Ewan shakes his head and sips his pint.

'And what did you say to that?'

'Yeah I bet you fucking do,' he spits back.

She'd blocked him after that.

Of course, her emails were professional, courteous. He didn't turn up for his dissertation meeting.

'I couldn't face it. I mean, I was pissed off. Not about the fact she didn't, you know, do anything. Just, the fact she seemed so shocked. I thought we had some kind of relationship. Friendship. And then it was over. She shut me down. Just like that. It felt cruel. Spiteful.'

'And you really didn't tell anyone about it?' I ask. My hand is twitching and I realise I want a cigarette for the first time in about five years. I want one very much. I wonder if Ewan smokes.

'Well, what was there to tell? I mean, what was I going to say? My lecturer was being nice to me and now she's stopped? I mean, she would probably have been applauded for not crossing boundaries. Doing the right thing.'

'And the appeal? So, did she not supervise you properly? I mean, that's not on. Just because she was offended by your advances. She still had a duty to you, to teach you. Or at the very least request another supervisor. She shouldn't have just ignored you.'

'Ah. Well. I guess we were warned we wouldn't be chased. You know, I didn't turn up for the first one and then I got an email asking me to book another. I never did. She never reached out. I was angry when I got my result. Really angry. But probably more at myself. I should have swallowed my pride and just manned up a bit. You know what you're like when you're that age. It's always someone else's fault. I blamed her for not trying harder. Still, I think she should have checked in, but whatever. You know. Maybe she was scared or something.'

'Of you?' I raise my eyebrow.

'The situation, maybe. I dunno. I feel like a dick now for the appeal, but those things. I never said those things they said I did. I may be a dick but I'm not a twat.'

'So . . . what, do you think someone did it to scare you off the appeal?'

'Maybe. Yeah. One of the girls I guess.'

'Did you say any of this to anyone? At the time?'

''Course I did. No one was interested.'

He looks back at me and something makes him uncomfortable because he shifts away and I am reminded of Jenny and the picnic bench. Do I always get too close?

I can still feel the warmth of his skin.

'Did you do it?' he asks me. 'Whatever it is you've been accused of?'

'No,' I say. 'I didn't.'

'What are you going to do?' He leans back in his chair. There is the hint of a smile playing on his lips and I notice how full they are.

'I have a hearing. Next week. I'm not letting anyone take me down.'

'Easy to say though isn't it?' Ewan says and I flinch. 'So what did you do? Or not do?'

'I didn't fuck my student in the toilets of a pub. I walked away.'

I watch carefully for his reaction.

But his eyes are dead and almost roll, like a shark's.

'But, now there's another girl. Who has come forward as well. A girl who claims she had messages from me. On social media.'

Ewan looks at me again.

'Well,' he says finally. 'That's just ludicrous isn't it?'

I drive for a while. The roads of Harrogate are annoying and twisty until I get to The Stray. There are lights hung in the trees that line the big expanse of grass that borders the fancy flats and Georgian houses. I wonder if Jenny lives in one. It occurs to me that I have no idea where she lives. I have always assumed she lives alone. But maybe she doesn't.

Or maybe she does. Maybe she is sat at home, laughing at me. Pouring her wine, that smug self-satisfied grin on her face. Texting Elodie. Evie. Fuck. Why? Why would they go along with it? I don't understand.

I know now it's her, without a shred of doubt.

Like she got Ewan to drop that appeal, using her coven, she used Elodie and Evie to get to me. Why Elodie too? Perhaps I was getting believed? Maybe it wasn't as cut and dry as I'd thought. Had suspicions been raised elsewhere? I'd heard about that toxic blogger being surprisingly on my side.

But what I really didn't get was why? A plagiarism case? Turning a blind eye to an essay can't be so bloody important that she was ready to ruin my career. My family.

I do a full circuit of the ring road before I remember that I actually have nowhere to go.

I miss Jamie so much my heart hums with sadness. I picture Becky doing his food. Him wondering where I am. What has she told him? Tears begin to cloud my vision and I begin to swipe the back of my hand across my eyes like a child, when something darts out in front of me. A pigeon maybe? I swerve and brake but I still feel that awful thud of my wheels going over something.

I glance in my rear-view mirror and feel sick. There's an animal lying in the road.

'Fuck.' I whack on my hazards and pull over, throwing the car door open while I am still slamming on the handbrake.

As I get nearer I realise it's a cat and horror sits in the pit of my stomach like a bowling ball. Another car is coming towards us and I wave my hands in the air at it to slow down and go away.

'You alright mate?' A young lad has wound down his window and is looking at me from under his baseball cap.

'I hit a cat,' I say, and squat down next to the wretched creature.

'Dead?' the lad says and pokes his neck out, trying to get a look.

'I think so,' I say softly. Its body is very still, and I see no signs of breathing. The kid gets out the car and motions to the car behind to stop.

Gingerly, I gather it up. It is still warm, but floppy and its eyes are wide open, but there is no light in them. There is a tyre mark across its belly and for a moment I feel like I am going to throw up.

'Do you know where there is a vet?' I ask the kid who is wrinkling his nose.

'Nah mate. It's dead. You just need to put it at the side of the road.'

I shake my head. 'I can't do that.' I hook my finger around its collar. 'I need to find its owners. It'll be chipped.'

'Seriously, you don't need to . . .'

'Look, just fuck off, OK?' I snap and walk towards my car. I hear him cursing me under his breath and the squeal of the tyres as he pulls off. I clamber into the driver's seat, still holding the cat, and everything starts tunnelling. I squeeze my eyes tight and Jamie flashes before me. Little chubby legs running. The stillness of his chest.

I almost feel the walls of the car crumple in on me, like a can being crushed.

I need to find its owner. There is a shiny heart on the pink collar. Her name was Enid.

CHAPTER NINETEEN

Evie

The campus was cold and the wind whipped the blossom off the trees on the quad. Evie walked past the memorial tree and picked up her pace. She couldn't bring herself to look. Harvey had texted her, said he'd be in tonight. She was beginning to think that he was looking at her for too long. His eyes too soft. Sitting that tiny bit too close. She couldn't bear it.

Last night he smelt different. Sweet and barky, like a B-list celebrity-endorsed aftershave. He had shaved too. His T-shirt looked less stained, and his breath smelt less of tar.

Oh Harvey, please no.

She couldn't bear to be the one to cause him pain. But when he'd suggested a film, and she'd made tired noises, the hurt in his eyes had been too much to cope with. So they had sat, watching some Netflix crime series where she had no idea what was going on, apart from there being a cop with no social life and an adulterous husband wandering around in light grey. There were flashbacks of a murder. Or an abduction maybe. She wasn't really paying attention. She had just been watching the clock and sipping at her vodka, praying for it to reach eleven so sleep could mercifully take her and for eight precious hours she could block it all out.

Liam and Finn had made awkward chirps of apology. Grimaces. Swear down Evie, we had no idea. What a nut-case. We never liked her. Is it OK with you if we tell our personal tutors about it all, because you know, the stress of it all – we need extensions and shit?

The hearing was set for Monday. She didn't have to be there, thank God. A written statement was enough. From her.

And Elodie.

God. Poor Elodie.

Evie had begun to shake until Harvey, thinking she was cold, had wrapped a blanket round her shoulders.

Jenny had slipped her a private WhatsApp. Just to check in. She wasn't meant to apparently. But she hadn't wanted her to think she was alone.

'I'm always here if you need me Evie.'

Now, as she walked back from another personal tutor meeting, where Jenny had held her hands and told her it was OK to feel anything, that she should allow the guilt to come, allow herself to feel it, accept it, and heal, she was almost starting to feel worse.

Jenny's office was like hot chocolate. Warm, soothing,

quiet and sweet. Her bright blue eyes that fixed on her face and didn't move throughout the entire conversation. It was as if she could read every thought going through her head. See every emotion that flickered across her face. She had nowhere to hide and she didn't want to. She found herself saying things, bad things, things that she hadn't even realised herself.

How before her boyfriend had left her, she had come to hate him. Hate those around him who had taken him away from her. That she had stayed up, late at night, scrolling through Facebook, Instagram, Snapchat.

She had online-stalked everyone in his pictures. She'd obsessed over who he was with and why he hadn't called her back.

'It got to the point,' she'd told Jenny, 'where it didn't even matter if I loved him or not. I couldn't lose him. Not after everything. I couldn't cope with him not wanting me. Not needing me.'

'I understand,' Jenny had almost whispered. 'It's a very hollow feeling isn't it? To not be needed?'

'Jenny, am I doing the right thing? Simon, I mean, I wish I'd known. More about his life and what he had been through.'

'Oh Evie.' Jenny shook her head. 'You can't look back there now I am afraid. I wish you could but you can't. It's all too late now. And think of Elodie. Without you coming forward, she never would have. She told me that. She told me it was you that gave her the courage.'

'But what if this destroys him?'

'Just because someone has been through something terrible, Evie, it doesn't automatically make them a nice person, or allow them to behave how they want. We all have choices to make. There's light and dark in all of us.'

'I feel like all I can see is the dark.' Evie started to cry and Jenny leant forward.

'I could give you some trite meme about it having to be dark for you to see the stars. But I don't think either of us are the live, laugh, love type are we?'

Evie shook her head through her tears.

'Remember that. Remember who you are.'

'Who?' Evie shrugged. 'My mother's daughter? I didn't even get the chance to know her.'

Jenny smiled. 'You're my favourite student. That's who you are.'

Evie quickened her pace now. Even though she knew it was over, all the creepy weird stuff, she still felt on edge. She still expected someone to grab hold of her at any time and whisper a slithery hiss in her ear.

You're not who you say you are.

Who could know? Who could possibly know? She thought of the picture. The four of them. Arms around each other, friends forever.

She'd been so careful. There was no trace of her on social media. She'd never done anything that would come up on a Google search.

There was only one place they could have got that photograph from.

Harvey was ringing her phone now and so she turned it onto silent and stuffed it in her pocket.

The halls were busy but there was a flash of pink ahead. Elodie Highfield was scuttling out of Castlegate Lecture Theatre, her head stooped.

Evie halted for a split second then began to follow her. She ducked and weaved, in and out of people, heading towards the underpass.

'Elodie!' Evie shouted. Elodie paused for a second, then looked back so briefly she wouldn't have had time to even clock a face in the crowd.

Her face seemed pinched and anxious, open-mouthed like a baby bird's. She didn't stop but instead she kept moving, snaking away through the throngs.

'ELODIE!' Evie shouted again and people started to look at her. She didn't care and began taking bigger strides, until she was almost running after her.

'WAIT!'

The sky grumbled and the clouds thickened, a sprinkling of fine rain began to spit and people started to move faster.

There was a tiny flash of Elodie's pastel, faded hair heading towards the stairs of the underpass. Evie jogged towards the crowd funnelling at the top of the entrance and tried to jostle down but she quickly became swallowed in a sea of Adidas and Superdry, people squirming up the stairs, weaving in with those going down, everyone ignoring the keep-to-the-left rule. Soon it was all limbs and bags, jabbing into Evie's side, backs of shoes being caught. Pushing and heaving, and the growl of the double-decker bus pulling in below. Evie was swept along by it all, her eyes still searching. Even if she spotted Elodie now it would be too late. She couldn't talk to her. Not here. Not with everyone around.

Dejected, she slumped her shoulders and pushed her way out of the throng, only to meet with the surge of passengers coming off the bus.

Dodging and sidestepping she managed to get to the grey concrete wall plastered with posters for bands, house shares and union elections. The bus seemed to swell as more and more students piled on, hanging off the handrails like monkeys, sitting on laps, the driver staring straight ahead so he didn't have to bellow health and safety rules into the echo chamber.

Once the last straggler had elbowed themselves on, the doors closed, with not exactly a whoosh, more a flat fart, and the bus pulled out on low tyres. The rain at the entrance on the underpass was coming down quicker now and Evie could smell the wet concrete and the grass verges either side were polished somewhat greener by the water. But now she was free to trot back up the steps, she realised she didn't really have anywhere to go. The underpass was creepily still, save for the drumming of the rain. It was getting heavier and darker up there and Evie leant back against the wall, and closed her eyes. It wasn't like anyone was waiting for her and she didn't want to get soaked to the bone.

The spectre of Monday's hearing was making her queasy and exhilarated all at the same time. At least this way it would be over. She could move on somehow. Get a flat on her own next year. Keep her head down. Pay her rent. Study quietly at the back of the room. It would be out of the question to transfer again. No one accepted final year students in a transfer. She'd made her bed. She would have to lie in it now. And it's worth it, she thought. Remember. It's worth it.

She didn't hear the footsteps. It wasn't until she felt the heat of the breath on her face that she realised she was no longer alone.

Her eyes flew open. They were heavy-lidded. Mascara was smudged under her sockets and her eye flicks had run down the side of each cheek.

Bronte.

'You're not meant to be near me,' Evie said tentatively. She could feel every scrape and bump and sharp edge of the wall behind her back, between her shoulder blades. 'You could get in trouble.'

'I'm way past that. The question is Evie ... how much trouble are *you* in?' Bronte snaked her face up to Evie's, but her balance was off.

'What are you talking about?'

'Because you're a LIAR,' Bronte shouted. 'You were meant to be my friend, and you LIED to me. It was all a LIE.'

'What was a lie? Simon? I didn't lie ...'

Evie heard an almighty crack and felt the back of her head scrape painfully against the concrete, the burn of her hair and a hot ringing sensation in her cheek. Her hand flew up to her face.

'You slapped me? Oh my God. Oh my God.' Evie felt her eyes well but Bronte's just grew stonier.

'Why did you transfer here Evie?'

'What . . . what are you talking about?' Evie stammered. Her face was starting to get hotter and hotter.

'Because you needed a fresh start after getting your heart broken. That's what you said, right? Because of a bad break-up?'

Evie tried to press herself further back into the wall. Oh God. She knew. How long had she known for?

'Oh, that's right. Precious Evie. Everyone's so obsessed with Evie. Queen fucking Evie. But what's your endgame? Why are you *stalking* us all? Do you think we had something to do with it? Spying on us and answering that house ad? I mean, it wasn't a fucking coincidence was it?'

'Bronte . . .'

'You didn't even come to his memorial.'

'I can explain.'

'I knew I recognised you Evie. The minute I saw you. But I just couldn't figure out where from. Remember? I even *said* it. It took me a few weeks. But then I remembered.'

Evie suddenly began to go very, very cold.

'Freshers' week. You were there with Josh. You're the girlfriend he was trying so hard to get rid of.'

'It's true. I didn't think you'd recognise me. Bronte, please. I can explain it all.'

'That picture. I kept it. When we cleaned out his room for his mum I found it in a drawer. He looked so happy. Then when we started finding nice stuff, for his memorial, I went and got it out of my drawer. And it was you. You lied to me. It was all a lie. Our friendship. Everything.'

'Bronte . . . let me explain.'

'I'd love to hear you try . . .'

'I . . . I didn't want you all to know, that's all. I didn't want you all to know that I was connected to Josh. I knew you were friends with him and I knew that I wouldn't be able to make a fresh start.'

'You are such a liar. You lied about this. And you lied about Simon.'

'But why? WHY? If you knew all this, if you knew about Josh and me, why didn't you just tell me that you knew? I don't understand.'

'Because I thought you were my fucking friend,' Bronte suddenly screeched. 'I tried EVERYTHING to get you to break. I wanted YOU to tell me. I wanted to know YOU needed ME. I tried to scare you. So you'd talk to me, confide in me. Even those posts.'

'What, what posts? What do you mean?'

'Oh Evie see it's just like you isn't it? Didn't you ever stop to think that maybe I could be noticed too? That people listened to me. That I had something to say? No. Because I'm a *sidekick*. I'm never the main character. Well when I was Village Vixen, I was. People listened then. Every word I wrote, people were talking about me. In the union. In seminars. I was someone.'

'It was you? All along. But . . .'

'Yes, it was me. I've been Village Vixen since my freshers' week when nobody invited me out and I spent the first three days sat in my room, crying. I even tried to tag along with the other girls in my flat to the pub quiz. You know what they said? Sorry, our team is full. With someone from a different halls. They just hadn't thought about asking me. I was invisible. I didn't exist.

'I only existed when I started typing.'

'So, you've been writing all those spiteful . . . vicious posts?'

'Not everyone thinks they are spiteful Evie.' Bronte came up close. 'There are hundreds of people like me.'

'What did I do? What did I do to make you hate me so much?' Evie couldn't stop the tears. They burned her cheeks before she even realised she was crying.

'I wanted you to be more. But you're just a liar, aren't you? And a cheat and a fraud. And a user. You used us all. And there is no way I am letting you go through with that hearing on Monday and bring down another man's life. You already destroyed Josh's.'

'What . . . what are you talking about?' Evie shrank back into the wall.

'He fucking killed himself Evie. It was all the guilt and pressure. We all heard his phone going at all hours of the night. We all saw the messages. He thought you were bat-shit. We all did.'

'He showed you?'

'He told us. How you couldn't accept it was over. How you thought there was something going on? Someone else? You couldn't just let him be happy.'

'Stop it.' Evie's hands flew to her ears.

'He thought you were CRAZY. You followed him here. Why? Are you hoping to see his ghost or something?'

'STOP IT.' Evie pushed Bronte's shoulders hard. The drumming of the rain and the pounding of her heart were deafening. Bronte stumbled back off the kerb and into the road. Her legs wobbled for a second and then gave way.

'See, you're mental.' Bronte's words started to slur and she pulled herself to her feet. 'You're mental. You lied about who you are . . .'

'No.' Evie stood over her. 'I never once lied about who I was. That was you. Come near me again and I'm calling the police.'

Evie's heeled boots clacked on the floor but she ran anyway, feeling the rain splatter on her back and drip into the waistband of her jeans. Her blood pumped in her ears and her breath was like knives in her lungs. Once she got out, away from the underpass, she turned. Bronte was sat, slouched on the bench, her shoulders shaking. Another drunk crying girl at the bus stop.

Pulling out her phone she ordered an Uber and by the

time she threw open the door to the house, she knew she must look unhinged.

'Evie?' Harvey half stood as she raced through the kitchen and into the hallway.

'Leave me alone. Please, Harvey.'

Evie threw open her bedroom door and started throwing clothes into a bag, wrenching them so hard off the hangers that the metal hooks span.

'What are you doing?' Harvey stood at the door, his foot wedged to stop it from closing.

'I've got to get out of here. I've got to go.' Evie reached behind her pillow and bundled in that The Who T-shirt that had once belonged to Josh.

'What's going on, Evie?'

She just shook her head, and threw in handfuls of underwear.

'Where are you going?'

'I don't know,' she said. 'I don't even know. Anywhere but here.'

Harvey looked behind him uncomfortably, then came into the room. The heavy door slammed but Evie didn't even look up.

'Is it about him? That guy?'

'Simon? No.'

'I don't mean him.'

Evie looked up sharply. 'What do you mean, Harvey? Just spit it out.'

Harvey looked down and sniffed. 'I heard Bronte a while

ago, when she was on the phone to someone. I think she was talking to that Tommy guy, the one that used to live with them.'

Harvey reached up and scratched the back of his neck. There was a slight damp patch under his left arm. 'But I didn't really know . . .'

'Wait. You knew? You KNEW all the time it was Bronte? And you didn't tell me?' Evie stepped towards him, still holding a pair of rolled-up jeans in her hand.

'I didn't know exactly,' Harvey snorted and looked at a patch of wall behind her head. 'And I did warn you to be careful.'

'I thought you were talking about Simon!'

'Jesus.' Harvey's hands came up to his temples. 'Why is it always about him?'

'What are you talking about?'

'You say you can't stand him, that you're mad at him. That he took advantage . . . but he is all you talk about. What do you know about me, Evie? When have you ever asked a question about me? You just like me here . . . don't you? I'm like, a pet dog or something. You're going to use me, aren't you? Like you use everyone else.'

Evie threw the jeans at his chest and watched them slither to the floor.

'What? Who? Who have I used?'

'You used Bronte. I don't know why. But you needed something. Didn't you? I could tell you didn't really like her. I saw you roll your eyes when you thought she wasn't looking. You never even noticed me, did you? Well I watched.'

'Harvey, don't. I can't cope with this right now.'

'*You* can't cope. Here we go. You can't handle it. Well, what about me? What about everything I have done?'

'What do you mean?'

'I fucking knocked him out for you.'

'What?' Evie whispered.

'By the football pitch. I was so mad at what he'd done. I thought, I thought he might get away with it. They always do, don't they. He said, she said. I wanted to scare him.'

'It was you?'

'Yes, it was me. And it was me who messaged you from his phone alright. Don't you get it? I did it for you. So you'd have more evidence.'

Harvey turned and kicked the wall and Evie sank down to the floor, her back against the bed.

'I can't believe this.'

Harvey leant forward and rested his forehead against the wall.

'Why was it such a big secret? That you knew this Josh guy? Why didn't you want anyone to know?'

Eventually Evie opened her mouth, her lips sticking to her teeth from the dryness, and her throat cracked as she swallowed.

'Harvey. I think I've made a really big mistake.'

He came to her and slumped down next to her, both staring ahead.

'Evie. I'm only going to ask you this once. Are you lying? About this? About Simon.'

Her breath was shallow as her head rolled limply to the side to face him, her jaw slack.

'Can I trust you, Harvey?' The words sagged from her mouth.

'Can I trust you?' he replied.

She looked at him and heard the rain begin to ease, dusting and sprinkling the window now. It could be three in the afternoon or two a.m. Time seemed to have no meaning anymore.

'Yes,' she said. 'I'll tell you the truth.'

CHAPTER TWENTY

Jenny

A week before the hearing

I open the door and scream.

Enid is there, limp in Simon's arms.

I don't know which part of this terrifies me more.

'What have you done to my cat?' I screech, and wrestle her out of his grip. I try to slam the door but the dead weight of her surprises me and she slips from my hands. Simon reaches out to catch her but I yank her away, holding her under her front paws so she is dangling down.

'Jesus. It's you? Jenny, I ran over her. I have no idea how. She came from out of nowhere.'

'You bastard. YOU BASTARD. You did it on purpose.'

'Jenny, I swear, I didn't even know she was yours. How could I know? I ran over her. This address was on her collar.'

'You're LYING.'

'I'm not lying Jenny. I would never hurt an animal. I would never hurt anything. You KNOW that. You KNOW it.'

'You hurt me.' I cradle the cat to my chest and the words are out before I even know it. Slowly I turn and walk to the kitchen like I'm in a trance. I hear the soft click of the front door closing and I think for a moment that he's gone. But when I sit at the bar stool, holding Enid up to my cheek, I sense he is still here. In the doorway. Staring at me.

'Please leave,' I say flatly and it occurs to me that I don't even care if he does or not. I feel numb. My toes are cold and my hands are hot. There's nothing in the middle section.

'Jenny. Let me help. The vet said we can bring her back there and they will take care of it. I didn't know if you had a garden or anything . . .'

'Take care of it?' I say. 'Take care of it? What, you mean, bring her back to life?' She is beginning to stiffen in my arms. I think of the kick to her stomach and I want to rip my insides out.

'OK. I'll leave,' Simon says.

Simon says.

Simon says come for a drink.

Simon says come to the theatre.

Simon says be my friend.

Simon says cover for me.

Simon says I have a secret.

I don't even realise that I am rocking back and forth until his hand comes out to steady me.

'Jenny, I'll say I made up the stuff about Elodie's essay. I'll say I got it wrong. I will get another job. I'll do anything.' His voice is beginning to sound desperate and I despise him for it. 'Just please don't do this. Please, stand them down. You know I didn't do it. You know it for a fact.'

I bring my eyes up towards him.

'And what makes you think I have that kind of power Simon?'

'You must have told them to do it, Jenny. I just don't understand why?'

'Because,' I say quietly. 'Just because I can.'

I raise my eyes towards him and force myself to keep them locked on his.

'You sick bitch.' He moves towards me suddenly and I duck fast, thinking he is about to hit me. Instead he laughs, bends down and softly kisses me on the cheek.

'I wouldn't give you the satisfaction.'

I watch him walk to the door and I can't help myself. I call after him and I hate the sound of my own voice, how high-pitched and needy it is.

'You've nothing on me Simon,' I say. 'And on Monday, everyone is going to know exactly the kind of man you are.'

He pauses, and turns.

'What is it Jenny? Can you not bear it? Can you not bear that they love me more than you? That I don't have to manipulate and control them for their adoration? That I don't tease them until they try and fuck me over a desk because that's how sad and desperate and gagging for attention you are.'

'GET OUT.' I reach for the nearest thing I can lay my fingers on and hurl it at his head. An apple. A fucking apple.

Simon catches it one-handed, looks at it, and then at me. He takes a bite.

'See you, Jenny.' He turns and walks towards the door and I can taste blood at the back of my throat.

He pauses at the handle and looks as if he is about to turn and say something to me.

'JUST GET OUT!' I scream again. 'GET OUT OR I WILL CALL THE POLICE.'

He shakes his head, but he does leave and I fly to the door to lock it. I run round to the back and lock that too, terrified of him coming back in. Terrified of the things he didn't say.

I can hear Josh in my head. I can hear his laugh, his cries. They are in every single room. I rush between them like a caged tiger, but he is there. He is everywhere. I can't escape him. I can't escape that night.

He was in my office and the tears wouldn't stop. Nothing I said or did could help. He had stopped the medication. He said it wasn't helping. His skin was chalky and grey and his hair was tar-like and crumpled.

'I can't go on,' he said. 'I can't carry on like this.'

'Josh . . .' I stroked his back. 'I need to tell someone. I'm sorry but if you're at risk of hurting yourself . . .'

'You can't!' He reached out and grabbed my hand so hard my knuckles went white.

'Josh . . . you need professional help. I'm not qualified.'

'No. Please. Jenny. Don't. Please don't. Please don't leave me.'

'I won't leave you,' I whispered as I pulled his crown towards me. 'I won't leave you.' He sobbed into my top and I rocked him like a child. I kissed the top of his head, then the swollen arc of cheekbone. I wanted to carry on. I wanted to kiss down his face, his lips, his collar bone. I wanted to kiss him down his chest and take all his pain away.

You see Simon.

I am just like you.

My phone buzzes and I grab it in annoyance. It's her again.

Part of me wants to throw it across the room and watch it smash, but instead I swipe it and answer. Her annoying, pathetic little voice whispers a hello.

'Elodie, stop calling me,' I say firmly. 'You can't back down now. Remember what we talked about? This isn't about you. It's about women everywhere. Women who have no voices, who can't be heard, who are just ignored. Men who think they can use us. Use us and throw us away. And nothing ever happens to them. When we break the rules, we are harpies, we are monsters. We are whores. When they break the rules, they are untouchable. Evie can't do this on her own.'

'But, Jenny, I feel like this is a really bad thing to do . . .'

'Sometimes good people have to do bad things. Sometimes we have no choice.'

I hang up the phone.

Enid's dead eyes bore into mine. My dead eyes bore back.

CHAPTER TWENTY-ONE

Simon

The hearing

I am surprised at the lack of drama when I arrive. I thought it would be like a courtroom drama or a John Grisham novel. I picture myself in a dock shouting like Jack Nicholson in *A Few Good Men*. He won an Oscar for that role. And he was only in three scenes.

Instead, the girl on reception makes me a decent cup of coffee and hands me a packet of fancy biscuits and we have an inane conversation about how the wind is picking up.

Becky let me back into the house so I could pick up my good suit. I have shaved. I am scented and my brogues are polished. Most importantly, I ate breakfast with Jamie and I told him about the book deal. Becky gave me that.

'Does that mean you can come home now?' he blinked.

I kissed the top of his head and told him how much I

loved him. Him and me. Two peas in a pod. Or, as Jamie says, two eggs in a pan. I don't know why.

Sitting outside the conference room door, balancing my coffee and saucer on my knee, for the first time I wish I'd joined the union. Although, to have anyone witness the next couple of hours would be degrading and humiliating. Jason asked if I wanted him to come. Bit of backup. Legal moral support. I said no of course.

I couldn't let him hear this before Becky.

Because I am going to tell the truth.

'Simon.' Louise opens the door and gives me a tight-lipped smile. I stand, my saucer vibrating, and she nods for me to follow her.

Not wanting them to see how much my hands are shaking, I think twice, place the saucer on my chair and button my jacket.

As well as Louise, there is a man in the middle of the panel with sunken cheeks who reminds me of Christopher Walken.

I consider telling him this as an ice-breaker, then quickly decide against it.

Another woman in her fifties, wearing an olive-green suit and the faint hint of a moustache, is to his left. I recognise her vaguely. Louise takes her seat on the panel. Two women one man. I bet that was deliberate. There is also a younger woman sat to the side with an open laptop. They sit on one side of the boardroom desk with me on the other. There is a glass of water already there in front of me and I take a sip.

I am calm. I know I'll remember this moment for the rest of my life. My hands have stopped shaking.

'Simon . . .' Christopher Walken opens and I sit up straight and smile.

'We'll start with a round of introductions shall we?' I nod as if it matters to me at all who these people are.

'My name is Anthony Howard and I am the chief investigating officer. I believe you know Louise Mushens from Human Resources?' I nod and smile again. I feel like one of those dogs in the back of a Fiat Punto.

'And this is Tracey Jannet, Faculty Director.'

Ah. That's where I remember her from. Dull three-line-whip away days and graduation ceremonies. A big gun. I feel flattered. I notice they don't introduce the note-taker though. I look at her and smile, to make sure she doesn't feel invisible.

'So, we are here today in order to explore two complaints made from female second-year students who allege you had a sexual relationship with them, which you did not subsequently declare to the department. By continuing to mark their work, these allegations are a direct breach of the interpersonal relationships policy.'

I nod again. There's a pause and everyone looks at me. I stay silent and he coughs and continues to read off his pad.

'Simon, as mentioned, I have been appointed investigating officer into the allegations. In summary, while forming relationships with students is strongly discouraged, due to the power imbalance that could be perceived, the university policy is that such relationships must be declared. Therefore, we would see this as potential misconduct.'

'I understand,' I say.

'We have statements here from both women who detail when the relations took place and previous and subsequent interactions with yourself. Have you had time to read through these statements in detail?'

'I have,' I reply.

'And we also have a statement from yourself, which denies these accounts. In a counterclaim you make a serious allegation about one of the witnesses, Jenny Summers. You allege you have not had relations with either woman, and therefore had no reason to declare anything at marking stage. You also allege that Dr Summers is making false accusations deliberately.'

'That's correct.'

'This disciplinary hearing seeks to address the misappropriation of your position and fundamental breach of trust. The hearing may result in a number of outcomes, including that of dismissal.'

I stay silent.

'Simon, we have two solid statements from two young women of good character and a witness statement from their personal tutor, who claims both of these women sought her counsel individually and unaware of the other. We also have your counter statements that allege these claims are entirely false.'

'That is correct.'

'Which leaves us in a rather unfortunate situation, where we have no choice but to look at the balance of probabilities.'

'You mean a "he said, she said".'

'Well. More of a he said, they said,' Louise points out.

'Don't you have to have evidence?' I point out calmly. 'Otherwise what is the point of an investigation?'

'This isn't a court of law. It is not a case of proving something beyond reasonable doubt.' I can't remember the man's name now. I wish they had name tags.

'It should be.'

'Simon, would you like to make any additional statements or retract anything you have previously said that you would no longer like to enter as evidence into the hearing?'

'Yes, I would like to make an additional statement.'

The younger girl taking notes wipes her palm on her thigh, her hands and fingertips obviously sweating with the nerves. I watch and wait until her fingertips are resting lightly on the keyboard.

'As I have said before,' I say, 'these allegations are untrue and an attempt to tarnish my reputation and my character. With the first allegation, it is true that I spent a lot of time with Evie, as she appeared to be suffering from severe mental health issues. One evening, at a bar, where admittedly I put myself in a position of vulnerability, which I regret, Evie tried to kiss me outside the toilets. She even attempted to pull me into the cubicle. I instantly backed away. After this, Evie seemed . . . irritated. I assumed, at the fact that I had rejected her advances. She came to see me on fewer occasions for one-to-ones and began to see Jenny instead. I thought little of it, and put it down to embarrassment at her behaviour, likely to be fuelled by alcohol. In terms of the second allegation, apart from teaching Elodie in seminar groups, I have had no interaction with her outside a teaching space. Certainly not, as she has alleged, in my car. I have never offered her a lift anywhere. She has never been in my car. I have never had sexual relations with either woman.'

'Yes. You have made this clear in your submitted statement . . .'

'And the reason I have never had sex with either of these women,' I continue firmly, 'is because . . .'

For a second I think I am about to lose my nerve. Once I say it I will never be able to take it back. I close my eyes and think about Jamie. About Becky.

About what they deserve.

I look up. Jaw steady.

'. . . is because I am gay.'

There is an uncomfortable silence. I let it run.

Outside the window a blackbird lands on the sill and taps its beak against the glass in surprise. I don't think it realises there is a barrier there for him to get to where he needs to be.

'Simon.' Tracey swallows and glances at her colleagues. I raise my eyebrows in anticipation. 'I am not sure your . . . sexuality . . .' She looks over helplessly but everyone is staring at their favourite part of the wall.

'Oh it does. Because I think that sways the balance of your probabilities,' I point out and for a second I start to rather enjoy this.

'But . . .' The woman from HR looks down at her files. 'Are you not married . . .?'

'I don't believe the relationship I have with my wife is any of your business,' I reply.

Becky knows of course. She's a very clever woman. She's never said it. Not out loud. But she knows.

Oh it's all so easy for celebrities to come out. Be applauded for being brave. Championed on social media. The papers don't look at the cracks left behind.

Would I be treated that way? Applauded for leaving my wife with a disabled son. Of course not. We would always be a family. That's not the issue. But not together. I wouldn't do it. I wouldn't do it to Becky. But mostly, I wouldn't do it to my son. I wouldn't put him through that. Some awful modern co-habiting hellhole of open beds and being called a 'modern' family. Jamie's life already isn't normal. He doesn't need any more stigma attached.

So the only other option would be to leave. To only see him at weekends. A night or two midweek. Find a flat that we could have adapted. Shuffle him round. I would always be the one that left.

Like the one who wasn't there.

I will never be that man again.

The past eight years have enveloped me in the kind of darkness I had seen only in my visions of hell. The months after the accident rolled into one, long, lucid nightmare where I felt neither asleep nor awake. It's hard to remember that time clearly, the beeps, the conversations with people in white coats who could have been speaking Latin for all I knew at the time. The words 'Locked-in Syndrome'. Becky curled up on the hospital bed, her face turned away with silent tears.

There is nothing wrong with Jamie's brain. He has no learning difficulties or disabilities. His body is completely frozen but his mind is on fire. It's like a sponge. He is so smart and funny. His school says he is at the reading age of a fourteen-year-old, the maths age of a GCSE student. His mind, his world, swirls in colours. His thoughts bounce off the walls of his skull. He lives a hundred lives in his head, in his books. In my books.

But he is there, trapped. Like the sun forced into a lamp, or a tsunami into a drip of a leaky tap. His soul always ready to explode from the prison of his own body.

I have always been gay. I know that now. I have clocked up hours in counselling sessions, joined support groups, had online sex in dark corners of anonymous dating sites where I have been able to close my eyes and pretend that voice is next to me.

When Becky and I married, Jamie was the size of a plum in her thickening belly and I thought of nothing but him. And her. This magnificent woman whose voice could always bring the fireflies out at dusk. I loved every inch of her buttercream body. The smell of her shoulder where it curves into her neck, the way I can see her fillings when she laughs, the taste of her supermarket shampoo when I kiss the top of her head. The way she leaves out water for stray cats on the back step and is the world's most terrible dancer. She can't reverse-park and she re-reads books until she can mouth the words along with the lines. She always has a packet of Parma Violets in her bag, even now, because they used to be Jamie's favourites. She speaks of his future like it is an ocean of possibilities. She can always feel the stars, even when they are not there.

Like I said. There are so many different types of love.

I have no shame, no embarrassment for what I do to keep sane although Mumsnet tells me differently.

The first time was in a pub. I'd been out with friends and he'd been looking at me all night. I was standing at the bar, he was at the pool table. There was something about his, his stance, the way he laughed with his head slightly cocked. The way his body moved around the pool table, his brown eyes met mine when he bent to pot the black.

When my mates hailed taxis I hung back. Went back.

I never found out his name. I put it down to too many beers and more than a year without sex. I have needs. The strange thing was, I didn't feel any guilt or disgust, just relief. Like, in the moment, that was what was right.

I thought about him for more than a year. I went back to the bar even, once or twice. But he was never there.

I started drinking more. Wishing for more.

I know she would stand by me, even though I don't deserve it. I have always known. She would hold my hand. But I can't put her through it. She shouldn't have to. She always has someone's hand she needs to hold. I can't demand she props me up to.

So I go on. It's a modern world and there are no taboos anymore.

Sticky, faceless, anonymous encounters. No names. No numbers. It's like a different me. Sometimes I don't even recognise myself in the mirrored walls of the club.

I started crying on the drive to work around two years ago.

The night before I'd been kissing a man with red hair. I told Becky I was delivering a paper at a digital learning convention. I even wrote it, did the slides. Then I drove to Manchester. Not Canal Street. Far too obvious. So much risk. The club was in a retail park. A shuttered-down warehouse. I had never been before and I had to fork out a membership fee and have a background check before I was even let through the door.

It was clean inside, men, couples, in towels. Making friends. Disappearing into private rooms. Watching. Spy holes. I got changed into my own towel and got a drink.

The man smiled at me. He looked like Ed Sheeran and Eddie Redmayne. His face and arms were freckled and his eyes were brown. No names. No numbers.

He tasted of liquorice.

And that's when I started crying. His mouth was wrapped around my cock and I loved every single second, his beautiful hair sprouting between my fingers. The tattoo of the tree on his bicep. His kids' names inked as the branches. Oliver. Jessica.

I wanted to know his name. I wanted to know him.

Jenny once said that I reminded her of that Stone Roses song. That I want so much to be adored. She's wrong. She's so wrong.

I want someone to adore.

Not in the same way that I adore Becky.

I want to love someone. I want to be able to love someone unconditionally and without barriers or shame. I want to sit opposite a man in a restaurant. I want to hold the door open for him.

I want to wear matching fucking Christmas jumpers.

But I want my son more.

Eventually it happened.

But it wasn't with the man with ginger hair.

'Right. Well, we have two statements here, and a witness statement testifying that you had sexual relations with both of these women.'

'And you have my statement that this is a vindictive set-up orchestrated by an unstable woman . . .' I take a deep breath. 'Who had an inappropriate relationship with a student. In fact, who has had inappropriate relationships with several students.'

'You think that Dr Summers would really go to such extremes?'

'It's not just her job. It's the . . . respect that comes with it. It's the validation. She never saw me as a threat until now. I'll admit, I knew she was perhaps blurring the boundaries with her student. And I didn't whistleblow. It seemed harmless. There was nothing to actually prove.'

'Can you please explain what you mean by inappropriate?' The man in the centre coughed.

'Not what you're thinking,' I say. 'The imbalance of power you mentioned? The breach of trust? It's not all tied into sex. That's a drop in the ocean. Jenny was different. She made her students trust her. She targets them. Vulnerable students. She picks her tutees lists. She sees where they have come from. Lower socio-economic backgrounds. Mental health issues. She reads their admissions files like a menu. Then she earns their trust, coaxing out secrets. Making herself indispensable to them. She gets off on it.'

Louise flinches.

'And it's all OK. While it's working. Then she might ask for a little favour back. Making a social media comment using someone else's phone. Making a complaint against a lecturer.'

'I really think . . .' The faculty woman holds up her hand but the man in the grey suit leans forward. I can taste the sexism dripping from my lips. But I don't care. I can't care.

'And that's what happened with Ewan Wright.'

'Ewan Wright?'

'He made a complaint against Jenny and then dropped it. She made sure he dropped it. He got it wrong you see. The trust. The bonding. His schoolboy mistake was that he thought it was sexual. It wasn't. He got angry. He stopped . . . adoring her. That upset her. She couldn't control him anymore. You can't control and mould and hypnotise someone who isn't thinking of what a wonderful, inspirational, leading figure you are. Not when they are clouded with visions of bending you over your own desk.'

'That's enough . . .' Faculty woman held her finger up. 'Please don't minute this Georgina.'

The girl stopped typing but looked at me apologetically. She believed me.

'She failed. He wouldn't be a monkey and she couldn't grind the organ. Neither got what they wanted. So they both got angry.'

'Simon. You can't make an allegation that a teaching member of staff is acting inappropriately by not having a relationship with their student.' Christopher Walken sat back in his chair.

'You are not listening. She is having relationships. Toxic relationships.'

'But what would even be the purpose of this?'

'I don't know,' I say. 'But I'm nearly there. I'm sure of it. Almost as sure as the massive discrimination case I will bring against you if you continue to pursue these false allegations made against me, along with damages claimed for emotional trauma.'

The silence is all the power, all the electricity I need.

'So, I think that about wraps it up for today. Shall I leave you my solicitor's details? I'd like to begin with negotiating my return-to-work date.'

Outside I look up at the window to see their three heads knitted together. The blackbird is still there. He pecks one more time at the glass, then turns and flies away.

Back at the airbnb I pack my case. I can't face another night here. Even if Becky doesn't let me through the door, the time has come for Carlos and I to part ways. I'm paid up. The bank account is so empty it doesn't even rattle. It's time to make some changes. I daren't even fill up the car with diesel in case my card gets rejected. I've got about twenty quid in my wallet and I dread to think of Becky trying to buy some milk and finding out I have left her high and dry.

She doesn't know the extent of the finances. Why I needed this advance so much. £10k might not be life-changing amounts of money but it is for us. The cost of the care for Jamie. My counselling. Private club membership. One salary. I hide it from her. She has enough to deal with.

It has to stop. It all has to stop.

As I zip up my case, I have a weird feeling in the pit of my stomach. Out of the wreckage comes a chance to rebuild.

I have become such a cliché.

I shake my head and for a second I hear him. I hear his

laugh somewhere inside me. It catches me off-guard. The way sometimes I think I see him in a crowd and I go to call out his name before I remember.

It's like he isn't dead, and for that minute it is as though everything makes sense, and I am whole and loved and the days can continue to tick.

And then I wake up and it's as if I have only just been told and the floor tilts and it's like my ribs are bursting and there is no air. There is no breath.

I zip up the case and try and imagine the words coming out of my mouth as I tell Becky. Her lovely face. What will I do? How will it all work? As if I haven't thought about this for every waking minute of every day.

A sudden pealing, angry noise brings me back into the room. An alarm in the street that sounds suspiciously familiar. Sticking my head out of the window, I see my lights flashing and I swear, assuming it's the dodgy lock again.

Grabbing my things, I haul out of the house, already clicking the beeper on my key fob but it's not making a difference.

I manage to silence the alarm by the time I'm on the street, but all of a sudden it is not the noise going through me anymore. It's the smell. The passenger window is smashed and inside the car it's him. It's absolutely him. His aftershave. It's so strong I start to shake. Hugo Boss. It's saturating the car. I reach over to the passenger seat and pat the fabric. It is drenched in it, the shattered empty bottle lying on the footwell.

I don't even see the glass in tiny beads, twinkling like diamonds in the sun.

I just lower my face to the fabric and breathe him in.

CHAPTER TWENTY-TWO

Evie

The day of the hearing

'What's happened?' Harvey said from the doorway. The smell of him turned her stomach. His sheets were an odd kind of damp. She hadn't resisted. After she told him everything, it felt futile. Arrogant, somehow, to refuse.

He was the only one left.

She just didn't have the energy anymore. Here she lay, in a vest top and period knickers, with the elastic torn. Her hair was matted and her armpits smelt of beef crisps.

'You need to eat.' Harvey came into the room and let the door shut. The lamp was dim and his face above it reminded her of her dad and his torch on camping trips. Telling ghost stories.

Evie shook her head and closed her eyes. She couldn't think of anything she would rather do less. Until she felt the weight on Harvey's hand on her thigh.

'You've got to stop this.' He was sat with his back to her. 'You've got to get up.'

He was clearly a virgin. Fumbling. Prodding, clumsy fingers and horrible hard squeezes.

Not like it was with Josh.

'I met him when I was fourteen,' she'd told him three nights ago, crumpled as a rag doll by her bed. 'I mean, I'd always known him. The way you do in school. We were aware of each other. Not enough to say hi to in the hallway or anything. Just . . . do you know what I mean?'

Harvey hadn't. Evie suspected he'd had a very different experience of school.

'Well. I met him in the school office. I volunteered after school for my Duke of Edinburgh award. He was . . . he was seeing a counsellor. Mrs Harrow. On Tuesday afternoons we started coming out of school at the same time, after everyone had gone. The school buses had gone. My dad didn't drive so we both had to walk into town to get the bus. We started walking together.'

Harvey just stood. Forehead against the wall.

'Bronte said . . . I was crazy. I wasn't Harvey. I was just . . . *heartbroken*. The Josh that would do something like this . . . that's not the Josh I knew. Something happened to him here. I was sure of it. I'm still sure of it.

'He wrote me emails. You see?' Evie pulled herself up to her feet. 'See, Harvey? If he'd thought I was crazy . . . he wouldn't have done that, would he? He wrote to me all the time. Even after he'd ended it. He wouldn't answer my calls.

But he would email. Check in on me. At first he'd sworn there was no one else. And then I saw him. At Christmas. I *saw* him. I told him, I emailed him and told what I'd seen. Demanded to know . . . who it was. And then he said . . . he couldn't tell me. That I wouldn't understand.'

Evie walked towards Harvey, her eyes beseeching. 'You have to believe me, Harvey. I'm not bad. I'm not a bad person.'

He turned and looked at her.

'I'm not using you, Harvey,' she whispered, her palm on his back. 'You're the only one I trust.'

In some small way she thought she deserved it, that he deserved it. The effort and pain and guilt of rejecting him yet again was so overwhelming it was just easier. His breath on her neck smelt of cheap vodka and the acne on his back was sore and lumpy as she ran her hands over it. She stroked him and patted him as if he was a child that needed soothing.

Afterwards she had let him sleep in her bed, and she sat hugging her knees to her chest, biting down so hard on her lower lip her bottom teeth were stained with blood.

She stopped sleeping after that and Harvey stopped seeming to notice.

The nights became the longest of her life. She would doze afterwards. Maybe for half an hour. And when Harvey's breathing became sour and shallow and his leg stopped twitching she would roll over onto her back and stare at the ceiling.

Food had no taste anymore. The idea of eating sickened her. There seemed to be no point in any of it. Her phone had not been charged, her body had not been washed. And still he wanted her.

He was a man of few words, but he was there. Always there. Licking at her shadow with his thick tongue. The weight of his stare was crushing her.

Josh. Josh. Josh. It was the only word she could see when she closed her eyes, a tattoo on the back of her eyelids.

On the third night she rolled out of bed and staggered back to her own room. Pools of clothes still spilling out of the case on the floor. A cold cup of tea that had developed a custard-like skin on the surface. She smelt of Harvey now and it was wrong.

Every night she dabbed Hugo Boss behind her ears. Every night since he had kissed her cheek instead of her lips at the train station.

She had noticed then, how the cloud in his eyes was back. The slightly vacant look. Oh he might have hid it well from his new friends. Bronte. Liam. Finn. But he couldn't fool her. His smile was the brightest in the room. The first on the dance floor. On the third night of freshers' week he told her how he had stopped a fight by jumping on a table, dropping his trousers and pulling his willy up high, leaving his scrotum to dangle, and shouting 'last chicken in Sainsbury's!' He always loved Billy Connolly.

He was like a rapid response unit when shit went down. Defused arguments with a well-timed joke. Chatted to waiters and strangers in bus queues. Shelled out for an extra coffee in Costa to pay it forward.

But he was a hundred hollow Russian dolls inside. That's how he described it to her once. Empty shell, after empty shell, getting smaller and smaller until he felt like he was going to just disappear.

He hated Christmas. As it approached, she could feel him tensing, alert, like a hare to a rifle. His head was prickly and sharp but he toasted and drank and danced as if with the devil.

But she knew. She held him. She felt every ounce of his pain as if it were her own. She knew, once he got through this winter, she'd have spring Josh. And he would come back to her. Because it was Evie and Josh and against the world.

And then, one day, the world just fell away.

'I'm not hungry,' Evie told Harvey now, turning away and fiddling with the plug socket extension on the floor.

'What are you doing?' Harvey asked as she groaned with the effort. Her fingers felt fat and sausage-like as she tried to plug her charger in.

'Phone's dead,' Evie croaked, making her wonder how long it had been since she had actually said anything out loud.

'I thought you liked it that way,' Harvey sniffed.

'I need to get up. I need a shower,' Evie said. The vinegary sheets felt almost wet. And she didn't want him getting into bed, to feel his hands on her. Inside her. She didn't want any of it.

All she wanted was for it all to go away. For everything to go away.

He leant forward and kissed her with his fat tongue roving around her gums, and she gently pushed him back after a polite amount of time.

'Seriously. I'm listening to you! I'm going to get showered.' She tried to smile. 'And I need the toilet.'

'Well. I'll come with you,' Harvey said flatly.

'No, come on . . .' Evie swung her legs out of the bed, but Harvey grabbed her at the top of her arm.

'Why don't you want me to come?'

'I need some privacy!' Evie swatted him in a way she hoped seemed playful. 'Let me be a girl for a bit.'

That seemed to soften him, although as he sat back she could see his ears pricked, his body tensed.

She ran the shower as hot as she could stand it. The mould on the ceiling was thickening. It had been three days since she'd seen Liam or Finn. She had no idea if they knew whose bed she was sleeping in or what they would think of her now. Kelly had all but moved out by the looks of her room. Was she with Bronte?

She thought of the lies she had told. She swilled them round in her mouth and felt like spitting them out at the wall, watching them splatter like black ink.

She dried and got dressed in the bathroom away from Harvey's eager eyes. When she went up, he was staring at her phone.

'Lot of messages coming through,' he said and tried to peer over her shoulder while she scrolled through them.

'Hang on, I've got a voicemail.'

Evie rang the message service. 'Oh, it's from HR,' she said to Harvey. Then, as the message began, she paled.

'There's been a development at today's hearing and we just need a little extra time. You'll get an email inviting you to an interview. Do feel free to bring along a member of the Student Union, or a peer for support.'

She played it again for Harvey.

'What do you think that means?'

'Just tell the truth.' Harvey sat down on the edge of his bed. 'I'll come with you. I'll tell them. You didn't even want to do it. He made you. You were drunk.'

Evie just shook her head. 'Fuck.'

'I want to kill him.' Harvey leapt up and kicked the foot of the bed so hard Evie felt the frame shake.

'Stop it Harvey, please.' She screwed her face up and buried it in the pillow.

'I won't let him get away with it.' He bent down so his face was next to hers and she could smell the Colgate on his breath.

'There's nothing left to do,' Evie muttered. 'What can I do?'

'We need to confront him.' Harvey stood up. 'I mean. He isn't going to lie to your face is he?'

'What do you mean?' Evie peered out under her sticky hair.

'I mean, let's go and see him. Make him stand there in front of you and deny that it happened. And this other girl. Let's find her too.'

'See him where? I mean, I don't even know if he's back on campus.'

Harvey went quiet for a moment.

'I can find him.'

'How?' Evie sat up on her elbows.

'Don't get weird but you know, when I used his phone? To call you? I enabled location services on his apps. He hasn't noticed yet. Or at least, he hasn't turned them off. So . . . here.' Harvey held up Find my Friends. 'We can find him. I always know where he is.'

'What? Why?' Evie swung her legs over the side of the bed.

'To protect you. So if he, you know, came back or tried to get near you, I'd know. I turned yours on too.'

Evie stared. 'So where is he now?'

It had been difficult convincing Harvey to let her go alone. She played the he-won't-admit-anything-in-front-of-you card. She'd promised to record him from her pocket. He'd even let her borrow his knackered old blue Volvo that smelt of a mix of ham and very old cheese.

She followed the map on the phone and found herself in unfamiliar territory. Far from the charms of the kitsch B & B, away from the scruffy but lively Groves. She drove into a labyrinth of streets lined with cut-price, refurbished white goods and mattress shops with wonky signs and metal shutters half pulled down still. A couple of boys, twelve or so, walked a tired-looking border collie cross, sharing a phone screen and laughing.

She kept her eyes peeled, a phrase of her dad's that had always revolted her. She knew his car. She'd been watching.

That night. When she had pulled him into the toilet. She was willing herself to be wrong. She had no idea which outcome would have been worse. If he had kissed her back, or if he hadn't. Both would have destroyed her.

The shops became fewer and the Bitmoji on the screen was still there. She was heading into a more residential area now. New trees in plastic cylinders. Buddha bushes. Shinier bus stop signs.

'Where are you?' Evie muttered, her neck craned, eye-balling all the cars she could see. She knew his. She had followed him to the car park before. At the start. When she still hadn't been sure.

Her phone began to ring, flashing Harvey's name. Tossing it into the backseat she carried on, left and right, until the icon was so close she could almost smell him.

There it was. Evie slammed both feet and the tyres span and squealed. His family wagon. Gun-metal grey. It looked somewhat out of place here, parked in a cul-de-sac to the left. Eyeing her rear-view mirror, Evie sped backwards and made a hard right.

He was here.

But where?

She parked up at the end of the road and climbed out, grabbing her bag with the phone ready and turned on, and caught a glance of herself in the mirror. Her hair wild and her jeans were hanging off her hips, her vest top loose and shapeless.

She approached the car cautiously. Where would he be? Circling it like a panther, Evie tried to take deep breaths but her chest was tight and her ribcage felt like it was bursting.

His car was so clean. All smooth lines.

No dirt. No mess. No splinters. No cracks.

Evie looked down and her eyes settled on a loose bit of brick in the wall outside a tall Georgian building. She grabbed it and wriggled at it, scraping her knuckles. Without thinking, without even looking around, she drew her arm back and hurled it at the passenger window. It hit and a cobweb immediately rippled out. But the brick disintegrated into pieces and fell at her feet.

A shriek and a wail and the car's lights began to flash aggressively. There wasn't much time.

Her hand reached into her bag and her fingers curled around the nearest, heaviest object in there, and within seconds Evie used her bottle of Hugo Boss to ram the glass through. It sliced at her wrists and blood began to seep down her skin. Howling in pain Evie dropped the bottle and watched as it tumbled into the car, filling it with the smell of Josh. Doors were opening, blinds being pulled and Evie staggered away from the car, tumbling back into her own, relieved she had been in such a rush she'd left the door open. She fell into the back and slumped down.

The blood was beginning to stream.

She heard voices, she thought, she wasn't sure. Noises, overlapping. Shrill. Sobs. The sound of sobs. Almost animal-like.

Pulling herself up Evie looked out of the windscreen. He was there. Simon. Crying into the seat, into the smell. Into Josh.

Her eyes grew heavy and the street in front of her began to look hazy and shimmer, the way the fields did in the summer when she would run through the wheat, before the skies had overcast with bruises. The sounds began to drift in and out, lapping like the shore. She could no longer smell him. All she could smell was her own blood.

CHAPTER TWENTY-THREE

Jenny

The day of the hearing

My hands are trembling so violently my coffee sloshes over the edge of my mug and scalds my thumb. I know that because it turns red and my skin starts to hum almost. But I can't feel any pain. When I was little, one of my foster dads used to run my hands under the hot tap after I'd played in the snow without gloves. I remember wondering what he was doing. Trying to warm me up.

Why? Why what was he doing it *for*?

Sometimes it hurts so far down, it scrapes and grates the iron chambers of my insides. My stomach, my lungs. Sometimes all I can taste is metal, black, dirty grinding metal, the taste of the rust on the pipes in the cellar.

The glare of my screen is hurting my eyes and I look away, outside the students are milling and my eyes search for Evie. She's late.

She's never late.

Where is she?

I bite down so hard on my lip I taste blood.

Another message last night. After Simon left.

The full song this time.

You can't take your money with you
And you can't take regrets.
All the pain will remain
With the shell that you left
What if the end is just the priest in your head,
What if the ground is a feather bed?
And you will awake to such magnificence,
Where everything's the same but different.

Listen to this. I had told him as I pressed the CD into his palm. Listen.

'Who's this?' He had looked at the cover, a blonde girl in blue jeans and her guitar across her knee. 'I don't really think it's my cup of tea Jenny.'

'Just listen.' I told him. 'Maybe you'll find the answers. We often do. In such unexpected places.'

The sudden buzz of my phone on the desk makes me jump and I snatch it up. It's a private number but I swipe fast anyway. No time to be cautious and coy anymore.

Let him come.

'Doctor Summers?'

I am guarded.

'Who's this please?'

'It's York Royal Infirmary.'

I grab my coat, order an Uber and explain to my colleagues, calmly and in crisis mode, there has been a situation with a student and I am needed immediately.

The accident and emergency department is relatively quiet, as would be expected mid-morning on a Tuesday. Monday isn't a big student night. I am ushered to Evie's cubicle and I peer around the pulled curtain. She is asleep. She looks so young, her hair all matted, her skin so pale. I reach into my bag and pull out a comb.

Her left wrist is heavily bandaged and she has a cannula in the back of her left hand.

'Someone from the mental health crisis team will be down as soon as they can,' the nurse whispers. 'We will have to wait for a bed in the ward, I doubt she can be discharged. She lost a lot of blood but she'll be OK.'

'And was she trying to take her own life?' I lean in conspiringly. 'What actually happened?'

The nurse pauses and looks at the clipboard by the bed. 'I'm not sure. The ambulance was called by someone in the area. They'd been at an attempted car break-in. That's all I really know.'

'A car break-in?' My brow furrows. 'Surely they don't think Evie had anything to do with it?'

'I don't know.' The nurse looks over her shoulder and

shrugs. 'The police have been notified. They'll want a chat when she wakes up. But best let her get some rest for now. Are you a family member?'

'No.' I smile. 'I'm her personal tutor.'

'Wow.' The nurse raises her bladed brows. 'I guess that's what they pay the 9k for then. You're her emergency contact? My lecturer didn't even know my name.'

Imagine.

'I'd do anything for my students,' I say, and pull over the plastic chair to start working out the knots in Evie's hair. 'They are just kids really.'

She looks like Snow White.

I pull out my comb from my handbag and I start to hum.

When she wakes up an hour or so later, her hair is smooth and wavy, although it could do with a wash, and I've wiped her face and neck down with baby wipes. Her eyes flicker and she squeezes my hand.

'Mum?'

'No sweetheart,' I say and lean in. 'It's Jenny.'

'Jenny?' Her voice is raspy.

'Jenny. From university.' My voice has developed a touch of impatience.

'Oh God.' Evie looks down at her bandage. 'Oh God. What did I do?'

'What can you remember?' I pull my chair close.

She is so frail, so spindly. Like an insect in a web.

'I . . . I smashed a window.'

I pause. 'Whose window?'

She starts to cry. 'Simon's car window.'

Letting out a long exhale, I blow out my cheeks. 'Oh dear. I heard from HR there's been some new information? Have they explained what is happening?'

Evie shook her head. 'No. He's going to get away with it. Isn't he?'

Her hair sticks to her forehead as she brings up her forearm to shield her eyes. It is bright in here.

'Evie,' I say slowly. I must tread carefully. 'We need to know what this new information is. Is there anything at all you want to tell me? Because I can help you, Evie. I can help you if you tell me. But if you're not honest . . . well. I'm afraid there's not much I can do.'

Evie turns her head and the tears begin to flow down her poor, translucent face. She looks like clingfilm pulled too tight.

'Evie . . . did you do this to yourself?' My fingers stroke her wrist and she pulls it away. Which I find a little rude.

'No. I sliced it on the glass. On the car.'

'Evie, you must be honest.' I pull my chair in closer and the scrape makes us both wince. 'I understand what you've been through, at home, in the past and now this. Simon facing losing his job. His son. It's so much pressure on you. I should imagine the guilt must be unbearable. Especially . . .' I pause. 'If you haven't told the whole truth.'

'What? What do you mean?' Evie looks horrified and for a second I wonder if I have got it all wrong.

'OK Evie, I am going to tell you something now. But you have to swear to me, swear you won't tell a soul.'

'I promise.' Her eyes are wide and I gulp. Is this worth the risk?

'The second girl. There is no second girl, Evie. I . . . orchestrated that. To help you.'

Evie's mouth drops open and I feel a flash of irritation.

'But why?'

'You're right Evie. The chances are . . . he won't get in trouble for what he has done. It was looking like he was going to get away with it. I couldn't let that happen. I couldn't let him walk away from yet another mess he has created.'

'But . . .' Evie's eyes are wide and she looks like an abandoned fledgling.

'I did it for you, Evie. So now you have to do something for me. Look me in the eyes. I know you lied. Because Simon is gay. We both know nothing happened between you. We are both implicated now. And . . . Elodie. That's a lot of people who could get in a serious amount of trouble if you back out of this now.'

'Oh my God.' Evie is properly crying now. 'Oh my God. Why didn't you tell me you knew? What? Why did you . . . go along with it?'

'Well, I don't know why you did this Evie. I should imagine it was attention? Perhaps your mental health isn't the best. But no matter the reason. He has done this before. He got away with it then and now he has to be stopped. Whether he did it with you or not, he deserves to be punished.'

I let her wrist drop and she cradles it, the sobs are thick and fast and I am nervous a nurse will come at any minute.

'Oh darling,' I whisper. 'I am right here for you. It's OK. Can you tell me why you lied?'

She shakes her head but allows me to stroke her temples.

'I can't bear to see you suffer like this. You poor girl. Those demons of yours really aren't letting go, are they?'

Her eyes are screwed up and the smell of the hospital, the sickness everywhere is like old school dinners and bodily fluids. It's too warm.

'I just don't know what to do . . .' she says.

'What do you mean?'

'I just can't face it, any of it. I just want to be far away from here. From everywhere.'

'Where do you want to be Evie?'

'Oblivion,' she says. 'It was all for nothing.'

'What was . . . what was all for nothing?'

'I told them.' She turns her head to me. 'I told them that Josh had been having some kind of affair with his lecturer.'

I stiffen.

'Who do you mean, Josh?'

'No one would listen. I emailed, I called. I even wrote to the vice chancellor. I just got stock replies. No one cared Jenny. No one cared. It was like, you know, in dreams, when you open your mouth to scream and nothing comes out?

Or you try and move but you're paralysed? It was like that. It was a nightmare.'

'I don't understand Evie. No one would listen to what?'

'I loved him so much. We'd been together since we were fifteen. That's why I transferred here. I could tell. I could TELL. The way he was talking, behaving. It wasn't him. He started using quotes. From a folk singer? I mean, folk? Josh? In his emails, he was spurting all kinds of stuff. I confronted him. He didn't even try to deny it. Said he couldn't tell me who it was. I suspected everyone. Everyone.'

I am so cold suddenly. My thighs are rigid. My neck is stiff.

She knows? How much does she know? Has she known all along? Has she played me?

'Someone was putting ideas in his head.' Evie's voice was becoming a hiss. I move my chair back ever so slightly.

'At one point, I even thought it was you Jenny. He talked about you all the time. On email.'

There is an iron fist around my heart.

'It wasn't me, Evie.'

'I know. I *saw* them Jenny. When I went home over New Year, I saw Josh and a man. A much older man. Kissing in the trees near, near a waterfall. Our waterfall. And his emails . . . he told me how he didn't understand who he was anymore. How he'd fallen in love with someone he shouldn't. When I saw him, I thought he meant, because it was a man. But then, Josh wouldn't think like that. He wouldn't think it was wrong, or he shouldn't, so he must have meant something else. I looked online. I looked at all the pictures of the lecturers in the department. It had been dark . . . but I was pretty sure it was him. And then, I don't know what happened after that. But Josh was in such a state. He said he couldn't eat. Or sleep. He was just like me. Like I had been over him. And I was HAPPY Jenny. I was pleased. I told him I'd seen him, that I didn't care, that we could still be together. But he didn't want me. Even after him. He still didn't want me he said. Not in that way. He said that he had changed. He was different now. A new Josh that didn't feel like he was holding his breath all the time. He was heartbroken. He wasn't happy. But there was some relief there. Relief in his emails. He wouldn't kill himself, Jenny. He just wouldn't.'

'But Evie, he did.' I sit forward.

'No. He was driven to it by him. He was someone he was meant to be able to trust. And he failed him. Josh was vulnerable. And loving. And sweet. And he was abused for it.'

'Evie . . .'

'I told everyone when he died,' Evie said, starting to sit up. 'Everyone. I wrote to heads of departments, deans, HR. Nobody wanted to know. I had no real proof. No one cared. No one would even talk to me about it. This was the only way. He deserves to be fired. I need to make him pay.'

All this time. We'd been doing exactly the same thing. We'd had exactly the same endgame.

When Josh first told me, about him and Simon, I'd gone

home and held Enid under the bathwater. Every blissful scratch and yowl. It had released me. He'd said I was the only one he could trust. How could I have betrayed that?

He'd fallen in love with the person, he'd said. It was horrendous. I'd had to listen to the details. The first time his hand had brushed his, the stroke so feathery he hadn't even been sure if it was real.

The kiss behind the lecture theatre.

I had lost him.

Before Simon, it had been me. Me who he trusted. I had been the one he'd respected. Admired. I would've been the one he thanked at graduation. I was the one who'd got him through.

He'd started to inch away from me. He'd made fewer appointments. My phone had become quiet.

He'd been making a mockery of me. They both had.

When Evie had come to me, I hadn't cared, to be honest, whether it was true or false. I should have whistleblown when I'd had the chance. But I'd been weak.

I'd watched. I'd waited.

One night, after I'd had a horrendous day with disruptive seminar groups, kids staring at their phone screens – such lack of respect, excuses – one girl had had the gall to email in that she wouldn't be able to make class because she had slept in her mascara and her eye was sore. By the end of the day I'd been ready to fling myself off that fucking tower.

My marking stack had towered in my mind as I went to the train station. And then my phone had bleeped.

It was him. It was you Josh. It was you.

I'd known if I waited long enough, he would break your heart.

The messages began again. The appointments. It was Christmas. The carols and the lights were so hollow to you. I'd met you for hot chocolate but you couldn't even raise your mug to your lips. The whipped cream and marshmallows were almost embarrassing. Like I'd bought you a Piña Colada with a paper umbrella and a fruit skewer.

Your eyes had been dim.

You'd gone home for New Year and he'd followed you. Told you he loved you. That he had changed his mind. You'd made plans. I'd held a match to Enid's tail.

But when you came back, he'd got cold feet. This time the pain was like a sledgehammer, you'd told me. You were like a teddy bear with all the stuffing ripped out of you.

You'd gone. There was no Josh anymore.

Every move you'd made seemed to cause you pain. You'd become bent and arthritic-looking, your fingers twisted in your hair. A sense of panic.

Your dad had called the department. He'd not heard from you in weeks. I couldn't even confirm to him you were a student here. Data protection.

It was only me. Only me who'd known where you were.

I'd started going to your halls. Remember. I'd come every morning until it was too much to bear.

'Josh.' I curled my body into yours. 'It's OK you know. If you want to let go.'

He hadn't answered. But he'd known what I meant. We were in tune like that.

'Just . . . let go. If you need to. It's not selfish. Not when you're in this much pain.'

He'd stopped bothering with his medication. It clearly hadn't been working. And he didn't even have the energy to pop the little white pill out of the silver rectangle. So I'd flushed it all away. It was time for him to think clearly.

That night he'd messaged me.

What if the ground is a feather bed?

I'd almost wept with relief.

We'd planned it together. Semester started and he didn't come to classes. There really was no point. I'd researched the best ways for him. Pills too risky. He didn't own a car, the exhaust pipe trick seemed to be the most gentle.

Some days he would waiver. Others he'd been resolute.

But I was there. I was always there to support him. I would help him see it through.

I needed Simon to stay away though. I couldn't have him interfere. Start making him promises he couldn't keep. I'd snuck into his office while he was teaching and wiped Josh's contact details off everything. I'd blocked Simon from Josh's phone.

Simon began to look harassed. Stressed. His usual too-cool-for-school demeanour was beginning to crack. I'd put more effort in. I'd kept him busy.

I'd whispered thoughts of oblivion into your ear. Of

restful sleep. Of universes and energy. I couldn't let you go on like this.

You were mine. Not his.

And then . . . you'd called.

'It's tonight,' you'd told me. I'd dropped my coffee and it had stained the carpet in the office. The stain's still there. Taking a deep breath, I'd closed my office door.

'OK darling.' My eyes had filled with tears. 'I understand.'

'I'm going to jump off the tower.'

'OK. OK.' I'd tried to be soothing. 'This is such a brave decision. I know it's not been an easy one for you to make. But you're doing the right thing.'

There'd been a pause. A tiny flicker of hesitation. And it was all there. It was mine. All mine to have. I'd let it fill my body. Could I do this? Could I really do this? His life was literally in my tongue, my throat, whatever words came out next.

'Jenny . . . are you sure? I am, aren't I? I mean, I just . . . my dad . . .'

'Sweetheart, if he could see you like this. They would understand. They will understand eventually.'

You'd started to cry and I let you. It had felt important.

'Will you be there? Will you come with me?'

'Oh Josh. I don't think I can. I think this is something you're going to have to do on your own,' I said.

Another silence.

'When are you going to do it?'

'When it's dark. When no one is around. I don't want to scare anyone, for anyone to see.'

'You're such a wonderful person Josh. You can do this. I know you can. And if you get up there, and you think you can't. Close your eyes and think of me.'

That night I'd sat in my office and watched the sun burn out and the reds and golds and pinks bleed over the sky. It had been the perfect night. High, on top of the tower, I knew you'd be there. Oblivion.

It cast a shadow in the view from my office. The tower. It was so poetic, a centuries' old act. Beautiful, in a way. He would be there so soon. Touching the sun. His eyes closed. He would think of me and I would pull the strings for the last time.

Because I would do anything for my students.

I'd waited from my office. For the sirens. But the dark wept and filled the sky and still there was silence.

Lights, just a handful, had peppered on in the tower, yellow against the inky sky, like a cheap thriller. Josh. Where are you?

Then, there was a rumble in the sky, and my phone, on silent, had lit up.

I'd grabbed it off the desk and knew it was you before I'd even seen the screen.

'I can't do it.' It hadn't even sounded like your voice. There was nothing left of you. It was skeletal. A rattle of bones.

'You can Josh. Of course you can. It's OK to be scared.'

'Please Jenny . . .'

'OK, stay there. I'm coming. I'm coming.'

I'd grabbed my bag and run, in between the shadows of the Student Union coffee shop and bars. Head down, I'd dodged and weaved like a rabbit. My hands were shaking so much as I'd swiped my card to get into the building. The lift was agonisingly slow and each floor I'd prayed for it not to stop. I'd prayed you would still be there.

I'd got out at the top floor and then out of the fire exit, into the dark narrow stairwell, the green exit sign at the top.

My heels had clattered as I'd taken the steps two at a time, when suddenly a sharp pain had made me stumble. I had gone over on my ankle and it was already beginning to swell. Crying out in pain, I'd limped the rest of the way up and thrown open the heavy fire door. My eyes had swept the roof but I couldn't see you at first. I'd thought maybe I was too late, that you had left. But there you were. Crouched by the wall, beautiful head in your hands.

'Josh.' I'd dropped my bag and gone to you. 'Come here.' You'd collapsed in my arms and I'd held your head to my chest. The sky above was too low. I could almost have traced it with my fingers and pulled at the night clouds. No stars tonight.

'I can't do it,' you'd sobbed. 'I can't do it.'

'You *can* do it.' I'd stroked your head. 'It's your choice. You don't have to do it. You don't *have* to. But you can.'

'I want to. I want to. But I'm too weak.'

Your face had felt clammy and cold, and pressed against my collarbone. Your breath was beginning to wheeze and you'd begun to gulp as you slipped down.

I'd pressed your face harder against my breast as if you were my child.

'It's OK . . . it's OK. You're strong. You're strong enough.'

But I wasn't sure. I wasn't sure he was. I pulled his face tighter into my bosom, until I felt his legs start to kick out.

Poor Josh.

'Feather beds sweetheart,' I whispered. 'Think of that beautiful, soft feather bed.'

It was hard, he was over six foot. I got on my hands and knees and dragged you to the edge. I didn't look down.

'Tell me.' I bent my head to your lips. 'What do you want Josh? What do you want? It's now or not at all.'

'Oblivion.'

At least, I think that's what you said. I couldn't be sure.

Evie is still staring at me. For a second I worry I have blurted it all out. Bless her, really. She thinks her little game is getting justice for Josh. She has no idea. No idea how far people can go.

Evie. Oh Evie.

I smile. 'Evie, I hate to see you in so much pain . . .'

CHAPTER TWENTY-FOUR

Simon

Six weeks later

Becky actually smiles as I pour her coffee.

There is the smell of hyacinths and wild garlic coming in from the garden through the open patio door. Jamie is sitting at the dining table, watching some YouTuber and waiting for me to play chess with him.

It's almost as if the past few months have been some kind of nightmare.

I'm home. My book is going to be published in February next year. I've got a three-book deal. Becky and I are seeing a counsellor. He comes to our house to make it easier with Jamie.

It will come out soon. I can feel it. It's there under my skin, like some kind of mythological creature clawing its way up my throat. I can feel it, really feel it bursting from my throat, out of my heart, oozing from my eyes. I have no idea how she doesn't see it too. I won't let it win though. I won't let it take Jamie from me.

Sometimes I picture a life. Jamie. Me. Some kind of cool ground-floor flat with bi-folding doors and blond wood. Light. Lots of light.

It's out of reach. Occasionally I can brush it with my fingertips. Each time I get a new round of edits. I'm working hard and fast.

The investigation seems to have gone quiet. I wouldn't say it's been dropped. But teaching is coming to an end anyway for exams and then it's the summer vacation. It's looking like I'll be back in September.

I'm sleeping downstairs with Jamie every night now. It works well. Becky gets a break, a bath, some time on her iPad. She's probably on Tinder. I wouldn't blame her.

I read the new versions of the book to Jamie and he tells me what works. What doesn't. What's patronising.

I think about Evie. Her face behind the windscreen. She has been through so much that I can't even be angry.

I'm nearly there now. I'm so close I can almost touch it.

'Are you in for dinner?' Becky asks as I get the chessboard out and start setting up the pawns.

'Yeah, yeah. I'll cook if you want?' I smile.

Jamie blinks, 'Thank God I'm tube-fed.' And I make a mock display of hitting him.

'It's just pasta, but sure.'

Becky shrugs.

'By the way,' she mouths and holds up her phone, 'what's a nipple caliper? Hope you're not getting any weird ideas? It came up on the browser history!'

'Just trying to spice things up,' I whisper and give her a wink. She really does have the most beautiful smile. Later that night, after we've fed Jamie, eaten my a-bit-too-firm-to-get-away-with-calling-it-al-dente pasta, I'm loading the dishwasher when my phone rings. It's an unknown number but I answer anyway.

'I'm going to jump.'

'What? Who is this?' I hold the phone screen up to my face as if somehow it will show me.

'I'm going to jump. I just want to be with him. I'm sorry. I just wanted to say . . . I'm sorry.'

The phone goes dead.

I don't even say goodbye to Becky. I grab my keys and the tyres squeal and I am flashed twice by speed cameras on the way. It's only when I pull up that I realise I didn't even ask where she was. I just knew.

I haven't been near the tower block since. I'd even got timetabling to rearrange my classes. I'd claimed I had vertigo. As I start to run, it all flashes before my eyes.

Kissing Josh around the back of the club. The weekend we had in the Lakes when I said I was at another conference. The way he read the classics and quoted Dickens and collected graphic novels. The way the sun on the lakes of Ullswater made me cry. The way he reached over in the Inn on the Lake over red wine and pigeon breast and held my hand. Laced his fingers through mine and told me he loved me. He'd said he would transfer to a different university just so he could be with me.

The ground-floor flat. The blond wood.

The next day we went to the falls and he kissed me by the crags and I felt it. Jesus. I felt it. He was my chance. He was my one chance.

I ended it on the drive home.

I didn't deserve a second chance.

The weeks after, I watched him fade. He blocked me from his phone. He stopped coming to classes. I would walk the campus searching for him, couldn't risk going to his halls. I just wanted to catch one glimpse of him. One look into his eyes. Just once. But he had become a ghost.

I got the news like everyone else in the department.

An email from Peter.

After all. He was just my student. And I was just his lecturer.

I won't ever let this happen again.

Busting through the fire door, panting, I bend over for a second, hands on my knees. I already know what I will see.

Evie is standing near the edge, shaking violently. Jenny stands a metre or so away, with a peculiar, calm expression on her face. Her face hardens in a flash when she sees me.

'Simon? What are you doing here?'

'Evie . . .' I ignore Jenny and reach my arm out to her. 'What's going on? Don't do this. You can't do this.'

'But I can,' she says softly. 'Tell him, Jenny. Tell him what you told me. It's my choice.'

I edge closer to her. 'It's not a choice Evie. This is never a choice. Please. Come away from the edge. It doesn't matter about anything. It's OK . . .'

'She knows, Simon,' Jenny says flatly. 'She knows about Josh. About you.'

I lock my eyes on her. 'What about Josh?'

'That you were sleeping with him. Exploiting him.'

'You don't understand. You've no idea what you're talking about.'

'How could you?' Evie starts to cry. 'How could you leave him like that? You used him. You broke him.'

'Evie . . .'

'I knew. He told me. He told me before he died that he didn't want to go on. He tried to be honest with himself. About who he was. He said it was like he had been holding his breath the entire time. I didn't understand then but I do now. You took it from him. You KILLED HIM.' Evie's last words ring out over the edge of the tower and fill the sky.

'No. Evie, please.'

She turns and looks over the side and I inch even closer.

'It was right here. Wasn't it? It was right here that he jumped. I wonder how he felt. Looking down. Did he hesitate? Did he think about me? Or was he just thinking about YOU?'

The look she gives me tears the meat from my soul.

'Jenny,' I say. 'HELP me.'

'Simon . . . why would I help you? You need to face up to

what you've done. To Josh. To Evie. It's time you faced the consequences of your actions.'

'Evie, look at me,' I say. 'Please. You wanted me to come. You called me here. Say it to me. Say everything to me you want to say.'

'I don't want to say anything to you Simon. I just want you to see me die.' She turns and I scream.

'JENNY. Don't let her.'

Evie is wobbling now, like a faun, her chin is jutted and her elbows jarred. My eyes dart between the two women. There's a look on Jenny's face. One I have never seen before, one so hawkish and raw. Her posture has changed. She suddenly seems taller, as if someone has pulled her up from between the shoulders with an invisible rope.

I don't understand why she isn't trying to stop her.

I don't understand.

But I knew. I knew it would be like this.

I knew she was at the top of the tower. I knew, because, nestled in the inside pocket of my jacket, I had Josh's phone.

It was a few days later. After the news came. After Peter closed the department for a day. I hadn't slept for forty-eight hours and I could barely remember the day, the hour. I'd sit at home each night, watching TV with Jamie, cooking with Becky, even laughing, but inside it was as if things, dark wraith-like beings, were tearing my insides apart, shredding my stomach, consuming my heart, sucking everything, everything light, everything good out of me. They shrieked and howled and rattled my bones, and every minute, every second I stood as still as a sentry guard, letting it happen. Not blinking. Not reacting. I wanted them to take me.

On the third day I went to the top of the tower.

There was part of me that felt perhaps I could.

But I had promised myself. Vowed. I would never leave Jamie again. Instead I sank down, my back against the wall, and I wept and rocked and clawed at my face.

He wasn't there.

I thought perhaps I would feel him. But all I felt was the wind that whipped through the gutter and rattled the pipes. I leant my head to the side, and that's when I saw it. Screen smashed. Battery dead. His phone, lying in the corner, by the fire door. As if it had been kicked away.

I picked it up. And brought it home.

'Why aren't you stopping her Jenny?' I say now and I take a step towards her. 'Why didn't you stop Josh?'

'I have no idea what you're talking about Simon,' Jenny says slowly. There is a hissy undercurrent to her voice and something squirms, serpent-like in my belly.

'Did you make him think it was OK? Did he confide in you? He did. I'm sure he did. In fact. I know he did.'

'Simon, why on earth would I tell someone it was OK to take their own life?' Jenny takes a step towards Evie, who flinches.

'Because you said it to me . . .' she whispers.

Jenny's eyes dart towards me. To the edge of the building.

'Jenny?' I stare at her. 'What did you say?'

'Nothing, no, it's all been taken the wrong way. Why do

you think I am up here? Why would I be trying to stop her if I thought it was OK?'

'You asked me to come here . . . you, you said I'd feel closer to Josh.'

I look between the two women in front of me. Now it's Jenny who is pale. Her skin almost blue. In her black coat she is almost crow-like. Wings fallen, eyes black.

'Were you here, Jenny? Were you here when Josh jumped?' I ask in horror.

'I was always here,' she replies. 'I was here. I was here when you weren't. When you left him to rot.'

'I loved him,' I say. It feels like an ocean, a mountain, an earthquake. 'I did what I thought was best for him.'

'SO DID I!' Jenny suddenly screeches and rushes at me, her wings spread. I jump to the side and grab Evie, wrenching her out of the way. Jenny stumbles and squawks on her ankle and starts to teeter. Her eyes fill with fear and her hands scrabble towards us, clawing. Reaching out I grab her arm and the sheer weight of her pulls me to the edge. I look down and see the pavement where the body and soul of the only man I ever loved lay crumpled, torn, broken. His eyes dim. His breath still. The pavement split. Just like my heart.

I look at Jenny. Her hands are trying to climb up my arm.

'Simon, help me,' she gasps.

I look down into the very depth of her eyes.

Then Evie grabs her fingers and starts to peel them back. One at a time, pushing and bending them. At first, I think she is trying to help but then, that second too late, I realise. That's not what she is doing at all.

There is a scream so distorted it could only come from the mouth of a monster. We both hear the horrifying sound of meat hitting stone.

But neither of us looks down.

CHAPTER TWENTY-FIVE

Evie

That night

'We should get out of here,' Evie said. Simon was standing, hair in hands, his jaw open. She yanked him back. 'You were right. You were right about everything. Don't let anyone see you,' she hissed.

Holding her phone up, she saw Harvey's name flashing up on the screen. 'Come on. Come on. Oh shit, Simon, what have we done?'

He turned, his shoulders up by his ears.

'I didn't . . . I . . .'

'Come on.' Evie tugged at him and pulled him towards the fire exit. Her legs felt like jelly and Simon was almost a deadweight. She put her arm round his shoulders. 'You've got to get a grip. COME ON.'

The screams were rising up like steam, a pounding of feet.

'Shit.' Evie held her phone to her ear. 'Harvey. As close as you can get.' Pulling her hood up over her head, she dragged him along as he stumbled down the stairs. She couldn't chance the lift. Down and down, the stairs looked like a rabbit hole as she turned each square corner further into the dark. Simon began to move quicker, his hand clung to the rail.

She could barely breathe. Her heart was racing as they came out of the doors into the cold night air. This time Simon pulled her back. The sounds of sirens and the blue flash of lights were on the skyscape. 'Careful. We've got to be so careful.'

'Harvey is waiting . . . he's behind the arts block.'

'Go,' Simon said. 'You go. I need to stay here.'

'No, Simon. You'll be blamed. This doesn't look like an accident.'

He grabbed his phone. 'I'll say I tried to stop her. She called me. Look.'

'But the recordings. On your phone. It'll sound like you did it deliberately.'

'I'll wipe it.'

'But . . .' Evie's face twisted in desperation. 'That's our evidence. That's all our work. These past few months. That's everything we needed to show she did it. That she coerced him. Just like she tried to do to me.'

Simon paused. 'I think justice has been done. Don't you?' Then he kissed the top of her head. 'Get out of here,' he whispered. 'I'll clean this up.'

Evie took a step backwards. Then another, shaking her head. Just hours ago, she had been trembling with excitement, positive she would get what she needed, what she'd been working to prove since she'd first heard her sing those words in the hospital, when she thought she was sleeping.

What if the ground is a feather bed?

The words in the last email Josh had ever sent her.

It might have been Simon who'd been sleeping with Josh. But with Jenny something much darker and so much more twisted had happened between them.

Evie took one last look at him, then turned and ran. All she could hear were Simon's beautifully executed cries of anguish ringing out through the dark.

The broken headlight of her car led straight to Harvey. He leant over and pulled open the door as she got in.

'Drive, drive, drive.' Her voice was strong, and for the first time, she felt it.

'What's happened? Why are the police here?' Harvey's feet didn't touch the pedals and the car engine stayed at a low purr.

'Harvey. Please, just drive,' Evie begged. 'It's . . . it's not gone to plan. I've got to get out of here.'

He sniffed, wiped his face with the back of his sleeve, and reversed out of the car park space. 'Where are we going?'

'Anywhere. Just drive. Just get us out of here.'

Evie slumped down in the car, her hood over her head.

They drove in silence through the streets, then through

the main roads by the castle gates. The groups of people, students, workers, gathered, limbs dripping off metal chairs, their eyes bright and their glasses full. Tourists were balancing on the walls, leaning over the bridge, over the river, out into the dusk.

When they reached the city gate, Harvey wordlessly turned onto the ring road.

Evie pulled her knees to her chest and turned her head to the side so she didn't have to look him in the eye. The old car rocked and shook as Harvey took it up a gear and they sped out, the Dales on the shrouded horizon.

'Where's Simon?' Harvey asked. 'Did you get him? On tape? Did you get him to confess?'

'No,' Evie said. And took a deep breath. 'Harvey. I need to tell you something.'

Six weeks ago

Evie pushed her jam sponge and powdered custard away untouched. It was nice being in a clean room. White, bright, no damp. No shadows. Shared ward of course but she'd pulled the curtains round her cubicle. Read. Watched the clock. Jenny had been in a couple of times. She'd told Harvey not to come. She couldn't face it. He showed up anyway, clutching some wilting lilies that weren't allowed on the ward.

She only had to stay a couple of days, just enough to convince them she wasn't trying to kill herself. That she was fine. The police had come. She'd confessed to vandalism. It had seemed pointless to pretend otherwise. She'd tried to tell them why. That Simon had slept with a student. They hadn't seemed at all bothered.

Like all the letters she had sent, the emails, all unanswered.

It felt like there was no chance of getting justice for the dead. That's why she'd tried to honey-trap him. She'd figured she would get justice by herself. Was Simon gay? Or did he fall in love with the person not the sex, like Josh said? Either way, he'd said no to her. He'd gently placed his hands on her shoulders and looked into her eyes.

'No, Evie. Don't.'

It was the second most humiliating moment of her life. She'd left with Bronte, drunk and mortified.

'Kelly said she saw you outside the loos with Simon, looking cosy,' Bronte had hissed in the taxi. 'Please tell me you're not going to become one of his groupies?'

'No! Why, what do you mean?' Evie had slurred. 'What did Kelly say?'

'That you were pressed up against him and he was whispering something?'

'She must be pissed.' Evie had laughed. But it was then she'd realised. It didn't matter at all whether she had slept with him or not. All she had to do was say she had. After all, her heart was still beating.

A complaint like that wouldn't get ignored. Not like it had been ignored when the victim was dead and buried, taking their secrets with them.

She wasn't going to be ignored again.

She'd sown the seeds with a few tearful 'confessions' in Jenny's office. She'd confided in Bronte and asked to move seminar groups. It had been her word against his. And technically, he was guilty. Let the punishment fit the crime.

Then suddenly, Elodie? That couldn't have been right. If it was . . . then she really had nothing to feel guilty about. But it wasn't true . . . it wasn't exactly a shock when Jenny had told her what she'd done.

She lay there, letting her brush her hair, and she wanted it. The touch of her hand on her head, the lullaby-like humming.

She almost craved it, without even realising. It was as if a part of her that was missing, that she hadn't even known she'd been missing, was suddenly there.

She wanted to close her eyes, and turn on her side, and cuddle into her. Let her tell her what to do. Protect her.

But it wasn't right. There was something off. The tug of her wrist as she untangled her hair. The way her features barely moved. Her eyes weren't focused, wouldn't focus. She seemed to be staring past her, looking through her. Every time she winced as the brush continued to pull, she could see a red flush paint Jenny's cheeks, her fingers worked quicker, her breath shallower.

Evie lay there, frozen, like a doll. And wondered if she had been very, very wrong.

Now, she curled her knees to her chest, waiting for her discharge letter. She wasn't exactly enthused to be going home, wherever that was. Suddenly, scraping together all her leftover cash and hopping on a train to the Lakes seemed like the best option. She didn't need a degree. What was the point? What was the point in any of it?

It was just at this moment that Simon walked into the ward.

'What are you doing here?' Evie scuttled back on her bed. 'Why are you here?'

Simon stopped, his palms held up, and looked around the ward. An elderly woman was asleep, her breath deep and ragged under her oxygen mask. The younger woman in the bed opposite had ear buds in and was painting her toenails, trying to avoid the tag round her ankle.

'I'm just here to talk to you. Is there somewhere I can buy you a cup of coffee? Are you allowed off the ward?'

'It's not a mental institution,' Evie said. 'I'm not strapped to the bed. Aren't you breaking some kind of rule by trying to talk to me? In hospital?'

'Probably,' Simon admitted. 'But I know why you're doing what you're doing. And you're really going to want to hear what I have to say.'

It's funny, Evie thought, how easy it is to break the rules when you have nothing left to lose. Or what you are capable of when you've stopped looking at yourself in the mirror.

Evie followed him. And in the hospital Costa coffee, amongst all the other shuffling zombies, she listened.

'I can't believe you've admitted all this,' Evie said after he finished and both their coffees had grown skin. 'How do you know I'm not recording you?'

'I don't,' Simon said. 'But I'm going full disclosure here, Evie. I'm trying to earn your trust. It wasn't me. It's true I broke it off. But I couldn't see a future for us Evie. I was so in love with him, I could barely see straight.'

Evie looked away.

'I couldn't do it. I knew the longer I left it, the more I would be hurting him. I couldn't be selfish. But Evie, please believe me, I don't think that was the reason. It wasn't . . . we weren't together long.'

'But you were the first man . . .'

'I know. I know, Evie. He . . . he wasn't well.'

'You think I don't know that?' Evie jabbed her finger to her chest and sprang forward.

'Of course, no. I know. Evie, he loved you. He loved you very much. He talked about you all the time.'

'No he didn't, he didn't love me.' Evie shook her head as the tears began to flow.

'There are many different types of love.'

'He didn't even leave me a note.'

'Evie, I don't think Josh had properly . . . I think it must have been very spur of the moment.'

Evie stayed quiet, a low buzz in her ears. The clinking of the cups was suddenly loud and painful.

'Aren't you angry with me?' Evie suddenly raised her head.

'No, not anymore. Not when I understood why you did all this.'

'How did you know?'

'Bronte came to see me.'

'What?'

'With a picture, an old picture of you and Josh. Then it all clicked into place.'

'When?'

'Just before my hearing. She wasn't doing well. She made contact with me on Facebook. I met her and she showed me the picture. She

tried to explain what she'd done. I think she was hoping I would help her stay in the uni. Stop her getting kicked off the course.'

'And did you?'

'No. What she did was unforgiveable. She may have had her reasons but reasons aren't excuses.'

'Isn't that the same for me?'

'Perhaps. And for me. No one is holding the hero card here.'

'So what do you want? You want me to admit I lied? Are you going to admit about Josh?'

'If that's what you want me to do then yes. But Evie, I think there's something else going on here. Something we need proof of. And I need you. I need you to help me prove it.'

CHAPTER TWENTY-SIX

Simon

The ambulance takes her but there are no blue lights. Police tape surrounds the tower. I am interviewed and wrapped in a silver blanket like the kind they give marathon runners, for the shock.

When I saw her body on the floor, her skull and face were smashed apart. Nothing but meat, lumps of tissues and her legs twisted so that she looked inhuman.

I thought I was going to be sick, right there. Right next to her body. The ultimate insult, the utter degradation. I looked at her body and I cried. For her. For Josh. Is this what his beautiful face had looked like too? This monstrous, demonic image? I fell to my knees and I howled until I thought I would pass out.

There were people, filing from halls of residence, porters ushering them back inside. Security were moving quickly, screening everything off.

I wondered for a second where her phone was. Would anyone go through it? See all the messages I sent her, pretending to be Josh? I just wanted to see. To make sure I was right.

The pigheart. I have to give credit to Harvey for that idea. He must have got inspiration from somewhere. But I can't think about Harvey now. Or Evie.

The night is blue with cold and I see the students in their little clumps shivering. I even recognise a few, huddled together, jaws chattering. The shock. The blanket is put over me and I am moved away by paramedics. Sweet tea is placed in my hands.

I look up and meet one student's eyes. She has straggly pink hair and skinny legs of a bird. She is clutching her chest, her books round her ankles, a wide silent scream on her face.

'Simon?' A paramedic bobs down in front of me. 'How you feeling now?'

'I'm OK.' I can't force my lips into a smile. It's like they are made of rubber. 'I just wish . . .'

'Don't start thinking that now . . . come on. Is there someone I can call?'

I think of Jamie. Of the warmth of my house. Of Harvey and Evie driving somewhere, back to their house maybe, scuttled up in a room, hiding from the others. Drinking cheap vodka until they disappear. Cold. Green damp bathrooms and mouldy shadows.

I look back at the paramedic and smile.

'My wife.'

CHAPTER TWENTY-SEVEN

Evie

She could almost sense the little hairs on the nape of his neck rising.

'I'm sorry I didn't tell you. I couldn't. I needed this to work and I wasn't sure you'd understand.'

He didn't reply. He just kept driving straight ahead. The trees were becoming thicker until Evie could no longer see the moon and their boughs were knitted above her head, like an arch.

'Where are we? Harvey, what are we doing? Where are we going?'

He didn't answer, but suddenly he pulled a sharp right and the car began to jostle and bump on the track underneath the tyres. The trees were even thicker here on her right and there was nothing but long, empty, dark fields stretching out on the left-hand side, and they seemed to be going faster than they should.

'Harvey, you're scaring me.' Evie fumbled for the door handle but she knew the car was going too fast and they were too close to the dry-stone wall.

'You lied,' he said flatly as they hit a ditch and Evie was flung against the passenger window, cracking the side of her head.

She whimpered and held her hand to her head. 'Ouch. Harvey, STOP.'

They were coming to the end of the track, she could see the fog ahead, blue and swirling.

Evie realised they were heading to some kind of quarry but Harvey made no efforts to stop and she let out a gut-wrenching scream as they headed closer to the edge.

'Harvey! Stop!'

Evie saw his knee jerk, but the car wasn't slowing.

The stones were flying, peppering the windows like bullets and Evie braced, throwing her arms over her head and her knees up to her chest when the brakes suddenly squealed and the handbrake screeched as Harvey yanked it up. Fumbling at her seat belt she managed to unclip it but the door handle still wouldn't budge.

'Harvey, let me out,' she demanded. Her heart was hammering and her mouth was dry. 'What was wrong with the brakes?'

But Harvey just sat there. His hands shaking on the wheel, looking out over the quarry. He looked pale, paler than usual. The line of his cheek was bone white in the moonlight.

'Let. Me. Out!' Evie reached over and tried to grab the keys from the ignition but Harvey's arm flew over her and pinned her back to the seat.

'Josh. Josh. Fucking Josh.' He spat and she felt the saliva land on her eyes, her cheeks. 'When are you going to understand that he's dead. He's dead. And he didn't want you. It doesn't matter if he was fucking someone. Or talked into jumping. Either way, he didn't want you.'

'Harvey!' Evie squirmed and tried to prise his arm off her chest. 'You're hurting me.'

'And you're HURTING ME,' Harvey yelled. Suddenly Evie felt the weight of his arm come away and her hair being pulled so hard she thought he might scalp her. His car door flew open and she felt herself being dragged, her side scraped the handbrake and she kicked out with her legs, but he carried on, until she tumbled out of the driver's door after him, feeling his hands under her armpits hoisting her up, ramming her against the side of the car.

'You used Simon. You fucking lied. You could have destroyed that man.' He grabbed her and slammed her back against the car.

Evie opened her mouth but her words wouldn't come out.

'And you used me, didn't you? All you want is that fucking . . . zombie.'

'He may not have done it to me, but he still did it, Harvey. He was sleeping with Josh . . . but I'm helping him. I'm helping him now see . . .'

The car rocked and Evie looked down. They were on the edge of the quarry. The floor fell away into perdition. The fog was silent. Watchful.

Harvey's hands were in a vice-like grip on the top of her arms. 'You have lied to me all this time, sleeping in my bed. Pretending you are someone you are not. You were just using me. I didn't want to believe it. But it's still him, isn't it? It's all about HIM.'

'No, Harvey I swear.' Evie tasted the lies as they fell from her lips. Sugary, sweet lies. 'Please don't hurt me anymore. I need you. I love you.'

'Tell me again and tell me like you're not fucking lying,' Harvey spat, rubbing his unshaved, sore cheek across hers. 'Tell me you love me. Look at me. Right at me. I want to see the whites of your eyes.' He grabbed her jaw.

'I love you.' Evie's words were strangled and coarse. She tried to look at his eyes. 'I love you Harvey. I need you.'

'What happened to Jenny?'

'Harvey. She's dead. She fell. It was an accident. I swear . . .'

She felt his hands loosen and he stepped back.

'I need to . . . I need to think. Harvey it all happened so fast. But she was attacking me. That's why I was there. She was trying to get me to jump.'

Harvey's eyes were so dark they looked black as he turned back to the car. She watched him walk round to the trunk, and pop it.

Her heart began to slow down slightly.

'We were there to get her to admit what she'd done. It's a

criminal offence, Harvey. She should have gone to jail. These past few weeks, she's been, planting suggestions. Telling me things like it's OK to let go. She's some sick, twisted kind of reaper.'

The boot slammed shut and something glinted in the moonlight.

'You both lied. I trusted you both.'

'Both? What do you mean?'

'He paid me,' Harvey said.

'What?' Evie took a step backwards into the trees.

'Simon. He paid me. To keep you close. To keep you . . . from doing anything too stupid.'

'I don't understand. What . . . what are you talking about?'

Evie watched in horror as Harvey lifted his rifle onto his shoulder and cocked the barrel.

'Harvey . . .' Evie whispered.

'Run rabbit. Run,' he replied.

His eyes were as dead as the animals he had shot and left to rot.

Evie turned and ran. The copse was thin and spindly but the crooked spindly trees scratched and jabbed at her as she hit them in the darkness. The fog by the quarry was tinged blue as the moon broke through the clouds.

'Run rabbit. Run rabbit. Run. Run. Run.' Harvey's sing-song voice drifted through the trees and she could hear the crunch, crack, crunch, crack of his boots on the earth.

Evie's legs were shaking but she carried on running, until she felt a sharp crack across her forehead. Her knees buckled and she hit the ground with a soft, wet thud. She tried to stand again but this time she was hit on the top of her head, a whack that scraped her scalp, and ripped her hair. This time she bit her tongue to swallow back the scream. Her fingers felt for the culprit, a thick, low bough, as her eyes searched the thicket for Harvey.

She couldn't see him, but she could hear his footsteps had slowed. The cracks were nearer now. If she started running, she'd give herself away.

Surely, surely he wouldn't hurt her? The boy who had so eagerly, if not clumsily, awkwardly, brought her into his bed. Who she would wake to see staring at her, stroking the curve of her waist into her hip, with a doll-like glass-eyed fixed stare.

Evie reached out for the trunk and was relieved to feel its sturdy thickness. On tiptoes and crouched she crept to it, and flattened herself against the back of it.

'Evie.' Harvey's voice was clear, and very, very near. 'Don't run. I was only joking. I'm sorry I scared you.'

Evie didn't dare breathe. The air was filling up in her lungs and her chest was bursting, but she didn't dare even let the tiniest amount trickle out of her nose.

'Bang, bang, bang goes the farmer's gun.' She heard him whisper under his breath. She could smell him now. If only he would move ahead of her, she could double back, back to the main road. Surely he wouldn't shoot her like an animal on the dual carriageway? Would he?

She heard it before she saw it. The thick crackle of leaves. The steel toecap of his brown Timberland boot.

He was next to her. Right next to the tree. Her lungs were on fire and her muscles were tight and cramping. Ahead of them both, the moon broke out again through the clouds and the arc of his cheekbone glowed with the palest of blue.

Evie began to inch the other way, back around the tree. Harvey was moving forward now, his gun still on his shoulder, his head and body not moving. Only his legs, moving slow, deliberate, as if through treacle.

She used the trunk to guide her, barely lifting her feet from the ground. Sliding in the mud, she manoeuvred back round the tree, her ears pricked for the slow in his footsteps. She was almost at the other side when it happened. Her ankle hit a root, one she wasn't expecting, and she tripped, and scrabbled against the bark to stay upright.

The footsteps stopped.

Evie's lungs betrayed her and she gasped, the sweet oxygen pumping into her lungs.

'Hello rabbit.'

It could have been a bluff, but Evie pushed herself from the tree and began to run, heading towards the fog of the quarry. If she could get back to the car, she could lock herself in, call for help. Maybe the keys were in the ignition.

Not even trying to keep quiet anymore, she blundered through the trees, not knowing if the thunder of the footsteps were hers or Harvey's.

Ahead, she could see the small clearing. The car stood

in a spotlight of moonlight, and the door, wide open. The ground underfoot was turning rocky and grey. Evie sprinted, her legs almost numb, and broke out of the woods. The edge of the quarry dropped sharply to her left, but it was the quickest route to the open car door.

She looked behind her, only for the briefest of seconds. She couldn't see him, but she knew he would be close.

She didn't even hear the shot.

One-Shot Harvey. That's what they called him.

CHAPTER TWENTY-EIGHT
Simon

One year later

The leaves are on the ground already. It's early for autumn, but this September has come on cold and unyielding. I lock my office door, say goodbye to a few of the stray lecturers, the odd feral student and head down the stairs. It's early, only just gone three, but you can tell the sky is trying to sully already. I'm done for the day.

I can pretty much write my own timetable now.

Jamie is in school, and won't get home for another hour, which gives me time to get back, to warm the flat. Get everything ready for him. We have an incredible view of the minster. Sometimes on a clear day, we can even see the river.

Thursdays are my favourite day now. Classics in the morning, small group after lunch, and then Jamie all to myself until Monday. I go over for dinner on Tuesdays. Becky has yoga then. She's looking good.

I can walk to work. Smell the conkers. The damp piles of russet and gold. The flat was expensive, but so was my settlement.

I have fellowship for life. I have a flat I could afford to buy outright. I have Jamie. I have my freedom.

Dreadful about Evie. Poor girl. It's funny isn't it? What love can do. It can drive you to the bitter end.

I've said it before and I'll say it again.

There are many different types of love.

But Harvey did what he was told. Kept an eye on what was going on for me. I'm not sure he believed me, or her, when I told him I hadn't done it. He said, she said. It didn't matter to him. Not when I handed over wads of cash for him to report back. To make sure she kept in line. To tell me what was going on in the house. That mad bitch Bronte. That's what really crippled me financially. But at least I knew what was going on. I had to think fast after that first meeting with Louise.

It could only have been Evie. The toilet incident. The party. I had to find Harvey fast. I watched her. Watched her house. I had nothing else to fill my days with. I took my chance when I saw him lumbering out of the house. Finn, Liam, they were far too clean-cut despite their lad-like image. Bronte, too hysterical.

Harvey. Well, I looked him up on the housing system and found his records. Colourful past. A bit of aggravated assault. I saw where he came from. Jenny wasn't the only one who knew how to pick her protégés.

I took beginner shooting lessons. We got talking. I said I was a private investigator for the university, looking into an abuse of power case. I said my name was Steve. He liked the feeling. The validation. The feeling of worth, of being needed.

He got greedy though. He wanted more and started telling me less. At that point I became worried. I thought perhaps she would maybe even drop her complaint.

I was nervous of Evie. Nervous she wouldn't be able to hack it. The guilt. The lies. Once we started working together, well, I didn't need Harvey anymore. But he stuck around. He was like a dog with his tongue hanging out. He threatened me. He told me he'd figured out who I was. Even whacked me over the bloody head. Tried to set me up.

Stupid, stupid boy.

One last payment. One last favour.

They found the bodies. Her and Harvey at the bottom of the quarry. His mangled in the wreckage of her car. Hers with a gunshot wound to her head.

They think he drove it over the edge. Murder–suicide. They do say it's like an epidemic.

And Jenny. The patron saint of pastoral care. The martyr of mental health. Best keep her up there. A beacon. A shining light. The blossom on the Joshua tree.

I unlock the front door and pour myself a glass of red. A decent one. I can afford that now. Forced into outing myself.

Emotional turmoil. Victimisation. Sexism. Discrimination. Jason's mate was incredible. Enough to buy myself the flat, to have it adapted. To pay for a part-time carer.

I have job security for life. I have the big office that used to be Jenny's. I have the flat with the blond wood.

I have Jamie.

I have my freedom.

You would almost think that I had planned it.

ACKNOWLEDGEMENTS

It's true what they say about follow-up fear. All the time writing this I had second album horrors. So a big thanks to everyone who loves me, for the reassurance, the wine and making me laugh until it came out of my nose.

A big thanks especially to Becky Mills, talented musician and wonder-friend. The character of Josh was inspired by a song of hers, 'Carols out of Season', which highlights the plight of mental health in men. Both Becky and I lost very important men in our lives to suicide, men we loved very much. It was an amazing experience to bring Josh to life together. She also penned the bespoke lyrics to 'Feather Beds' for me, when I couldn't find a single song that worked the way it needed to. Who would have thought all those years ago, sleeping in your pig pen and listening to the mouse-traps snap all night, drunk on Mad Dog 20/20, we'd be thanking each other in our album and book acknowledgments. Thank you. I hope you know how much you inspire us all.

This book was written over a very difficult time in many people's lives. I don't think I would have got through the pandemic without my awesome friends. Ruth Lockwood who, when I mentioned I had a cheesecake craving mid-writing, baked me a biscotti delight and delivered it to my door the next morning and has always – since the day I met her in the playground of the village school when neither we, nor our kids, knew anyone – has always kept my glass topped up and my soul propped up.

Karen Cockerham, who I met at age 18 when we were housed next to each other in halls of residence, these uni stories should ring a bell. Sadly – the rotten fishhead story is not entirely fiction. Thanks for always having my back and putting up with my general madness and making my Lancaster years the best ones of my life. I'm always telling my weeping final year students when they graduate the story of us. Bridesmaids. Godmothers. When the world ends it'll be me and you in a car listening to Blink 182. Speaking of which, a shout out to B-Floor County College 1996. Thanks for all the love you've shown me, even though it's 21 years on . . .

Lucy Mizen, my oldest friend (not my *oldest* friend as she likes to point out, but the one I've known the longest). It's been 39 years since I first knocked on your door and asked if you wanted to play out. All my stories, somehow, lead back to you. This summer I was cleaning out my garage and found a collection of short stories I wrote for you for your sixteenth birthday. I was only thirteen, I'd like to point out, so it wasn't completely tragic and uncool. I gave you them back this year. You are the definition of unconditional love. Don't try and ditch them in my garage again bitch. The Lost Boys forever.

Carolynn Williams, another soul sister, who never appears to tire of my dramatics, is always willing to have one last drink and makes me laugh until I wee, my Hepworth Village mums and fat bitches, my Sheffield Uni sanity girls and all the incredible friends in my life, I am so so unbelievably grateful that there are too many to list – but I'm going to give it a go . . . Cat, Sarah G, Becca, Lisa, Kate, Nicola, Yvonne, Katie, Lynn, Joely, Michelle, Arlene, Polly, Will (not a woman but still a bestie), Lindsay, Lily, Emma, Emma, Caroline, Kate, Sarah, Anouska Kemp for the HR and legal advice – I genuinely wouldn't have kept going without your love and support. Sorry if I forgot anyone. I'll get you next time.

Dad, for reading me *The Hobbit* when I was tiny, all those Sunday trips to the cinema, your old copies of *Empire* and your incredible vinyl collection. Storytelling comes in many forms and you introduced me to worlds that I have always been able to escape into, even now.

To escape the horrors of lecturing full-time as well as having to home school my sons in the height of the pandemic – a huge thanks goes to my mum and my stepdad Dave, who let me move into their shed so I could knock out the mid-section of the novel without various children telling me how stupid I am for not knowing the longest river in Africa or what a fronted adverbial is.

I mean it. I slept in there, ate in there, wrote in there and did various press interviews for my first book, *Paper Dolls*. I was also delivered pate, cheese, wine and tea in flasks. I highly recommend my mum's shed for your next mini break. It's technically a summer house but I think that makes us sound pretentious, so we'll go with shed. Mum – seriously. Sometimes I don't know where you end and I begin. Thank you. For everything.

A shout out for my big sister Suzanne who hates reading my books because she's a massive wuss after being scared of an episode of *The Waltons* when she was little. I kid you not. But she ploughs through them anyway. You're the best sister anyone could have.

Huge giant thanks to my wonderful editor Florence Hare. I couldn't ask for a better person to knock my books into shape. Even when she makes me chop out my favourite bits, she is always right. And a mahoosive thanks to my agent Jo Williamson. We are always, excuse the pun, on the same page. Thanks for always having my back and being the best person ever to have in your corner. It's been a rollercoaster – and you're so much fun to scream with. I couldn't imagine anyone else along for the ride.

And to all the students who I have ever taught – don't read this looking for you! I promise . . . it was always confidential.

I really believe it is my privilege to have had some small part in shaping you as journalists, and as people. I'm proud of each and every one of you.

But, as ever, my biggest thanks goes to my husband Mark and my sons, Tommy and Oscar. You are the best stories I have ever told. I love you so much boys.